The Vulture's Bargain

Nicholas W. Armington

For Caroline, whom I could not have written this book without.

- CHAPTER 1 -

They were sitting idle two miles off Mauritius. The crystal-clear tropical water lapped at the sides of the deep-sea fishing vessel, as two lines extended into the ocean passively awaiting a bite. Lifting his Mai Tai to his lips, ice clanking in the glass, the sudden jolt of being yanked out of his seat from behind sent the cup tumbling to the deck where it shattered at his sandaled feet.

"What the hell?"

Without a reply, he was effortlessly lifted off the deck chair and his feet dangled for a moment before the thud of the boat's rail against his back rattled him again.

"What the fuck are you doing?"

Again no answer as he remained pinned against the rail, his expression quickly shifting from mere shock to panic as the stiff fiberglass side of the boat dug into his spine. His frantic eyes focused on the third passenger who was emerging from the small cabin under the front of the vessel.

"What is this, a joke? Call off your goon. I'm going to need a lot more rum to get my buzz back. And then a chiropractor."

Silence from the third passenger and a growing dread replaced the man's panic.

"Okay, this is killing my back. Seriously, call off your dog. What is going on?"

"You talked to the feds." said the third man, between long drags on the cigar that was dwarfed in his large hand. His sunglasses sat easily on his heavy cheeks under the searing hot mid-day sun.

"What? What do you mean?" the man stammered, struggling to keep his composure.

"Don't play dumb with me, Rust, we've worked together too long for that."

The man's head and upper back now teetered over the side of the boat.

"Stop this! I have no idea what you mean. Where is this coming from?" Rust's voice was now driven by sheer panic. In desperation, he remembered the fourth occupant of the boat, and frantically searched his field of view, craning his neck. He spotted

1

the figure standing at the front of the boat, back turned to the commotion and scanning the horizon.

"Two days ago my guys saw you walk through the front door of government house. Then right into the FBI legal attaché's office. That can mean only one thing - you're cooperating. That's bad for me, but it's worse for you," said the third man with an icy tone that sent a shiver through the captive, despite the tropical heat.

"That's what this is about? That was nothing. I was just checking on that tax issue for our LLC. Why didn't you ask me? This is crazy!"

Cigar smoke tumbled out of the third man's nostrils as he chuckled to himself.

"You were never a good liar, Rust, and you haven't gotten any better. My source is the legal attaché's assistant. She heard everything through the door. It's over."

"You bastard! It's over for you too. You've been stealing from our clients, and from the rest of us. I had no other choice. You betrayed us." Rust exclaimed, indignantly.

The third man shook his head and exhaled deeply.

"You underestimate the reach of my influence. Law enforcement will not be an issue for me. Anyway, you should have protected yourself better when you found out. Always too trusting, Rust."

He turned away. The fourth man, now at the wheel, revved the engine to life.

"Make it look like an accident," said the third man, as he stepped back down into the cabin.

Rust's screams were lost in the laboring of the two massive outboard engines as his legs were thrust into their speeding propellers. The red blood slick on the surface was the only evidence of the deed and the reef sharks it attracted the only witnesses.

- CHAPTER 2 -

Noah was hitting his stride after three years at the firm. His goal throughout law school had been to become a hard-nosed trial attorney, and he was well on his way. He averaged twelve-hour days, but the long hours did not faze him. Winning was the important thing. The pay that went along with it didn't hurt either. After burrowing deep into a hole of debt putting himself through law school, he was now digging himself out – little by little.

"I'm a litigator." That was his response when anyone asked him what he did. That title implied expertise – that he knew what he was doing and had seen it all before. With each year, and each new case, he was acquiring a skillset that would allow him to run cases on his own. To devise the winning strategy and put it into play. One day his abilities would make him the lead counsel that everyone wanted to hire. His future was preordained. It had been since shortly after he decided to become a lawyer, and he had spent each day since working toward his goal.

The constant work of a litigator is draining, and Noah's walk to the office each day provided a momentary respite from the never-ending demands of his cases – to clear his head before the onslaught of the day. That morning, he was observing the moon pale against a lightening blue sky, and was lost in an absent-minded reverie when he arrived at the entrance to his office building. At the revolving doors he reflexively reached for his entry card and his mind began to focus on the morning's tasks when he felt a firm grip on his shoulder.

"Noah Ellwood-Walker?"

It was less a question than an accusation. Noah turned and was confronted by a navy-blue jacket emblazoned with three capital letters, "FBI". The jackets had always looked so cheap to him on the news, but up close he could tell they had quality to them – odd your first thought when being apprehended by a federal agent. The agent

3

was enormous, with stern, chiseled features. His eyes said, "stop right there," and Noah did. Panic overtook Noah, and his mind started firing shelved synapses formed while studying criminal procedure in law school, but all that he could summon in the moment was the familiar *Miranda* warning:

> "You have the right to remain silent, anything you say or do can be used against you in a court of law. You have the right to an attorney, if you cannot afford one, one will be provided to you. Do you understand these rights?"

That recollection was not helpful, as he realized the agent was in the middle of reciting these same instructions. In response, Noah managed only, "Ok, I understand."

The click-click of hand-cuffs followed, though unnecessary given the agent's imposing figure. Then they were on the move, with the agent ably leading Noah toward an SUV that appeared out of nowhere. The door opened, and Noah saw that he was not alone. Three of his colleagues were already crammed into the back of the vehicle. He was relieved by this sight – at least he was not the only target of the round up. The agent guided Noah into the back seat, and the door slammed shut, leaving him with an obscured view through a heavily tinted window.

He was afforded no welcome by his colleagues. Each was frozen in disbelief. The only sounds were the muffled drones of the morning commute seeping in through thick windows. Each stared ahead or down at the floor, all entirely in shock. The outside world was miles away. The air still, and thick. After sitting in confused silence for a few moments, frustration overtook Noah.

"Hey, what is going on here?" he exclaimed to the group. No reaction and the silence in the vehicle persisted. He didn't press further, but instead turned his gaze to the exterior of the vehicle to take in the scene unfolding outside.

The otherwise normal Tuesday morning commute was accented by the conspicuous presence of federal law enforcement. Like predators amongst schooling fish, the agents moved swiftly to their targets surgically apprehending them and leaving their fellow

4

commuters undeterred. Noah observed one of his co-workers after another falling prey to agents moving from the cover of black SUVs. Apprehending these individuals took little more than a heavy hand and those few terrifying words. These were not hardened criminals; it was like sheep herding.

Markus Stillfield Brice LLP was a boutique litigation firm well known in Boston as a high intensity shop where hard work and long hours were expected, but generously rewarded. All they handled was civil litigation, and Noah had never had an inkling of illicit activity during his time there. It was a well-respected firm, revered in Boston and known throughout the country. He kept plumbing his psyche for any clues – anything he could remember, but the incessant sniffling of the man sitting behind him made it impossible to focus.

"Shut up, dude!" Noah thought to himself.

The SUV was sweltering now, fueled by the anxiety of four adults pondering their futures. Beads of sweat formed on Noah's brow and his shirt stuck to his back. The windows were closed and the doors locked. Continuing to peer outside, Noah could see the intensity of the roundup slowing.

The front door of the SUV popped open and a linebacker sized agent slid heavily into the driver seat. He was followed on the passenger side by another agent wearing a suit.

"Fuck, it's hot in here," said the second agent.

"Yeah, it is," responded the first, then to Noah and the others in the back, "here we go boys."

The engine roared to life with the sound of a machine built for high-speed pursuits, and the SUV accelerated away from the curb into the roadway ahead of stopped traffic, proceeding to weave through the city streets. The prisoners jerked violently side-to-side with each turn. As part of a convoy now, the SUV merged onto a highway heading north before exiting and quickly turning into a subterranean garage under a medium sized non-descript office building with tinted windows and "FBI – AUTHORIZED VEHICLES ONLY" emblazoned on a sign by the entrance. The

5

prisoners lurched forward with the steep down slope, then the SUV leveled out. The engine cut out.

"Alright boys, we're here," signaled the driver.

- CHAPTER 3 -

It was the quietest he had ever heard a room full of lawyers. Some had their head in their hands, others were pacing. The man who had been behind Noah in the SUV was still softly weeping. They had been instructed to, "wait here until your name is called," and were all dutifully obeying that directive. The cell sat in the middle of a larger room and was demarcated by steel bars on all sides. Just inside the bars on three sides were low metal benches that were as comfortable as indestructible slabs of metal could be. There was a putrid stench in the air that he couldn't place. It was either that smell or his current predicament that was turning Noah's stomach.

Many of his co-workers had already been called back to the labyrinth of interrogation rooms in the basement of the FBI's Boston field office and none had returned to the holding cell where Noah was one of the last remaining detainees. He could do nothing but wait his turn. Without warning he was brought to attention by his name being announced for the second time in a span of hours.

"Ellwood-Walker, Noah!"

He shot up bolt straight. The guard narrowed his eyes and beckoned Noah to move to the door of the cell. As he approached the door, it was opened just far enough to let him slip out. The guard's hand grasped Noah's elbow and before he realized it, he was unthinkingly following the guard's lead down a brightly lit corridor lined with windowless doors – each with a red light above it. What could be happening to his colleagues behind those closed doors? What could they be talking about? Stopping abruptly, Noah was ushered through an open door into an empty room. It closed heavily behind him and he could hear the red light click on as the guard walked away.

The tiny room contained a small table and four chairs. The chair he pulled from the table was lighter than it looked, and more comfortable than the benches in the cell, and he sat and stared at the white perforated hardboard on the opposite wall – alone again for the first time since his commute that morning. His heart was racing, but couldn't remember when that started again or if it had been working this hard throughout the whole ordeal. He could hear the pounding from his chest clearly in the silent room.

The door opened without warning, and two agents entered. The first had ridden shot-gun in the SUV that transported Noah to the FBI field office. The second was younger, and she carried a stack of binders. They moved as a unit to the table and sat opposite Noah, with the younger agent placing the large stack of binders with a plastic slap on the metal table.

"Good morning Mr. Walker, I'm Special Agent Robert Moody of the Federal Bureau of Investigation, and this is my colleague, Special Agent Eve Rust. I want to ask you some questions about your firm and your work there. Before we get started, let me remind you that you have the right to remain silent, and anything you say can be used against you in court. You also have the right to a lawyer. Do you understand?"

"Yes, but why am I here – why is my whole firm is here. I've done nothing wrong and work for a respectable law firm. I'd like some answers. What is going on here?" demanded Noah, surprising himself with his exasperation.

"Noah, I understand the shock this all must be to you, and to your colleagues. You've probably never even spoken to an FBI agent much less been arrested by one. Look, we'll get to all of that, but let's start with a little background if that's okay with you. Where did you go to law school?"

Noah paused, but decided to cooperate for now, and answered.

"Essex Law School, in Massachusetts."

"No way," responded Agent Moody, "me too. When did you graduate?"

"About three years ago."

"We definitely didn't overlap then. My fifteen-year anniversary is coming up. Amazing how time flies. Is professor Ryan still there, did you have him?"

"I did," said Noah, feeling all of a sudden like he was at a networking event.

"What an asshole, right?"

"Yes!" said Noah, surprised to be finding common ground with the federal agent.

"I don't want to go too far off topic here, but one time in Professor Ryan's class I was talking with the guy sitting next to me, and I was laughing about something and Professor Ryan walked all the way up to me and he grabbed my elbow and escorted me out of the classroom – in front of everyone – and told me in the hallway that kidding around in class would not be tolerated. I told him his actions constituted a battery – he didn't like that."

"I can't believe that," responded Noah, snickering. All of a sudden, Noah and the special agent interrogating him didn't seem so different.

"Okay, so how did you find your way to Markus Stillfield Brice?"

The firm had interviewed Noah on campus at his law school and he had been impressed by the two associates he spoke with. He was in awe when he visited the firm's immaculate high-rise office and flattered when the hiring partner explained how good a fit they all thought he would be there. She explained that they only made offers to those they viewed as "top prospects" and that Noah's high grades and recommendations reflecting a strong work ethic put him in that category. The salary they offered him was exorbitant and he jumped at the opportunity.

"What type of cases do you typically work on?" continued Agent Moody.

"It's really a wide range of business litigation, from contract disputes to products liability cases. I basically work on whatever they give me."

"I'd like to drill down a little bit and ask you a few more questions about specific cases you worked on and the people you worked with. Okay?"

"That should be fine." Said Noah. He had nothing to hide. So far, the interrogation hadn't been so bad. Nothing like he expected.

"Let's start with *Three Lynden Holding Corp. v. National Train Corp.* You were involved in that one, right?"

The question surprised Noah and reminded him that he was not having a friendly conversation. He was certainly involved in that case, but no one could have known that based on publicly available information. He never entered an appearance in the case, and all his work was in the background.

"Yes, but how did you know that?" asked Noah.

"People are starting to talk Noah, they're really starting to talk."

Who was starting to talk and what were they saying? Everything the firm did was by the book. What could the FBI want with him and his colleagues?

"Who did you work with on the *Three Lynden* case?" continued Agent Moody.

"The partner on the case was David Markus. He was the only other lawyer on the case that I can remember."

"And what about *Front Road, Inc. v. National Automotive Wheel Manufacturers, Inc.*, and *Broken Atrium Co. v. Southrise Financial, Corp.*, you worked on those cases too, correct?"

Noah had no choice but to answer in the affirmative.

"And who did you work with on those cases?" continued Agent Moody. He was now leafing through a small binder that Agent Rust had slid across the table to him. Noah felt like his entire life was documented in that binder, though Agent Moody seemed to have already committed its contents to memory.

"Well, that would have been Mr. Markus again, and also Frank Stillfield on the *Broken Atrium* case."

So far so good, thought Noah. He still had no idea what was going on, but none of the information he had given to Agent Moody pertained to the specific work he had done on the cases. Noah was wary of getting into the specifics of what he did on the cases or into his communications with the partners. He didn't have anything to hide, but he did have ethical obligations. The rules of professional conduct for lawyers prohibited him from disclosing confidential client information and that included conversations he had with the partners concerning his cases.

"So, how long did those cases last?" Agent Moody continued. He was now physically inching toward Noah with each successive question.

"The cases were all fairly short – that's my recollection," continued Noah, "they may have settled, but I honestly can't remember."

"Well, they were all dismissed very shortly after being filed, none of them lasted more than a couple months."

"That could be right. I just don't remember."

"Well, don't you find that odd, that sort of pattern?"

"No, I wouldn't really call it odd or a pattern – lawsuits settle all the time, in fact most lawsuits settle, sometimes it happens very shortly after the case is filed. I wasn't told much about the strategy in these cases, and I never spoke with the clients about why the cases were brought or why they were dismissed."

The tension building within Agent Moody was now unmistakable. Noah had to pull back from the table to keep his distance from the advancing agent.

"Okay, well let's go back to the *Three Lynden* case. Tell me about the first conversation you had with Markus about it."

11

It was just the type of question Noah was dreading. Agent Moody had crossed the line and was seeking privileged information that could not be shared. Noah could not answer without breaking the oath he had taken when becoming an attorney. He paused and could feel sweat collecting on his brow again. He wondered if Agent Moody could see it. He noticed his heart still racing.

"I'm sorry, but I can't tell you that without breaking my obligations of confidentiality and that I will not do," Noah said with as much conviction as he could muster.

Silence again. Agent Rust was now looking directly at her colleague, trying to anticipate his next move. She leaned forward, and opened her mouth to ask a question but Agent Moody put up his hand to stop her. He pulled back from the table, retracting his elbows into a crossed position on his chest. He leaned against the back of his chair. Agent Rust followed his lead.

"Look, Noah," he said in a frank tone, "this is a serious situation. We're not just questioning you as a formality. We think your firm has been regularly involved in fraudulent securities transactions and many of the cases you worked on are at the center of these allegations. And I'll be honest with you, Noah, your colleagues *are* talking and they don't seem to be so worried about breaking any confidentiality obligation. If you're really innocent here you shouldn't be so shy about talking either. I'd hate for an indictment to be leveled against you just because your bosses were doing something illegal without your knowledge. Your colleagues are talking Noah, it's time that you do too, so you don't get wrapped up in this mess."

All Noah wanted to do was cooperate with the FBI, but he also didn't want to lose his law license. He had spent an incredible amount of time and money becoming a lawyer, and he was not ready to give up on his career.

"I'd like my lawyer now." Noah would not risk his own future by making a knee jerk decision under pressure from the FBI.

"OK, fine," retorted Agent Moody, obviously frustrated, "If you want to speak further, please give us a call." He got up and headed for the door. Agent Rust hastily gathered the binders, but paused and reached into her jacket pocket and placed her card on the table.

"Please call if you decide to talk. We're not after you. You don't want to get caught up in this if you don't have to." She turned and followed Agent Moody through the door.

The room fell silent again save for the incessant beating in Noah's chest. He immediately second guessed his decision. Looking down at his hands, he saw that the ink on his fingertips from fingerprinting had rehydrated because of the sweat on his palms and was beginning to run.

A moment later the door swung open and a guard stood in the doorway. He beckoned for Noah to stand up. Noah complied and the guard led Noah down another hallway away from the interrogation rooms. They stopped at a door at the end of the hallway without a red light above it. The guard opened it and a warm breeze mixed with the hallway's recycled air.

"We'll be in touch," admonished he guard, and Noah was let out onto the street.

– CHAPTER 4 –

Glassware is not used in restaurant kitchens because it breaks too easily. When tempers flare, as they often do in those cramped, hot, and charged environments, it's dangerous enough to have knives always at hand rather than to also have drinkware constantly within reach that will explode into a million shards when thrown in a fit of anger. Anger is forged within these tight spaces among high-strung and overworked artisans. The energy can be harnessed into productivity, but at times it is uncontrollable. Because one smashed glass ruins all the half-prepared meals within the blast radius, lid-less plastic food containers are the go-to drink receptacle for cooks. These receptacles can be abused to no end and survive to be refilled and thrown again.

Noah used these ubiquitous containers so much during his two years as a line chef that it was odd to drink from a regular glass again after he decided to leave the restaurant world to begin his quest to become a world-beating attorney. For months after he made the career change, his mouth oddly craved the sharp lip of the container and its association with long nights in a busy kitchen amongst a team of close friends, and the celebratory drink that would replace the water in the cup at the end of almost every long night in the kitchen.

Working in a kitchen was a function of Noah's indecision after graduating from college. He had done well in school but had no idea what he really wanted to do with his life. He wanted to make an impact, and wanted to make some money doing it, but beyond that did not have true direction or any more specific notion of what a rewarding and successful career for him would entail. Without the luxury of being able to live off his parents while he decided, he needed to find paying work quickly to support himself. That work would serve as a placeholder while Noah kept pondering what he would be when he grew up. Luckily for him, restaurants were everywhere in Boston, and especially in the North End where Noah moved with a group of friends after school. He assumed he could get a job in food service quickly with a college degree, especially since he wasn't picky about his employer or even what he did in his first job. The idea of working in a restaurant had a certain excitement to it as well. There was a cache to being a part of the hidden world of restaurant kitchens that the public only glimpsed through reality television. It was as good a first stop as any while deciding what to do with the rest of his life. He applied to every restaurant he had patronized in his neighborhood, but invariably faced the same obstacle.

"I'm glad you've enjoyed dining at our restaurant in the past. What experience do you have working in a kitchen?"

"When did you graduate from culinary school?"

"Do you have any cooking experience at all?"
There were other variations on this theme during his interviews, but the outcome was always the same.

"Thanks for your interest, but we're looking for someone with more experience."
Noah adapted, and was eventually able to get his foot in the door. Because he had no problem doing menial work and working hard at it, he had no qualms about accepting a job as a dishwasher at a large, upscale restaurant just two blocks from his apartment. He wasn't discouraged, but instead committed himself to being the best at this simple job. He quickly earned a reputation as a good-humored hard worker, and he soon had the opportunity to advance. He became friendly with the cooking staff and they taught him some basic skills on slow days in the kitchen. He learned the proper method to cut onions and pare fruit, and the fundamentals of cooking vegetables. He showed his willingness to learn and improve and the cooking staff kept giving him more responsibility. Within a year he was promoted to line chef, and he was put in charge of cooking all vegetables that were in any dish served at the restaurant. Parsnips and celery became his domain and he became known as a discerning apprentice at the local vegetable markets where he would go each morning after a 5:00 A.M. squash match to gather the best produce for that evening's dinner service.

Restaurant life was exciting, for a time. It was fast paced and intense and kept Noah focused throughout each shift. For almost every minute he spent in the kitchen he was paying attention solely to the ticket in front of him, cooking the food that was ordered, and anticipating the next ticket coming down the line. It was like his daily game of squash in that way – the constant flow of tickets was the squash ball pinging around the court demanding all his attention. There were other perks of the job. The free food constantly on offer was delicious, and he had the chance to meet the celebrities that visited the restaurant on occasion. As a kitchen staff member in one of Boston's culinary establishments, he was also automatically inducted into the informal underground association of cooks in the city, which meant that he could get a table – in the back – anywhere that might otherwise take a month to get a reservation. When things were slow, the kitchen staff would bet on what the next order to come in to the kitchen would be, with the losers buying drinks at the end of the shift.

"It's hot out, and when it's hot out people love to each crab cakes, it's going to be crab cakes, no question. Nine times out of ten it's crab cakes."

"No, dude, muscles, it's the summer of muscles."

"$100 that it's going to be a dozen little necks, any takers?"

The antics were fun, but Noah knew almost immediately after ascending to the position of line cook that work in a kitchen was not a long-term career for him. He grew tired of many aspects of it quickly. The multiple burn scars on his forearms from reaching into a searing oven too quickly he could have done without. The marks would forever be a reminder of his time laboring in a hot, cramped, and windowless room for nights on end. He could not be confined to that sort of cave for the entirety of his adult life. The long hours were excessive for the pay. He stayed for the experience, but knew he had to get out when the right opportunity came along. Noah was constantly looking for that next job and primed to jump once he decided what direction it would be in. A chance encounter sent him on his way.

The restaurant was owned by a group of investors who were each professionals in other fields but lived the rock star life vicariously through their venture and the celebrity chefs they hired to run it. Around the holiday, the ownership group treated the staff to an extravagant dinner at another of the restaurants they owned. It

was a debaucherous spectacle – a time for the staff to let loose and
let off steam built up over a year of long nights in the pressure
cooker of a restaurant kitchen. After two years of letting go himself,
Noah had begun to largely abstain. He found it made the beginning
of the following year less awkward. Instead of letting loose, he
began to talk to the owners during these dinners to get a sense of
their lives and determine if their careers were to his taste. One was a
young corporate lawyer, who was confident, and brash after a couple
drinks. They drank a top shelf scotch that Noah recommended and
set off talking, with the lawyer doing the lion's share. He regaled
Noah with stories of his day-to-day.

"I just got back from a week of depositions in Osaka. Man,
the food there is incredible. You should really go if you ever get a
chance. And make sure you get to Kyoto, that place is incredible."

"When I was a prosecutor, I did over 50 trials and put most
of those criminals behind bars. There's no feeling like getting your
first guilty in a jury at trial."

"You don't need to be afraid of judges. I haven't been since I
got yelled at by one of them the first time I stood up in court."

"Well, I drive an A7 now, it's just better looking than the 5
series, and it's faster too."

"It's not all corporate work, I do a lot of pro bono too and
have been able to help a lot of people who couldn't otherwise afford
it. That's really the most rewarding part of the job."

Noah was smitten with the idea of becoming an attorney after
that encounter and started the law school application the following
morning.

His life was spartan after that, with a daily routine consisting
of a 5:00 A.M. wake up, followed by an hour of squash at the
YMCA where the courts had concrete walls that dripped with
humidity by the end of a match and a wooden floor that was warped
at the service boxes. A quick stop at the market before breakfast, and
then hours of LSAT study before reporting to the restaurant at noon
and toiling into the early hours. He got precious little sleep each
night. Outside of the restaurant, he was a hermit. When he wasn't
chopping onions and poaching green beans, he paced his apartment
for hours running logic drills through his head. LSAT study even

began to meld with his work. Analogies like artichoke is to paring knife as pork shoulder is to cleaver flitted through his mind as his hands worked preparing vegetables at his station. His inquiry of the sous chef as to whether steamed vegetables were sufficient or necessary to be added to the special got a large soup ladle thrown at his head.

The test was on a cold Saturday morning and was a blur, but he scored high enough to get into a top school and was able to relax a bit during his final months at the restaurant. With his mornings free from LSAT toil, Noah volunteered a few hours each week at a legal clinic, providing practical advice to the homeless. The kitchen staff celebrated with Noah on his last evening with a toast at the end of the night.

"And don't forget that you are always welcome to a meal at the chef's table whenever you need a break," were the parting words from the head of the kitchen.

Noah appreciated the offer, but knew he would have hardly any free time over the next three years.

- CHAPTER 5 -

The Beantown Court Reporter

BOSTON – Federal prosecutors announced today a new case against a prominent Boston law firm allegedly engaged in criminal activity. In a recently unsealed indictment, the three partners of the law firm Markus Stillfield Brice LLP are accused of perpetrating securities fraud by artificially causing the value of certain stocks to fall and making millions off the stocks' slide through a short selling scheme.

According to the indictments, the Markus Stillfield Brice partners created shell corporations that were used to "short" certain stocks, in other words betting that the stocks would lose value. The partners are accused of then manipulating the value of the stock after betting against it. After the partners made a bet that the stock would fall, they sued the companies that issued the stock. These suits were immediately publicized, driving down the share price. The artificial drop in value of the stocks they bet against allowed the partners to reap millions in proceeds that were funneled to the partners through the shell corporations that they created. This scheme went on for years and funded the partners' lavish lifestyles, that included vast real estate holdings, and expensive automobiles, yachts, and wardrobes.

The prosecution has a number of cooperating witnesses, including a principal at one of the shell corporations that brought the lawsuits, as well as associates at Markus Stillfield Brice who worked on the cases filed to artificially tank the shorted stock.

At a press conference today, the U.S. Attorney for the District of Massachusetts expressed confidence in the case and underlying investigation, stating that "we are sure we have identified and apprehended the bad actors here and are committed to bringing them to justice."

None of the partners were able to be reached for comment in response to these allegations or this story. The allegations underlying the indictment were investigated by the FBI's Boston field office and well as the Boston office of the Securities and Exchange Commission.

The arraignments for the three Markus Stillfield Brice partners are scheduled for two weeks from today at the U.S. District Court in Boston. All are expected to plead not guilty.

The Beantown Court Reporter

BOSTON – The Defendants in what is now being referred to in the Boston legal community as the "Short on Law," scheme made their first appearances in federal court today. David Markus, Frank Stillfield, and Mary Brice arrived at the courthouse this morning accompanied by a phalanx of white-collar criminal defense lawyers. The three partners led one of the more prominent boutique law firms in Boston and their first appearance in answer to serious criminal charges leveled against them drew crowds of reporters and lawyers to the courthouse today to learn more about what is becoming the most talked about case of the year in Boston legal circles.

The lead counsel for the partners is Cutty Barton, a game cock of a defense lawyer who has defended a long list of Boston's most prominent criminals. At the first opportunity, he shot to his feet during the hearing today and fired a volley of white-hot accusations at the prosecution, complaining about delinquent discovery from the government and exclaiming that the prosecution was withholding evidence. The lead prosecutor, Wylie Schoenheight, waited out Barton's attacks serenely, his pencil frame unperturbed by Barton's bluster. When it was his turn to respond, he coolly rebuked each point.

"Your Honor, the government has fully complied with its obligations to disclose all discovery, including all exculpatory material to the defense and will continue to abide by those obligations for the entire case."

The judge was satisfied with the prosecutor's assurances and Schoenheight segued into the merits of the bail arguments, arguing that the defendants were wealthy and well connected and with those resources could flee at the drop of a hat. Schoenheight asked for $2 million bond, each.

"Do you have a response to all this, Mr. Barton?" the Judge inquired.

Rising to his feet once more, barrel chest extended to its fullest, Barton unleashed a second tirade denouncing the accusations against his clients and broadly accusing the government of improperly unleashing the FBI on the sanctity of a "well-respected" and "highly-regarded" law firm that had never once been accused of wrongdoing. Judge Halderman was unmoved, and, seeing through this smokescreen, peered down at Barton from the bench and contritely implored him to "please get to the point, counsel." After clearing his throat loudly, Barton pivoted quickly to an explanation of each of the defendants' close ties to the community and then onto a catalogue of their immaculate records before these "misguided accusations by the government."

After hearing the arguments, Judge Halderman decided to split things down the middle, and ordered that the defendants each pay $750,000 bail, and that their passports be seized and that each not be allowed to leave the state for the duration of the case.

"Note my strong objection, your Honor," responded Barton, but no further bluster echoed from his tired lungs. Judge Halderman set a date for the completion of discovery and for trial, with a curt admonition to the prosecution that all relevant discovery be turned over promptly.

The trial is set to begin in six months.

The Courthouse Steps

BOSTON – Opening arguments took place today in the "Short on Law" case. Assistant United States Attorney Schoenheight was first up, as is customary in criminal proceedings. He calmly rose to his feet, introduced himself as the attorney that would be representing the government in the case, and stepped forward and paced deliberately before the jury while expounding the outline of the government's case.

"The defendants perpetrated a complex scheme with a simple goal in mind – to get rich off of other people who followed the rules and trusted the system. The defendants wantonly manipulated the stock market for their own gain. Using a series of shell corporations, the partners of the law firm Markus Stillfield Brice – the defendants in this case – "shorted" the stock of certain companies, essentially betting against the stock price of those companies, and at the same time sued those companies to ensure that the value stock of the stock they bet against would fall. This type of activity violates a number of United States securities laws and caused the honest shareholders in those companies to lose millions, while the defendants became rich. You will hear from a number of witnesses who had direct knowledge of the scheme and in some cases actually participated in it. You will hear from a principal in one of the shell corporations established to bring frivolous lawsuits against the unsuspecting companies. You will hear that he was a 'principal' in name only and that the company he purportedly presided over was not run by him, but by the defendants, and that he filed and then withdrew lawsuits at the defendants' direction. You will also see email correspondence in which the defendants discussed shorting stock immediately before the frivolous lawsuits were filed. The evidence will clearly show that it was the partners, not anyone else, that directed this massive financial fraud. Ladies and gentlemen, I ask you to listen to the testimony, pay attention to the evidence, and use your common sense. I will have a chance to speak with you again before you deliberate and will ask you to find the defendants guilty. Thank you."

After finishing his opening, Schoenheight glided back to his seat, and faced forward with his hands clasped before him and the slightest of smiles on his face. Cutty Barton was next.

"Ladies and gentlemen, I also want you to listen and to use your common sense, but I want you to do it while keeping in mind the heavy burden that rests on the prosecution. It is only the government that has a case to prove here, not my clients. And the prosecution has to prove its case 'beyond a reasonable doubt.'

You've all heard that term before but what does it actually mean? It means the highest level of reasonable certainly possible. *The highest level of certainty*. Ladies and gentlemen, that is a *very* high bar!"

When making this point, Cutty extended his right arm high above his head with such force that his cufflink ejected from his cuff and tumbled to the carpeted floor where it bounced forward and came to rest just before the front wall of the jury box. He was too enthralled in his own speech to notice and continued to plow forward with his monologue.

"I ask each of you to keep that heavy burden in mind when listening to the evidence and testimony." Cutty went on to explain that the partners were not criminals, because they had all been conned themselves. His clients had just been following directions from one of their clients and had no inkling that a crime was being perpetrated under their noses. His clients had no hand in masterminding the scheme, and the government had not even made an effort to try to apprehend the true perpetrator of the crime.

Cutty closed with a flourish, admonishing the jury to "listen to your intellect and your hearts," and then turned and returned to his seat.

The trial will resume tomorrow with the government's witnesses.

The Boston Crime Tattler

BOSTON – The government's trial presentation in the "Short on Law" case has been efficient and effective throughout, with each witness chosen to give testimony specifically tailored to support a key fact of the government's case. The government's first witness was Art Fussilini, the head of a shell company that allegedly filed a multitude of meritless lawsuits meant solely to crater the stock price of the companies being sued. Fussilini was crew cut and had eyes that were perpetually in shock. He testified that he had fallen on hard times when he met David Markus who offered him a sweet deal to become the head of a small, litigious company. He needed the money, so he took the job without much investigation into the company he was meant to run. As he soon found out, his only responsibilities were approving the filing of lawsuits when he was told to by one of the partners. In almost every case, he was instructed to dismiss the lawsuits shortly after they were filed.

"Well, yes, I did think that was somewhat odd," he answered in response to a question posed by lead prosecutor Wylie Schoenheight, "but I didn't read too much into it, or dwell on it, honestly. From my perspective there was nothing wrong with the lawsuits being filed and no harm done as far as I could tell as they were almost all withdrawn shortly after filing. I didn't completely understand it – I'm not a lawyer – but the pay was good, and I needed the money, and didn't want to mess with a good thing, so I didn't ask too many questions."

The government then summoned a string of senior attorneys from Markus Stillfield Brice who corroborated Fussilini's account and explained how almost all the cases filed by the firm lasted for only a short period of time and that the filing of the cases was publicized to the greatest extent possible, using a collection of public relations firms that were kept on retainer for specifically that purpose. All this was accomplished at the direction of the partners.

Next, through a financial services expert, the government admitted documents showing how only days before each of the lawsuits, a second company systematically shorted the stock of the companies against which the lawsuits were filed. Using large and color-coded charts showing the stock prices of the companies that were targeted by these lawsuits, the expert explained that in each case the filing of the lawsuit caused the company's stock to drop, allowing the short sale to be incredibly profitable. The nail in the coffin for the partners was the most unassuming of the witnesses – a clerk from the Massachusetts Secretary of State's office that confirmed that David Markus and Frank Stillfield were named as principals for the company that shorted the stock of the companies that the firm was simultaneously suing.

Cutty Barton did not sit idle through the government's case. He valiantly cross-examined the witnesses on a wide variety of topics from their own background and relationships with the partners to any deals they struck with the government in exchange for not being indicted themselves. With many of his questions he appeared to be pushing the theory that the partners were not the drivers of the scheme, but that they were being led by another individual who had not been charged or even pursued by the government. His clients were only pawns in a larger conspiracy that the government had completely ignored. The disbelieving expressions on the jurors' faces during these inquiries on cross-examination demonstrated that the theory fell on deaf ears.

The defense elected not to put on any witnesses in rebuttal. Closings will take place tomorrow, after which the jury will be charged with deciding the fate of the three partners.

The Beantown Court Reporter

BOSTON – The jury came back today in the "Short on Law" case and issued their verdict just over an hour after going into deliberation. It was a complete victory for the government – each of the three partners on trial was found guilty of each of the securities fraud laws they were accused of violating and each of the partners received fifteen-year sentences for their part in the financial crimes perpetrated by the law firm that they ran. Cutty Barton, the defendants' animated lawyer, made a string of objections upon the announcement of the verdict and made a motion for a directed verdict that the court overturn the jury's decision. The judge was unmoved by Barton's pleas and denied his request without explanation. Barton vowed to appeal as soon as possible, but for now the defendants are all looking at long sentences in federal prison. When asked by the judge if the government expected that any further indictments would issue in relation to this case, Assistant U.S. Attorney Wylie Schoenheight explained that the government was still weighing its options in that regard. The partners were all cuffed by Federal Marshals at the end of the proceeding and led away from counsel table and toward a small door at the side of the court, all still displaying blank stares of dismay and confusion at the verdict returned by the jury and the sentences immediately imposed by the judge.

- CHAPTER 6 -

Noah hadn't set foot in his attorney's office since the day after his interrogation by the FBI. It had been over a year since Noah's arrest and his frantic search for a criminal lawyer in the moments after being released from custody, and echoes of fear and anger still coursed through him when he thought about the event. He remembered every moment of that encounter despite his lingering shock, including his attorney's advice to him that day:

"Noah, I would advise against talking with the FBI any further right now. Your best move is to wait and see if the government is going to indict you. The government's real target is obviously the three partners in your firm, but if they think you have information that will help their case, they'll indict you. They probably already know that you didn't have much to do with this scheme – you're too junior in the firm – but if their inquiry suggests you were complicit enough that they can convince a grand jury to indict you, they'll do it to try to get you to testify against the partners. But from what you're telling me you really don't have any information. And you already told them that, and they probably know it anyway. My guess is that they were just fishing in that interrogation. They just rounded up everyone and grilled you all to see if anyone would give up something they didn't already know. At this point you have nothing for them, and you don't have anything to lose by waiting to see what they'll do. We definitely don't want to reach out to them to see what they're thinking – you don't poke the bear! If you get indicted, we can have a conversation about how much you can tell the Feds to try to cut a deal, but for now you just need to wait."

That was a tough pill for Noah to swallow – to just wait and see whether he was going to get indicted and maybe get a look at the inside of a federal prison. Thoughts of that prospect haunted him, day and night, for weeks.

After a month without any further communication from the FBI, and without a paycheck from his now defunct former employer, Noah went back to the restaurant where he had worked before law school to see if he could help at all in the kitchen. They greeted him warmly with a free meal, and a job, and for the next month he was back to dish washing duty. It was the only position the restaurant could spare on short notice, but it wasn't long before Noah impressed the new kitchen crew, and was promoted back to his old position at the vegetable station. It was an odd feeling to be doing this work again, just now with a law degree, but the manual labor was cathartic and Noah again found respite in working during the dinner hour and having time only to worry about the next order coming from the dining room.

When he was not occupied in the restaurant kitchen, Noah continued to be troubled by fear of the unknown, and convinced that a federal prosecutor was busy putting the finishing touches on a grand jury presentation designed to produce an indictment naming Noah as the defendant. He became an avid reader of the various Boston legal news publications in order to follow the progress of the prosecution of his former bosses. He thirsted for new articles from *The Beantown Court Reporter* and *The Boston Crime Tattler*, constantly checking their websites from his phone at the restaurant whenever he had a free moment – hopeful for any article suggesting who the government might be pursuing next in their investigation. He also continued to call his lawyer for updates. But, as time passed, and as each call with his lawyer produced the same advice – "just keep holding tight, you're doing great, no news is good news" – the waiting got a little easier. After three months, and the issuance of the indictments against the partners, Noah got a dose of confidence, thinking that the government must have their case buttoned up and would not be announcing any further indictments. As the partners' trial approached, Noah felt almost certain that he wouldn't face criminal charges himself. Now, with the trial over and the partners headed to prison for fifteen years each, and his lawyer's recent request that he come into the office to get some "good news," he was cautiously optimistic.

The Law Office of Martello Vaniscovsky was located in an old wharf building abutting Boston Harbor that housed a collection of small criminal defense firms, and other assorted small businesses. The man at the building's reception desk was snoozing more often than not and the single elevator in the four-story building, that ran the length of one of the old harbor piers, was exceedingly slow and clicked ominously when ascending. Noah's lawyer's suite consisted of two small offices, for Vaniscovsky and his partner, a receptionist's desk, and a small conference room, all with brick walls and exposed beams overhead. There was a kitchen just off the reception area where a long broken hot water heater commanded a small counter and dirty dishes collected in the sink.

The receptionist was beautiful and Noah remembered that too. She was thin, almost brittle, with long, dark hair and glasses and when he saw her Noah wanted to hold her, and take care of her.

"Hi, I'm Noah Walker, here to see Attorney Vaniscovsky."

"Sure, let me see if he's available. Wait, oh hi, I remember you from last year, how is everything," she stood from her desk and extended a hand, "I'm Alana."

Noah's heart jumped and for a moment the saga of the last year was out of his mind. He moved toward her but was interrupted by an office door behind her bursting open. A large, potbellied man with a receding hair line and shirt sleeves rolled up entered the room.

"Noah, my boy, come right this way," greeted Vaniscovsky.

Noah was whisked away from romantic fantasy and back to business by an aggressive hug from the animated attorney who ushered him into the small office. It hadn't changed at all. The walls were adorned with framed prints of nineteenth century court room scenes and the room was stale with the smell of decomposing leather bindings on obsolete law books inhabiting every flat surface. In his first encounter with the space, terror induced tunnel vision kept Noah from noticing the disarray of the room. Had he noticed it initially, he may have second guessed his choice of counsel. As it was, he had retained Vaniscovsky. Now, incredibly, good news was promised.

"Have a seat, have a seat," directed Vaniscovsky. "Now, I know it's been a long wait, and I've told you to be patient and you have been and I'm proud of you. As you know all the partners were found guilty last week, and quickly – I don't know if I told you this,

28

but the jury was out for only about an hour, just enough time for them to take bathroom breaks before voting on the verdict. Can you believe that?"

"Just get to the point," thought Noah to himself. Vaniscovsky, a seasoned reader of people, could see that Noah was in no mood for small talk, and moved to the issue at hand.

"I spoke with the Assistant U.S. Attorney responsible for the case yesterday morning and he informed me that they did not expect to seek any further indictments related to this case!" Vaniscovsky had both his hands raised to the ceiling, as if in praise to the legal gods. Noah sat back in his chair in a sort of half relief – his body and mind had been girding for bad news to follow bad for months and it was difficult to release that strain on a moment's notice. His subconscious was unable to immediately accept this proffer of potential relief and reverted to an analytical response.

"They do not expect to seek further indictments – what does that mean. It sounds like I could still be in danger of indictment."

Vaniscovsky was still caught up in his own delivery of victorious news, arms still extended, still relishing the moment, and was caught off guard by this reaction. With the skill of an experienced trial lawyer, he collected himself quickly and proceeded with a calm and comforting tone.

"Noah, trust me, this is the best you are going to get. The U.S. Attorney is never going to commit to not indicting anyone – he has to leave that option open, but if they went back and indicted you now, it would be the first time I've seen something like that. They didn't have anything in the first place, and they still don't. They also wouldn't have even spoken to me if they were considering indictment. Head-up, head-up, my friend, this is really good news!"

Vaniscovsky moved from behind his desk over to Noah and sat next to him and put his arm around him in paternal fashion and, with an even more frank and comforting tone continued.

"You can get on with your life now. This chapter is over."

The physical contact of an arm around his shoulder brought Noah around and he turned to Vaniscovsky and said,

"Yes, thank you."

He felt exhausted. He didn't realize the extent of the burden he had been carrying around for the last year. He had been perpetually in limbo, glued to the media coverage of the trial, but not daring to go close to the court house, instead keeping the spectacle at arm's length. He thanked Vaniscovsky again, earnestly, then rose and walked to the door. Vaniscovsky's voice trailed behind him,

"Now, don't forget to stay in touch. Let me know how you are doing. Don't worry, you've got your whole life still ahead of you."

Noah was again tuning him out, his head once again confused – now with relief. He found himself standing at the reception desk again with Alana who was looking up at him intrigued because clients usually didn't stop on the way out, especially when they got good news – it was usually a rushed "thanks again," lost in the wind of escape from trying circumstances. But Noah was in no hurry. He stopped and looked at her, not staring, but enjoying her stunning face and her inquisitiveness.

"Can I buy you dinner tonight?" he asked. The inquiry hung in the air for a moment, and just long enough for Noah to brace himself for rejection.

"Um, no, sorry, I'm not free tonight," she replied. Noah started to turn toward the door, disappointed but not dejected. He was still enjoying a high from the news he received from his attorney, and was starting to utter some comment to the receptionist to excuse himself on his way out when Alana interrupted him.

"But, how about tomorrow?"

Noah stopped. They exchanged smiles, and phone numbers, and Noah left with a wide grin on his face, already planning the night in his head. He was finally looking forward to something again.

- CHAPTER 7 -

The seaside town of Manchester is picturesque in almost every season. The beach and harbor bring fervent activity in the warm months, while the cooler ones see the town return to quiet repose until the warmer seasons arrive once again. In the Gilded Age, Manchester was a resort destination for wealthy residents from Boston and New York, some of whom built large residences, termed "cottages," along the rocky coast punctuated with a half dozen sandy beaches. This wave of vacationers included presidents and other notable people who enjoyed the natural beauty and sporting pastimes offered on Boston's gold coast. In the hundred or so years since that time, Manchester has transitioned into a more understated and close-knit community. The town offers a suburban haven, and while it is still home to a small but industrious commercial fishing and lobstering community, it is defined by beautiful residences and a picturesque downtown splashed with restaurants and shops that skirt an acclaimed beach, removed entirely from the bustle of the city.

Removal was what Noah required after the notoriety of the trial and the shadow of infamy it cast on him and all the other former associates of the former law firm of Markus Stillfield Brice LLP. Like a scarlet letter, the words "dishonest," "criminal," and "conviction" were indelibly associated with his name on the internet, and with so much media coverage, some of which exposed all the names of the lawyers that formerly practiced at the firm, one could not conduct a search for "Noah Ellwood-Walker" without pulling up some news of the case. Personally, Noah recovered from this public disgrace quickly because he knew that he had done nothing wrong. He had known nothing of the schemes and was not a central figure in the firm or at all responsible for its downfall. But the news did not delve that deeply into the causes of the firm's implosion. They did not parse those accountable for its demise from those that were collateral damage. Instead, the press characterized the outcome as the partners being convicted for the criminal activity of *the firm*. Noah had been an employee of that firm and so a cursory review of the news made him guilty by association. Though the news coverage did not bother him personally, he could not get around the fact that Markus Stillfield Brice was permanently inscribed on his resume. There was no good solution for that. He could leave it off his resume, but then how would he explain a three-year gap in his work history? Even if he lied, any employer worth actually considering would conduct a background check and learn of the fate of his former employer.

Despite this impediment, after learning he would not be indicted, Noah began to search and apply for legal positions again after having spent the last year working as a line chef at his old restaurant to make ends meet while he awaited the outcome of the trial. He started big, thinking big firm lawyers would be able to see through the morass of the criminal proceedings that enveloped his old firm and would intuitively know that a young associate could have had no active hand in whatever sinister misdeeds his former bosses may have undertaken. He soon found he was wrong in that assumption.

His first interview was at an international firm with a large Boston office, and he felt it went quite well. He spoke with two partners and an associate and they all seemed nice and sharp, and none of them asked any questions about his prior firm and what had transpired there – ticking all the boxes as far as Noah was concerned. The associate, five years into her time there, was blasé about the big firm life in a way that made Noah miss the security of it all. The young partner was energetic in an inviting way and spoke passionately about his cases and the people working on them, and the senior partner was accomplished but accessible and even had a formidable pro bono practice. All the interviews went on longer than scheduled and Noah left the office upbeat. The human resources person said that they'd be in touch soon and she was, but with a request that they be allowed to conduct a background check. He consented, but in reply got only weeks of silence. Frustrated and with little else to do, he finally reached out and almost immediately got a succinct response.

"Thank you for your inquiry and for following up. While you were an exceptionally qualified candidate, we ultimately decided to go with someone else for this position. We wish you the best with your search and career."

Noah took that to mean a candidate without a federal arrest on his record. Later interviews followed a similar arc, ending in the same denial. In one, at a smaller firm, where the lawyers tend to be brusquer and more forthcoming, an older partner was disconcertingly frank with him.

"Noah," he said, "I like you. You seem like a very good person, and I think you probably had nothing to do with this mess and I'm sure you want to get passed it and leave it all behind you. But, I'm sorry to say that that is going to be very hard for you in this profession and in this day and age. Lawyers do their research, and it's too easy to pull up information about your old firm. The name Markus Stillfield Brice is all over the internet, and yours probably is too. No one is going to want to take a risk on you – that's just the sad truth. Let me give you some advice – it might

32

be time to consider striking out on your own. It might be time to put out a shingle and start your own firm. I'll be honest with you; it will be hard at first. But you'll get a chance to see what you're really made of. You might fall on your face, but that's fine too. You'll learn something about yourself. You're young, now's the time to do it."

Noah brushed this idea off at first, finished the interview, that predictably ended with no offer, and began his trek home once more in defeat. As he walked, his mind reverted automatically to thinking of the firms he had not yet applied to and strategizing how he might tweak his presentation during interviews to get around his past. As he did so he found that the partner's words hung in his mind. At first, they echoed with pangs of frustration as he walked from the office building to a nearby T station. Standing on the subterranean platform waiting for the next train, his initial rejection of the partner's ideas turned to cautious contemplation as he eyed a travel advertisement touting "freedom" in the Caribbean and displaying a broadly smiling couple who Noah thought looked like they worked for themselves. The train arrived with an ear-piercing squeal, and a gust of putrid hot air that blasted the side of his face. The car he climbed into was sparsely populated and he shared it with only a small gaggle of students at the opposite end who chatted loudly amongst themselves as the train pulled away from the station. Noah listened to them passively and caught pieces of a conversation about a roommate that apparently no one could stand, as he continued to weigh the advice he had just received against his preconceived notion of what it meant to be a successful young lawyer. He had always believed that working at a prominent firm after law school was the mark of a lawyer who was going places. The firms hired only the best students, after all. But the conversation he just had was starting to make him question his whole premise of success.

Two stops later the group exited and Noah found himself riding alone. The train came out of the tunnel and crossed a bridge over the Charles River and he took in the view of small sailboats backlit by the afternoon sun and the warm glow of the sun reflecting off the line of brownstones lining Storrow Drive in Boston's Back Bay. Noah continued to turn over the partner's comments in his mind, now more seriously than before. A plan of action was beginning to form in his subconscious. What if he did strike out on his own? Now would certainly be the time.

"It needs to be somewhere outside the city," he was actually talking out loud to himself now. And then his head started to lift with the excitement of a potential new opportunity. In a moment he had made up his mind. He would start his own firm. The partner was right – now or never. By the time he arrived home to his small apartment he had already decided that his new firm would be a small-town general practice one and that he would just take anything that came in the door. He would learn the new law he needed on the fly as he adapted to what local quibbles his clients brought to him. He would think on his feet again. He would rely on his wits again and grind out a living. It would be hard but he was ready for a challenge. That night, he stayed up late researching the various Boston suburbs to determine where he would start a burgeoning practice. He identified Manchester as a town north of the city with relatively few solo practitioners, and he had his destination.

Alana went with him. By the time he made his decision to start anew, she had become a fixture in his life. She was just getting out of a bad relationship when he asked her out and in a way he was too, having spent the better part of a year saddled with uncertainty about his future, and they spent that first dinner complaining to each other about past hardship, and mistakes, and listening to each other. They had another dinner three nights later and then breakfast the following morning and were then together for a trial period. She supported him through his failed job search, and advised him, and comforted him and they began to rely on each other. The move to Manchester was a bigger ask because she had always wanted to live in the city, and had only lived there for a short time when she began seeing Noah, but she went because she was sure she loved him. No one had listened to her nearly as well as Noah did, and she realized that she hadn't ever really loved anyone before.

They found an apartment – two-adjoining rooms with a small bathroom, and a galley kitchen – in the center of Manchester over a vacant storefront that became Noah's law office. It used to be a clothing boutique and when he first saw the space it still had a white washed boxy check-out kiosk and shuttered changing rooms in the back. The checkout kiosk was traded for an enormous dark wood desk that Alana paid too much for at a flea market; the shutters on the changing rooms were removed and filing cabinets replaced the space where customers once tried on their new looks. A scale was stenciled on the glass storefront, bordered on the top and bottom with "Noah J. Walker," and "Attorney at Law," in bold, bronze lettering. They drank champagne at the desk when the renovations were complete, and then, when it was quiet, Noah proposed to her, revealing a simple ring hidden inside a hollowed-out old law book on his desk. He didn't tell her that the ring represented the last of his savings. She kissed him and they were blinded by excitement for the future. They were married shortly after at a small-town hall ceremony amongst friends and family and enjoyed an informal barbeque reception in a park by the Manchester

34

Harbor with a view of the sun dipping into the Atlantic amongst waving sailboat masts. A larger celebration was put off until they had the money for it. Their cost-conscious honeymoon consisted of a string of hikes through the White Mountains in New Hampshire where they camped or stayed overnight in rustic hiker's cabins that they sometimes had to themselves. Upon their return to Manchester, they took long walks during the summer evenings, watching the people and listening to the chorus of peepers that habited the small stream that coursed through downtown. They were happy and fiercely believed in each other and were excited for the next steps in their lives.

And then they waited – and waited. And then a month went by with no clients, and then three. And then they started turning off all the lights at night except for those in the room they were occupying to save money. The bills piled on the table by the door in their apartment grew so high that it could not support its own weight. To avoid it cascading to the floor they created three smaller piles for first notice, second notice and final notice – the first two were never opened and were instead shoveled into a trash can at the end of each week. Noah had suggested that Alana could leave her job in the city so that she did not have to commute each day, having initial confidence that he could provide for them both and that clients would pour through his office's entryway. Alana had volunteered her services to administer the law office and they loved the idea of working together, and seeing each other every day, but if no work materialized, she would soon need to seek a paid position elsewhere. That still would not be enough to keep the lights on.

Noah and Alana were chasing a dream, but the time was coming soon where grasping for it would put them in such a financial hole that it would be difficult to ever get out. With the combination of Noah's law school loans, his unpaid legal bills from his arrest, and the cost-of-living piling on them monthly, the interest alone was enough to guarantee that they would never qualify for a home or car loan in the future. Because they were still young and did not have many responsibilities beyond feeding themselves and trying to pay the most delinquent of their bills, they felt they could chase destiny a bit longer. But they knew that if Noah's work did not pick up – and soon – they would both have to pursue employment that actually paid a reliable wage. Where and how to do that, neither had taken the time to consider. Given even their current rate of spending, they would be out of money in two months.

But then finally a trickle, as small stuff started traipsing through the door here and there. The first was an old widow who wanted to specify a grandchild in her will. She brought Noah freshly baked cookies with her check when the work was complete. Her neighbor needed a purchase and sale agreement drawn up for a new home and Noah did that too. And then the small trickle of engagements began to flow like the small stream that ran behind Noah's office. Like the ocean tide into which the stream flowed, the work rose and fell, but it was never very much. Noah's and Alana's life molded to these ebbs and flows like sand shaped by the tides. During times of plenty, when Noah had a paying client, they would treat themselves to small luxuries, like takeout, or a nice bottle of wine – something more expensive than whatever was in the $5 dollar barrel that week – and Noah would try to chip away at his loans and they would choose which bill to pay. In bust times, all this affluence came to an abrupt halt and austerity measures were adopted again and they ate ramen in the dark until another client walked through the door.

In recent weeks, Noah and Alana found themselves in one of those rare times of plenty. They decided to celebrate by getting pizza and a "fancy" bottle of cabernet. In a game they played, one was tasked with finding food and another with finding drink and with the food responsibility Noah had settled on a joint down the street that had recently opened its doors and was wildly popular with locals. Noah knew that Alana would be occupied for some time getting the wine because she was close with the owner of the bottle shop she preferred and the two would talk and taste at length before settling on the winning candidate. With some time on his hands, Noah decided it was a good time to reflect, and to do it with a drink in his hand. He made the quick walk to the pizza joint, took a seat at the bar and ordered a scotch and a beer to enjoy while weighing the topping options for that evening. The restaurant was busy, with a din like a hungry flight of seagulls perched atop a piling awaiting the day's catch. Noah was flanked by first dates, clear to him by the loud introductory conversations between the couples and the awkward positioning of bodies. He listened for a few moments but then tables opened up and he lost his free entertainment. The seat to his right was quickly filled.

The first thing he noticed about the man was his watch when he laid his wrist lazily on the bar next to Noah. A metallic Rolex. Noah was intrigued enough to gather more information and looked down to see that the man had nice shoes too – leather loafers, the type with a brass bar across the top. Noah had no idea whether they were a designer pair, but they certainly looked expensive. He continued his observations and looked up to see a middle-aged man with crew cut hair and days old graying stubble. He was slightly overweight in the way that suggests an affluent, leisurely lifestyle. He wore a light blue button-down shirt with the sleeves

36

rolled up, and was intently studying the drink list. Then he startled Noah with a direct question.

"Okay, son, what's good here," he said without lifting his head or even perceptibly moving, like he could sense Noah's examination of him.

"Um, sure," stumbled Noah, looking away quickly before answering "well, ah, I'm having the Bruichladdich Port Charlotte – scotch whisky – unpeated – it's pretty good."

The man studied the list again.

"Ok," he answered, signaling the bartender in the same action, "give me two of those Port Charlottes, and keep it open." He flipped a black credit card from his wallet that landed heavily on the wooden bar with a metallic slap. The bartender immediately pulled two glasses, placed them on the bar and poured generously. The man grabbed both, claimed one for himself and slid the other to Noah.

"Oh, thanks, really, but I'm short on time. I'll probably finish mine and head out – plans tonight with my lady. Enjoy this one though," said Noah as politely as possible as he abashedly attempted to slide the drink back to the man.

"You know what I've learned," said the man, at the same time pushing the drink back to its original position before Noah, "you always have more time than you think. Have a drink, tell me about yourself."

Noah thought this was somewhat odd, and direct, and if it had come from someone less put together, he may have been more forceful in his rejection of the offer. But, as it was, Noah did have a little extra time and he did like what he was drinking so he decided to go along for a bit. He finished his first drink and pulled the second refreshment toward him, and then launched into his story – his whole story. That wasn't his intent, but when he started to tell it, it felt good, and soon he couldn't stop. He started with law school and then the offer from Markus Stillfield Brice, and then the saga of things falling apart. The man listened intently, and without interruption, and continued to provide alcohol when necessary. Noah launched next into his present financial turmoil fueled by a slow small-town law practice, his overwhelming law school loans, and the crushing pile of bills that was growing daily. With his tale complete, Noah reached for the freshly poured glass before him and took a long sip while looking wistfully at the multicolored wall of libation displayed brilliantly before him, like Hong Kong at night in the rain.

"Well, that is one hell of a story," said the man, smiling wryly into his glass. Noah noticed the smile and thought it an odd reaction to his sob story but he could not keep hold of the momentary thought as it was quickly lost in his inebriated haze.

"But, chin up Noah," continued the man, "I'm quite sure we can help each other."

That stopped Noah mid-sip and he felt a small jolt of adrenaline brought on by what sounded like a potential opportunity. He began to smile himself as he listened to the man's next words.

"I happen to be in need of a litigator myself, well, actually a colleague is in need of one and I act as an advisor to him. What he needs is a lawyer to file a case for him that is basically for breach of contract, but has a bit of a finance spin to it. From what I'm hearing, I think it's something you could easily handle. I'd be glad to mention your name. No guarantees, but he tends to follow my advice. Is that something you'd be interested in?"

It wasn't really much of a choice for Noah. Faced with a client looking to file what could be a lucrative breach of contract case the answer was clear.

"I would be happy to take on that matter for your colleague," he managed without sounding too excited. The acceptance was welcomed by a firm slap on Noah's back from the man, and a boisterous commendation.

"That's the spirit," said the man too loudly for the small restaurant, causing some of the patrons to turn inquiringly.

Noah sat back after touching his glass with the man's and put down another cool sip of scotch. Then he pulled out his phone to take down the man's name and number and then he saw it – a string of calls, voicemails, and texts from Alana, that increased in their intensity of anger from one to the next and Noah was suddenly panicked and needing to leave. He quickly opened his phone and took the man's name, Duncan Shaw, and number and gave him the reciprocal information and excused himself, throwing a crumble of old bills onto the bar in his wake. In a flash he was out the door and to his apartment. It was only after entering and seeing Alana's fuming countenance that he realized he had forgotten to even order food for them.

***

38

Duncan Shaw watched after Noah as he rushed out, then waited five minutes to leave a generous tip of his own for the bartender before pulling back his chair, rising languidly to his feet and strolling to the restaurant door. He exited and pulled out his phone and stood just outside the restaurant dialing as the keypad washed his face in a sickly blue light.

"Hey, yeah, we just finished," said Shaw in a hushed tone, "yeah – mission accomplished. He bought the whole thing, and no question he'll go for it. I'll contact him first thing tomorrow to keep him on the hook. No, no suspicion I could see from him – he was too drunk to think through it much anyway so we'll have to seal the deal when we meet with him. Okay, speak to you tomorrow."

Shaw slid the phone into his pocket, then took out a cheroot cigar and a lighter and upon igniting it his face was bathed in a flickering of warm tones. He took a long draw, exhaled, and then smiled to himself as he began the short walk to the apartment he had rented directly across from Noah's and Alana's.

- CHAPTER 8 -

Noah woke and almost could not see because of the pain. He hadn't consumed that much alcohol since the night after the bar exam, when it had the same effect the following morning. Initially he was dazed and blissfully unaware of his actions the night before, but then faint memories started filtering in broken pieces to the forefront of his mind like a damaged film strip. Alana was understandably angry when he arrived late and empty handed, and was entitled to the "what the fuck," stance she adopted upon Noah's return to their apartment. Noah's slurred apologies had little effect.

His only defense was to explain himself and the potential work he had found that evening. He attempted time and again to lay out the "huge" opportunity he had stumbled upon but it had no effect on Alana's understandable anger, and after enjoying the last word, she informed Noah that he would be sleeping on the couch that evening. She left it to him to find bedding, knowing that he would not know the first place to look. She then steamed into their bedroom and slammed the door. Noah stood in deafening silence with Alana's anger echoing horribly in his head. Then he heard her sobbing quietly to herself in the bedroom and it was everything he could do not to break through the door and comfort her, but he knew that would only ignite the argument once again and he was able to contain himself and rein in his impulse. He was not surprised that she was upset, but he was surprised at the magnitude of her irritation and wondered if there was something else going on.

He moved to the kitchen and could then hear the shower turn on in their bathroom as he took some bread and peanut butter out of the refrigerator to fashion a makeshift dinner. As he ate, the shower stopped, and he could see the light turn off in the room from under the bedroom door. There was silence again. Their interaction was over for the evening, and Noah lopped slowly back to the living room like an embarrassed puppy. Without any hope of finding a sheet to cover himself, he flopped onto the couch and turned on the first sports he could find – a rerun of a baseball game played earlier that evening. It took him only seconds to pass out.

He awoke to a damp spot on the throw pillow below his face where his drool had collected. He wiped his face and sat up slowly to a room that was quickly spinning around him and the pain of a pounding headache. He barely made it to the sitting position with his head cradled carefully in his hands, but then he smelled something wonderful and peaked up just enough to see wisps of fresh steam playing above a hot mug of coffee sitting on the small table before him. A beauty to behold for any hangover wracked brain. He reached for it aggressively and downed a large gulp before he saw a note also resting on the table. His heart stopped for a moment wondering if the fight the night before had really been so bad to warrant a follow-up writing, but then he read it:

"Your breakfast is ready."

He was relieved and confused, and also suddenly starving. Coffee in hand, he slowly pulled himself up off the couch and steadied himself before continuing down the hallway to their small kitchen. There was a hot pot of coffee waiting to refill his cup when he arrived and also a neatly wrapped wax paper package on the counter containing a breakfast sandwich from their favorite café down the road. Then he saw her sipping coffee by the kitchen window and admiring the tidal stream behind their apartment. She looked beautiful and he wondered to himself what he had done to deserve all this and if last night had been a dream.

"I am so sorry about last night," Noah pleaded, assuming the whole event had not been a concoction of his own imagination.

"It's okay, I'm sorry too, I should not have exploded like that," responded Alana, who stood to hug him. They embraced, as they always did after cooling down from a heated argument, and suddenly everything was okay again. Noah went to refill their coffee cups and then noticed three paint samples in pastel colors neatly lined up on the counter.

"What are these?" Noah asked, still too wracked from the evening's inebriation to internalize any symbology, "are you planning the brighten up the kitchen a bit?"

41

"Well, I thought after you finished your breakfast that we could discuss what color to paint the nursery, or, I guess, the bedroom, which will have to double as the nursery for now. I don't think we can have the baby all the way out in the living room, and definitely not the kitchen…"

Alana continued to ramble, nervous, and unsure of what Noah's reaction would be. Noah was stopped in his tracks.

"Huh?"

She smiled, shyly, "I'm pregnant."

Noah was dumbfounded, but he knew better than to let his face betray it for too long, and it wasn't hard to mask his surprise because his other overwhelming feeling was pure joy. He had never realized it consciously, but the pride he was feeling now felt like it had somehow always been there. He was beyond excited to be a father and his face showed a beaming elatedness. That made Alana happy. Noah swooped her up and kissed her vigorously.

"How far along are you? When are you due? Are you hungry?"

Noah went to the refrigerator before Alana could even answer and grabbed a half-eaten loaf of banana bread that Alana had made the day before. He also reflexively grabbed a bottle of sparkling wine he had stashed so that they could celebrate, but then stopped himself.

"Wait, can you have any of this? Maybe we should just go out for lunch later?" inquired Noah, ashamed again at his own thick-headedness.

She smiled, and he was relieved, "I'll have a sip, but it looks like you need it more than I do."

They both chuckled, and he went for a tool to open the bottle. Suddenly a pang of fear overtook him as he was easing the cork out of the bottle's neck – how in the world was he going to be able to support the baby and Alana without steady income?

Pop!

He was jolted momentarily back to the jubilant moment and poured two glasses, one tall and one short, adding orange juice. He turned back to Alana and consciously hid any concerning thoughts with a broad grin on his face. They toasted and stood together looking wistfully out the kitchen window to the morning light glimmering on the water as it coursed toward the ocean. Alana took his glass to refill it, and he absent-mindedly turned to his phone which he had neglected so far that morning. His intent was to check the weather so that they could dress for a long walk to fully discuss this news. What he saw caused another dose of adrenaline to inject into his bloodstream.

He turned to Alana and said, "I am so sorry, but I have to go. It's that thing I told you about last night. It's really promising and could be the kickstart my practice needs so that I can support us – all of us. You're amazing, all I really want to do is celebrate, maybe I can put them off for a little while…" But Alana, prophetically understanding the situation didn't let him finish his sentence.

"Go," she said, "I understand. You're working to provide for all of us now. I will see you when you get home. But you're going to owe me a leg rub – the first of many. And grab some ice cream while you're out, please."

∗∗∗

He had missed a string of communications from his new acquaintance, Duncan Shaw. They had piled on the screen of his aging phone – first a missed call and voicemail indicator showed up, then scrolling down he saw a text message.

"Please call me. My friend would like to meet this morning."

Noah was startled with the panic of immediate responsibility. He set aside his mimosa and downed a huge cup of coffee too quickly, burning the top of his mouth in the process. He leaped to the shower for a douse of steaming water that promised to open his pores and let the excesses of the night purge from his system. He left the shower in less pain, and considered his wardrobe – a suit and tie would be too formal for this initial meeting, especially given Shaw's appearance the night before. He opted for khakis, a button down

43

with rolled sleeves, and loafers. He spun to the kitchen and embraced Alana grandly once more with a hug and kiss and professed his love and excitement to her again. He then devoured his sandwich in four bites and stepped out the front door while engaging his phone to contact Shaw.

"Good morning, sir!" Shaw greeted him warmly, and it sounded as though he was on the water with wind intermittently obscuring his voice.

"Good morning. Thank you again for the drinks and conversation last night. I got your messages. I'm ready to meet your friend anytime this morning to discuss the opportunity."

"Excellent, my boy, excellent," replied Shaw, and then to some unfortunate deck hand, "hey, trim the sheet will you, Jesus!"

That Shaw was taking the call from a boat legitimized him even further for Noah, who was eager to solidify the initial meeting. He was already dreaming of the lucrative opportunity it might bring.

"Just tell me where to go and when and I'll be there!"

"Excellent, I'll text you the address, it's in the Farms, right next to Manchester, so it won't be too long a drive for you. My friend is very interested in engaging you and wants to meet in an hour. See you then."

"No problem, looking forward to it," said Noah, but Shaw had already hung up. Moments later Noah's phone pinged with the address. Noah was elated and turned his mind to preparation. To say that Noah was rusty in the area of contract law was an understatement. He had touched it only tangentially in his small-town practice and even then for very simple matters, so he took the next half hour to dive into the thick contracts treatise that occupied a forgotten section of shelving in his downstairs office. He sipped coffee at his desk as bright morning sunlight poured in through his expansive storefront windows. He flipped through the pages, stopping to read sections that were relevant, and felt like a real lawyer again. He had always been an ardent note taker and the surface of his desk was soon covered with scrawled thoughts on a dozen yellow sticky-notes – errant thoughts about potentially useful law to be used later on.

His time was up before he knew it. He hadn't gotten to all he wanted to, but knowing he could never be fully prepared, he closed his book and exited his office through a back door that led to the parking lot behind the building. He hopped into his aging Audi A4 that he bought when he felt flush in his first year with Markus Stillfield Brice, and pulled onto Manchester's main drag. It was a hopelessly impractical vehicle given his financial straits, but he had kept it, telling himself that it presented an air of success in first impressions with potential clients. The car hadn't produced any clients for him so far, and had become painfully expensive to keep in working condition, but observing the address Shaw had given him, Noah was glad to be arriving in a luxury car, even a late model one.

Noah's foot was heavy with excitement as he sped along the ocean road and he opened the front windows and moon roof to let the sea air course through the vehicle's interior. The meeting location was one of many sprawling mansions that lined West Beach. Noah knew of the palatial abodes only from the removed perspective of an outsider. His closest look at any of them had been over hedged fence lines while driving by and comprised only distant and fleeting views of gabled roofs and tall chimneys zipping past. Upon arrival at the address he had been given, he pulled through an understated entrance that revealed a flowing lawn split by a crushed shell driveway lined by young silver beech trees. After proceeding slowly up the driveway, he pulled into a courtyard before a grand brick mansion reminiscent of a gothic castle and was immediately struck by the amount of activity on the grounds. People were rushing to and fro across the courtyard like a colony of ants under attack, carrying flowers and trays and furniture. Noah paused to let a couch carried by two of the workers slowly pass in front of him before parking on a grass spit next to the courtyard, as far out of the way as possible. Noah exited the vehicle and surveyed the landscape of scurrying workers trying to figure out where he should enter the building. Then Shaw appeared from a side entrance as if on cue and approached him. Shaw was wearing a suit and Noah now felt woefully underdressed.

"Noah, great to see you again," he said jovially, "welcome. And, nice car – you know what, I think I had the same model ten years ago," Shaw laughed and Noah now felt doubly unprepared, already making plans to sell the Audi the first chance he got.

"Just kidding, just kidding," Shaw continued, "come this way, my friend is very excited to meet you, and please don't mind the hustle around here, the big man's wife has decided to have a cocktail party on short notice and the kind of cocktail parties these folks put on take some serious preparation – and dough." He rolled his eyes in welcoming jest as he ushered Noah into the grand entrance of the building. The level of activity inside matched that of the exterior and the two weaved amongst an army of orderlies into a side room off the main entrance. It was a wood lined office with thick shades drawn across the tall windows causing the room to be very dark despite the brilliant daylight outside. It took a moment for Noah's eyes to adjust, but when they did, he could make out the figure of a man sitting behind a heavy looking wooden desk.

"Noah, meet my good friend Roth Casimir," said Shaw extending his arm toward the man in introduction. The man sitting before Noah was grotesquely large, and each of his individual facial features seemed somehow oversized as well. He extended his arm and Noah's own hand was lost in a handshake that left his fingers crippled.

"Please, sit, Duncan has told me so much about you," said the man in a deep, gravely tone as he beckoned to a plush chair. "Let's get right to the point, Noah. I trust Duncan here and he likes you, and thinks you can do the job. That means I like you and think you're up to the task, understand?"

"Yes, absolutely, and I just wanted to say …," but Noah couldn't finish his thought because the man continued speaking over him in a commanding tone that almost echoed in the wood paneled room.

"Good, I'm glad you're on board, so let me tell you what I need. Noah, my business is taking aggressive positions against large companies and then collecting when those companies don't pay up. In the matter I need your help with, I bought bonds from a large

46

foreign company – one of the largest private companies in Africa – and now they're not paying me what I'm owed so I would like to file suit against them." The man paused long enough that Noah felt compelled to fill the void. He opened his mouth to begin to explain that that was not exactly the type of work he had done at his former firm, or ever, but Casimir bulldozed on without letting Noah utter a word.

"It's really very simple. It's called distressed debt. A private company can sell bonds to whoever is willing to buy them, just like a government can. A bond is just an investment. When I buy a bond from a company, they are committing to pay me some interest on it, and in exchange they get to use my money for the term of the bond. Sud-Coast and Company, the company I bought the bonds from, is refusing to pay the money it owes on the bonds I bought because it's going bankrupt. I need you to file a lawsuit against Sud-Coast and get the payment that's owed to me, with full interest." The man sat there, looking pleased with his explanation. As the silence extended beyond a few seconds, Noah took the opportunity to interject.

"That sounds like a really interesting strategy, but it sounds high risk? How do you know they will even have capital to pay when they are going bankrupt?"

"He speaks," thundered Casimir, "you're right, Duncan, this kid is sharp. Yes, Noah, there's always risk in anything that's worth doing, but I've got a strategy that cannot lose. I've put almost all the pieces in play to guarantee payment, and the last important piece is you Noah, and the lawsuit you will file against Sud-Coast to compel them to pay their debts to me. Can I count on you?"

Silence again reigned in the small dark room. Sensing hesitation, Casimir continued.

"And perhaps Duncan didn't tell you, but we'll be giving you a $100,000 retainer and covering all expenses. That retainer gets refilled when necessary and we'll be paying you twice the hourly rate you charged at your former firm. And trust me, Noah, there will be enough work that you will earn that retainer many times over."

* * *

47

Noah was in a daze driving away from the bustling grounds of the mansion and found himself unconsciously taking the long way home in silence. Half his mind was triumphant – he had secured a client with a case that was likely to take him and Alana out of debt and on the path to financial stability. Perhaps one day they could have a comfortable life after all. But there were also misgivings lurking in his mind about the propriety of the lawsuit he had been asked to file. The premise of the case was deplorable – suing a failing company to squeeze money from them is not what he went to law school for. But he was now going to have to provide for a family, and his small-town practice had so far proved unable to generate sufficient income. Soon he and Alana would be facing an inability to cover their basic living expenses, not to mention those additional costs of getting their space ready to bring a new life into the world. He struggled with these thoughts as he drove absent mindedly along the winding seaside roads. Then he grasped at the memory of something he heard in law school, that every client was entitled to a zealous lawyer to represent them, even those accused of crimes. For some reason, that mantra made this client a little easier to stomach.

He got on the highway and headed north, to Gloucester, driving fast and listening to the rhythmic thuds of the joints in the Annisquam River Bridge under his tires as he crossed into the next town north of Manchester. He then turned off onto local roads and enjoyed a meandering crawl around the Cape Ann coast. Rounding Rockport, he turned back toward the highway and his mind was at ease. He would continue with the representation he had just accepted, but scrupulously make sure everything he was doing was by the book, no matter how much money they were dangling before him. He would then take the money he earned and provide for his family. He had no steady clients and could not afford to be picky about who he took on. No client was ever going to be perfect. He convinced himself that this was typical corporate litigation work, and nothing to be too worried about pursuing. The opportunity had the potential for great monetary upside for his family and for Noah to grow his skillset and become more marketable to the next potential client. Satisfied with his decision, he called Alana to tell her the good news and sped back, buoyed by the promise of some money, and the security of a busy case.

* * *

"Well Duncan, we got him, at least for now. Good job bringing him in – you were right, strike quickly and overload him with opportunity – and money!"

"Yeah, you know, he's a really good kid actually, he just picked the wrong firm, that's all – and he couldn't have known what he was getting into. And I know he's got no idea what he's getting into here. Just kind of too bad, I guess. Maybe we can do something to help him out when it's all over."

"Hey, don't get soft on me Shaw! We knew what we were doing when we hatched this little plan of ours just like we knew what we were doing when we engaged his old firm to do our dirty work on the last scheme. It's not our fault we had to feed them to the feds after they tried to screw us behind our backs. Noah's a part of our scheme now, he just doesn't know it yet. When the time comes, he's either going to embrace it, or we'll get rid of him. That's how we've always done it, and it's proved a flawless business plan thus far."

"Yeah, yeah, I know. I was just saying that he seems like a good kid, that's all. Just wrong place, wrong time for him, I guess."

"Duncan, get over here and have a drink, you're worrying me. C'mon, we should be celebrating, this will be a huge deal for us."

Casimir swiveled in his chair to an oak cabinet and pulled down an expensive whiskey and poured two hefty drinks and the men sat there for a moment, sipping and contemplating what they had put into motion.

"Now, you still have that place across from his office and apartment, right?" asked Casimir.

"Yeah, I've got it, great view of both places and especially the office with its huge picture windows. And I've got a directional microphone trained on the window all day and all night, so I can hear everything that's going on in there."

"Perfect. We've got everything in place. Just keep watching and make sure he stays in line. We can always intervene again if he doesn't do what we ask."

"You got it, boss," said Shaw, standing, "alright, I'm taking the rest of the day on the water, and this is staying with me." He grabbed the bottle of expensive whisky and ambled away.

Casimir sat for a moment, in the darkness where he felt most comfortable, smiling obscenely into the inky void.

– CHAPTER 9 –

Sailing came easy to Shaw, but that wasn't surprising given his upbringing. His father sailed, as did his grandfather, who found he preferred travelling under the power of the wind after two tours of duty in the navy, serving on a collection of destroyers and smaller attack boats. Shaw had grown up on the water learning to sail various types of racing and cruising boats, and became accustomed to the movements of a sailing vessel on choppy seas at a young age, such that the gentle heave of a swell effortlessly lifting a vessel perched atop it was an innately welcome sensation to him. It was sailing – not his grades – that got him into college, where he led the varsity team to three league titles. Upon graduation he had a long sailing resume and a mediocre academic record. He accepted an office job, but it was only six months before he knew that life spent in a cubicle was not the one for him. He made a change, and went to teach history at a prep-school and took the helm of the sailing team. He loved it. After two years, he knew the history curriculum backwards and forwards, and so he could focus his mind on coaching his team. He lived for the afternoons spent on the water racing sailboats. In his spare time, he poured hours into the restoration of a twenty-two-foot wooden sloop that he bought for pennies at a local boat yard where it was scheduled to be dismantled and sold for scrap. He had diverted almost all of his disposable income into replacing rotted planks and filling holes in its hull.

Most of the teachers at his school were young and recently graduated, and all were still full of the collegiate impulse to seek a good time whenever possible. One evening Shaw joined his colleagues as they partied into the night. In an attempt to impress a friend of a friend attending the gathering whom he found beautiful, witty, and probably just out of his league, he did a keg stand too many. She was ultimately not impressed, but in the process of unsuccessfully wooing her with his athletic drinking, Shaw forgot that he had to drive himself home. He couldn't have known about the bombshell sitting next to him when he climbed into the driver seat later that evening. He had driven one of his colleagues to the party, and she had a bag of cocaine in her back pocket. During the ride it had slipped from her pocket and lodged in the gap between the seat and the seat back cushion. She didn't notice it was missing when she got up, and he didn't notice it when he drove away a few hours later.

The blue lights that illuminated behind him and the blast from the cruiser siren ignited a feeling of pure panic that coursed through his body. He knew immediately that he was too intoxicated to drive. His interactions with the officers were a blur but he remembered clearly the moment when one of the officers pulled the bag of white power from his car and the officer's deflating words,

"What do we have here?"

Shaw guessed immediately where the bag had come from, and at the same time knew that no story he told the police would get him out of this predicament. He was the only person in the car with those drugs, so they were as good as his.

The rest of his case was academic. He was arrested, then released on bail and got an attorney whom he saw twice in person – once at his arraignment during which he was told not to utter a word, and again at his plea, his next court appearance where he was counseled to accept responsibility for the charges against him – to plead guilty – in exchange for a light sentence. It was his first offense and the young prosecutor assigned to his case offered probation in exchange for pleading guilty. To Shaw, this seemed like an incredible windfall as he was thrilled not to be facing jail time, but the real fallout of the plea manifested in the days and weeks that followed. The prep school where he worked learned of the conviction and promptly terminated Shaw's employment. This was a huge blow. No more breezy mornings in class and long afternoons of getting paid to sail. Worse still was that with a criminal record he found it impossible to find another teaching job. Without income he had no choice but to sell his project boat, half-finished and at the expense of all the time and money he put into it.

Months passed and he became desperate for work, and he had no choice but to take the first opportunity that presented itself – a handyman at a marina. The owner was a reformed felon himself with a record far longer than Shaw's single misdeed. He was not scared away by a measly DUI and drug possession conviction and so Shaw was given a chance. Over the years, Shaw had acquired extensive skill not only in handling sailboats on the water, but in maintaining them as well, and Shaw was soon promoted to a position working on some of the most expensive yachts at the marina.

In addition to his skill maintaining sailboats, Shaw was also an able conversationalist and made friendships with the owners of the vessels that led to further opportunities. The most lucrative of which was the opportunity to transport the incredible vessels down to the Caribbean for the winter sailing season. The owners would pay handsomely to have their prized possession arrive safety in the warm climes of the islands each year. After a couple years at the marina, Shaw landed his first client. With the help of one of his co-workers, Shaw got the boat down to St. John in one piece, and a few days early after two weeks of calm seas, and free food and wine. The owner was well connected in the yachting community, and word of Shaw's abilities to ferry yachts spread quickly.

That first transport job turned into three the following year, and continued to multiply. Soon he had to hire additional hands and skippers to handle the increasing business, and before he knew it, he was the manager of a steady stream of yacht traffic from New England to the Caribbean. Shaw Transport was born. He spent his winters in the tropics and his summers in Boston and truly felt he had the best of both locations. With his team in place, and growing, and word of his business spreading, he found himself with something he had never had before – free time and steady cash.

***

Poker was his game, or so that's what he told himself. His clients always seemed to be winning huge pots and rubbing elbows with celebrities in the process, and Shaw needed part of that action. Like all addicts, he convinced himself that he was better than he actually was.

He started small with the storefront casinos that dotted the beachfront boardwalks of the tourist centers of the Caribbean. They knew him well at Captain Jack's Poker Parlor in Nassau, and The Palace in Freeport. He also supplemented his poker education with internet gambling, taking longer and longer breaks from his days at Shaw Transport to play "just one more game," at his desk. The business didn't suffer. He had done an excellent job hiring skippers and the logistics were relatively simple.

But he kept losing, and losing big, and to the wrong people. Besides legitimate gambling houses, Shaw also ventured into the

53

world of unsanctioned games thinking his luck might change. It didn't, and he learned quickly that when you owe money to organized crime, they will do whatever it takes to get that money back. He had just been leaving his office late one night after completing the staffing for the next season's transports when two large men approached him as his back was turned locking his office door.

"We're going back inside," said the first, and the second grasped his upper arm in a vice grip and ushered him back to his desk. Shaw sat as the two men stood at the door. Then another man walked into the room. He was shorter than the two thugs and had a large face that looked almost swollen. The man's piercing eyes struck Shaw and made him shudder with fear. After sitting across from Shaw, the man took out a gun. Shaw knew this was the end. He closed his eyes and gripped the arms of his chair and braced himself, but was still alive moments later. When he opened his eyes again the man was talking. The firearm was on the table before him.

"Look, I know you're not a bad guy – some of my friends use your transport service. And I know you're not trying to screw me on purpose. But your addiction has gotten the better of you. You owe me a lot of money, and I can't just let you walk away with it. The underworld is not a forgiving place. If I let every guy with a gambling problem get one over on me, the wolves would come out and tear me apart. I'm feared because everyone knows I'll follow through when someone crosses me."

The man started tapping his gun on Shaw's desk and Shaw started praying silently to himself for the first time in years.

"I asked myself, what do I do with you," the man continued, "I could kill you, but that seems like a waste. You're not inherently bad, you just have a weakness. Besides, if I killed you there is no way you could pay me what I'm owed. I thought about it for the last couple days and have decided that I could use your help."

Shaw started breathing again and listened to the proposal that he had no choice but to accept. Shaw Transport now stewarded a steady stream of yachts down to the Islands each fall, and took them back to their home ports each spring. The second leg of the trip was what interested the man with the gun. At the end of the winter, when the yachts headed home, they were destined for small seaside hamlets most without much of a police presence. There was no

54

process for "checking-in" these boats when they made it back home for the summer – they just pulled up to their moorings like they had never been gone.

"Your clients' yachts are the perfect vehicle to bring my cocaine to the United States. Your business is well known to the authorities by now so I doubt they will ever check your boats. I'll be able to pack lots of product in the large holds of those boats and it can be offloaded at any small port on the eastern seaboard. It's perfect."

"But what about my skippers," managed Shaw, "I don't want to get them wrapped up in this – they've done nothing wrong."

"Don't worry about that. I will provide the men you need, and they will all be comfortable with the cargo they are transporting. All you have to do is continue scheduling the transports. I will take care of the rest."

Shaw's hand was still unsteady when he extended it to shake the man's.

"Don't worry, you're going to enjoy being my business partner. I've never had an unsuccessful venture. We will be in touch," said the man as he stood up to leave with his thugs and started discussing a fishing plan for the following day, "he must be the only guest on the boat, it's the only way we can make it work…"

"Wait, I don't even know your name," Shaw interrupted.

"It's Casimir."

***

Shaw spent the first months in abject terror. Each day he expected the police to break down his door and take him into custody. Then months went by, and things were little changed. Shaw Transport continued to run smoothly. The new crew members supplied by Casimir were all able sailors, and prompt and professional. The business continued to grow.

After six months, Shaw found an envelope in his mailbox containing a stack of $100 bills – his first cut of the profits of the new partnership. He was surprised at how easy it was to take the money, and the subsequent payments, to upgrade his lifestyle. His gambling compulsion had disappeared after having a loaded gun in his face and he began to see more of his mysterious business partner who brought Shaw more and more into the business as time went on. Shaw told himself he had little choice in the matter with the specter of a quick demise if he ever disobeyed Casimir's directions.

If there was a single moment that marked the beginning of his rise within Casimir's organization it was after drinks and cigars on the deck of one of the yachts that was awaiting transport back home. The dispute between Shaw and one of Casimir's thugs began after Shaw struggled momentarily to open a hatch.

"I can call my niece if you think you need a hand with that," was the snide comment from the thug.

"I'll take you any day of the week, you clown," snapped back Shaw without pause. It would have taken a lot less to get the thug going and he was on his feet in a flash and at Shaw's throat a beat later. Casimir let them tussle for a few moments before calling the first round and suggesting a more gentlemanly contest to decide the dispute – an arm-wrestling contest with the loser having to buy dinner for the three of them that night.

The thug saw this as a foregone conclusion and grunted his assent. Shaw was just as quick to reply in the affirmative. What the thug didn't know, and Shaw knew all too well, was the physical strength it took to bring large boats into and out of the harbor, and to turn the winches on them in heavy seas, and to hoist huge sails while underway. The contest was quick and painless for Shaw, and Casimir saw a side of Shaw he didn't realize existed – one of strength and brash confidence in the face of a man twice his size. In that moment Casimir's mind hatched a new career path for Shaw inside his organization.

**

Shaw learned Casimir's businesses one rotation at a time, and his ascent was swift. Casimir's narcotics operation was vertically integrated in that he controlled the production and distribution of his product at every step in the process. Shaw Transport had been an important addition to Casimir's supply chain, but Casimir eventually introduced Shaw to all facets of his business. He started Shaw at the ground floor, running a small marijuana and cocoa farm in the Blue

Mountains of Jamaica. After living in a one room shack for six months in the dripping humidity of the region – and increasing the farm's production by fifty percent – Shaw was promoted to a refinery for cocaine on St. Kitts and Nevis, before later being introduced to Casimir's distribution network, and eventually becoming a top advisor to Casimir as time went on. When the U.S. Drug Enforcement Administration moved to curtail drug smuggling from the islands, Shaw was instrumental in pivoting Casimir's operation on the islands to loan sharking where he set up the most extensive illegitimate loan operation the Caribbean had ever seen. Shaw continued to be paid handsomely for his work and he continued to earn money for Casimir's organization. He poured money into an opulent lifestyle, but a part of him was always reminiscent of his time teaching sailing, and he periodically made large anonymous donations to youth sailing programs throughout the islands.

When local authorities curtailed the loan sharking business, Casimir already had Shaw's next assignment planned. Over cognac one evening, he explained that he had made the acquaintance of a partner in a law firm in Boston who had a plan to make money off of stock trades and related lawsuits. Shaw was on his way back to his hometown to put the scheme into play.

- CHAPTER 10 -

Noah was a subscriber to the religion of work again, and he was astonished at how quickly he fell back into a steady cadence of labor. The morning after his meeting with Casimir, as Noah was enjoying his second cup of coffee and preparing to pour over the relevant statutes governing purchases of bonds from foreign corporations, Shaw surprised him at his storefront office with a heaping box of papers.

"This is what you'll need to get you started, but if you have any questions or need additional documents or things just call or text me – the boss prefers that I be the go between if that's okay with you. Good luck, and keep us posted on progress."

Noah took delivery of the box with open arms, ready to begin work in earnest – he didn't have a chance to ask Shaw how he knew where his office was, but figured he'd found it on the internet and didn't think more of it. He examined the papers ravenously – he hadn't dug into such complicated material since his time at Markus Stillfield Brice, and his mind had been yearning for a challenge. He also immersed himself in the law of bond purchases and the contracts that governed them. He brushed off his corporate finance books, made another strong pot of coffee, and dug in.

Purchasing a bond is basically lending money to a company or a government. The purchaser of the bond pays the issuing entity an amount of money for the bond and the issuer can use that principal for the term of the bond to fund its operations. The term of the bond is a time period set at the time of the purchase and once it expires – once the bond is mature – the issuer must pay back the bond principal to the purchaser, plus interest.

Bonds can be risky, because there is no guarantee they will be paid back. If the institution that issues the bond is in poor financial health and it does not have the capital to pay the principal and interest due once the bond is mature, the purchaser of the bond is out of luck. There are a select few who specifically seek to purchase bonds from financially troubled institutions because the bonds can be bought very cheaply and with massive interest rates. If the bonds pay out at the end of the term, the profit is huge. This strategy comes with enormous risk, however, because in most cases companies struggling enough to sell bonds at huge discounts will never be able to pay on them once the bonds mature. But if you can find the sweet spot – a company selling bonds at bargain prices that will pay out in the end – you stand to win big once the bonds mature. Bond purchasers that pursue this strategy are called "vulture funds."

This was the type of bet Casimir appeared to be making based on Noah's review of the papers. Sud-Coast was in financial straits and in serious risk of going bankrupt. Casimir bought his bonds at the height of Sud-Coast's financial trouble, so he got them at a huge discount and a steep interest rate, but with that cheap purchase price came the risk that the bonds might never be paid off.

Sud-Coast had in fact recently informed Casimir that they could not pay what they owed on the bonds, but Casimir was not accepting that position, and wanted Noah to sue Sud-Coast for full payment on the bonds. Casimir expected that when he pressured Sud-Coast with a lawsuit, they would cave and pay all that they owed. This was beyond a long shot from what Noah could tell – after all, if Sud-Coast was bankrupt, where would they find the money to pay the hefty sum owed to Casimir? Noah didn't have a good answer, but his client had insisted that he sue, and he intended to do what his well-paying client asked him to.

Casimir had bought the bonds through a holding company and Noah filed the lawsuit on its behalf. While Noah had the bond purchase agreement that showed the company's name and address, the box of materials Shaw had given him contained no further information concerning the make-up of that company. He knew this was something Sud-Coast would ask for during the course of the case, and something they were entitled to. And he also knew he should confirm this information for himself. He assumed the principals of the holding company were Casimir and Shaw, but made a note to confirm that information.

Noah drafted up his complaint – the document that would initiate the lawsuit – and filed it in federal court in Boston, and served it himself, the same day, by walking over to a small office Sud-Coast maintained in Boston. Sitting under an oversized Sud-Coast logo just inside the simple office was a young receptionist with her eyes dutifully looking down at a stack of papers she was carefully sifting through.

"Good morning," began Noah, "I hereby serve Sud-Coast, through you, with this complaint for breach of contract filed at the U.S. District Court in Massachusetts, just down the road. What is your name please?"

"Um, good morning, my name is Karla Franz-Bloemfield, but I don't understand, what is this document?" said the receptionist after looking up in surprise.

"Your company is being sued and this is the complaint in that lawsuit."

Noah handed the packet of papers to the confused receptionist who asked to whom she should give the papers. Noah told her that copying the packet and forwarding it to her boss and the company's legal department would be a good start, but could not direct her any further as her employer was now his opponent in a pending lawsuit, and so he turned and left, leaving the still confused receptionist in his wake still staring perplexed at the sheath of legal documents. He returned home and waited for the inevitable nasty letter from Sud-Coast's lawyers.

In federal civil litigation, the party accused of wrongdoing in a complaint has twenty-one days to file an answer, admitting or denying the allegations made against them. It was twenty days before Noah heard anything from Sud-Coast and the response he got was in the form of a surprisingly cordial letter from their lawyer asking for an extension of time to answer the complaint. While Noah had only limited experience interacting with opposing counsel in his time at Markus Stillfield Brice, he had learned that the opposition was only polite when they needed a favor from you. Noah was willing to assent to this request, however, hoping that his leniency would be reciprocated in the future if he ever needed a favor. Before calling opposing counsel to make first contact, he looked up his opponent.

Mike Sledge was a proud double lion, attending Columbia for both undergrad and law school, and taking four years in between to serve in the U.S. Army as a company commander – an aggressive one. His on-line firm profile described him as a "seasoned" litigator. Noah rang the direct dial on the website and got an immediate answer.

"Sledge here," he said abruptly. Noah could hear him typing away absent mindedly on his computer keyboard.

"Hello, my name is Noah Walker, I represent Undertow Acquisitions Group LLC in an action against Sud-Coast and Company and I'm calling about your request for an extension of time to respond to the complaint."

The typing stopped and Noah heard a click as Sledge picked up the receiver taking the call off of speaker phone.

"Pleasure to meet you over the phone and thank you for getting back to me so quickly. Really looking forward to working with you on this case. Have you had a chance to consider my request?" The charm was turned on full. Noah explained that he was amenable to the extension and Sledge was pleased, and thanked him. But then Sledge pivoted, catching Noah slightly off guard.

"Look Noah, let's be real here for a second. Sud-Coast doesn't have the resources to pay all that money your client is looking for on those bonds, and I think you and your client already know that. What Sud-Coast does have is an insurance policy for lawsuits that will provide money for as much litigation as you can handle, and more. Noah, lawyer to lawyer, I can guarantee this client is going to buckle down and go scorched earth on this case – they're not going to pay you a dime or give an inch, they are going to litigate every point and spend any money they have to do so until the bitter end. And then, even if you win, they won't have the money to pay you. You're going to lose here either way, so I say we make a deal right now because my client doesn't want to go through the slog of this litigation unnecessarily. We are willing to settle for the cost of litigation - $2.5 million – what do you say?"

Noah had never heard anyone honestly offer that amount of money to anyone, much less to him and one of his clients, and his palms started to sweat a little when he heard those words. He managed to keep his cool and resist the temptation to accept because he knew Casimir was looking for much more than what was on offer.

"I appreciate the offer, and will take it back to my client, but you and I know that this case is worth ten times that so I don't expect that offer will be accepted."

"Okay, Noah, have it your way, but trust me, that route will only bring you pain and will get you nowhere. Thanks again for the extension," he hung up as abruptly as he had begun the call, but no longer seemed so grateful for the extension. Sledge was just looking for an opportunity to fight. Noah settled in for a battle.

* * *

Shaw chuckled to himself in the dark throughout Noah's conversation with Sledge – he had his directional microphone perfectly trained on Noah's storefront office window and because the call was on speakerphone, he could hear both sides of the conversation. He felt that Noah actually did quite well given that he had never been in charge of a case this large before and was opposite a first class and experienced trial attorney. After the call ended, Shaw took a brief intermission from his constant surveillance to fill his bowl of kettle cooked popcorn – an obsession of his since childhood. Relieved and restocked, he returned to his dark perch inside the lightless room. He settled back into his recliner by the window, donned his headphones, and tuned back in. The sun set over Manchester's harbor and Noah's storefront office lit up like a movie screen for its captive audience of one.

* * *

On the day Sud-Coast filed its answer to Noah's complaint, Noah received another gift – dozens of requests for discovery from Sud-Coast's attorneys. In civil cases like this one, the parties are obligated to collect their own evidence from the opposing party. Sud-Coast asked for everything under the sun – all documents and things related to the lawsuit and Noah's client's purchase of the bonds; all communications related to the matters in the lawsuits and the bonds; every shred of paper related to the lawsuit, the bonds, and Noah's client. Noah knew that many of these requests were overbroad and he would object to them, but there was a category that worried him. One set of requests dealt with Undertow Acquisitions, the company he was representing, and specifically asked for information concerning its make-up and formation. This was not a surprise to Noah as it was a typical request to make by the defendant, but what worried Noah was that he didn't have the information from his client yet, so he sent a quick email to Shaw asking for the corporate formation documents related to Undertow Acquisitions, including information about who founded the company, and who controlled it. All this information was responsive to Sud-Coast's requests, and not something Noah could withhold from them, so he hoped Shaw would respond with the information quickly. That would allow him to answer Sud-Coast's requests, but would also allow him to put his own mind at ease concerning who he was actually representing.

The next weeks were blissful for Noah and Alana. Noah had work to do and was getting paid to do it. He spent his days contentedly buried in legal issues, something he never thought he would get the chance to do again after he was arrested by the FBI. That ordeal was all a faint memory now as he worked away, hour after hour, in pursuit of a result for his client. With no commute, he was still able to end his days at a reasonable hour and make the short trip upstairs to see the lovely Alana, and while away the night together. They had started to allow themselves some of the luxuries of having a steady income and grew accustomed to getting takeout at least twice a week and going out to eat at least once each weekend. They talked together for hours when Noah was not working and were in love with each other unquestioningly. In the mornings, Alana struggled with intense morning sickness and fatigue that often sidelined her for the first half of the day, and made it difficult for her to assist in the office as Noah's paralegal as she had hoped to be able to do. But, by mid-day, Alana would typically be feeling much better and would often come down to the office when Noah needed a break, and she could use the company. They would plan where his future associates might sit, and how the office might be expanded, and where they might travel someday to get away from the long and frigid New England winters.

It was during one of these interludes that Noah got a surprise call from his opponent.

"Ugh! I'm sorry, this is from opposing counsel in the Sud-Coast case. I have to take this."

"I know, don't worry – I understand. I'll see you tonight. Love you." Alana rose, and headed back up to their apartment while Noah girded for a skirmish.

Calls between lawyers always start tranquilly and even cordially and in response to Sledge's mundane first question about the weather Noah reported briefly on the climate in Massachusetts and reciprocated with an inquiry concerning the weather report from Washington, D.C., where Sledge was based. The litigators then turned to the issues at hand.

"Noah, you've given us just about nothing in discovery and we're entitled to all we've asked for, as you know, so if you're going to dawdle any longer, we're just going to have to bring this to the judge and file a motion to compel all the things we've asked for." threatened Sledge.

"You know that's premature," countered Noah, "this is our first conversation on the topic, so you can't threaten to go to the judge now. I haven't even been given a chance to finish my document production, so you don't even know everything you're going to get yet. Just so you know – we are going to produce the information you're looking for, as long as it's reasonably within the scope of our obligations. It's just going to take some time to collect the rest of it."

"Well that's just not reasonable, Noah. You brought this case and you should have had your documents ready when you filed it. You knew these discovery requests were coming – you must have done your research when you filed your complaint, so you must already know the information we're seeking. It is unconscionable, unethical for you not to have. It's high time you coughed up the information we're asking for."

Noah gulped because Sledge was partially right. The extent of his research into the case prior to filing the complaint were the documents in the box he got from Shaw that didn't include corporate formation documents. But that didn't stifle Noah in the moment – he had read the documents he was given, and they were extensive and comprehensive, and he made his own determination that the legal theory proposed by Casimir was sound. He also wasn't going to let himself be pushed around by a blowhard, so he pushed back on Sledge without any misgivings.

"Look, Sledge, your requests are incredibly broad, and you chose to draft them that way. You're going to have to live with that decision. We're going to answer your requests, and we're going to answer them fully as far as we are obligated to, and we're going to produce documents, but it's going to just take some time because you've asked for a lot here. And you can't just go to the judge and declare an impasse on this issue now, and you know it. It's too early and I've told you I'm going to give you what you want, so we have no dispute and the judge will just get upset with your bringing a non-issue to him."

"You have two weeks – you have two weeks Noah and then I am going to move to compel those documents and the court will agree with me. They are vitally important and you should already have these collected and ready to go. You brought this suit and you should have had your ducks in a row when you did."

"I don't know what to tell you," responded Noah, "I'll do my best, but two weeks probably won't be enough time to get all you asked for. You asked for so much, it's not unreasonable that it will take me some time to collect it. You know that, and the judge will agree."

"And that includes all support for any contention that the group action provision doesn't control in this case," continued Sledge undeterred, "because we think that provision preempts your claims and entitles us to summary judgment."

That caught Noah's ear for two reasons. First, the term group action provision was new to him and so he had no idea what effect it could have on the case, which was scary. But second, the mention of summary judgment rung in his ears because that is a potential death nell to any case. In summary judgment, a party asks the court to rule on the case without going to trial. Noah wanted to avoid that at all costs.

"Well, we certainly disagree that you are entitled to summary judgment." Noah extorted.

"I can't say that I'm surprised to hear that. We look forward to your discovery."

"Hey Sledge, we need to talk about the documents you owe me." followed Noah, but it was too late, Sledge had already hung up.

"What a jerk!" Noah yelled to himself in a fit of anger. He went to dial Sledge's number to continue the conversation before realizing that another call would only lead to another frustrating waste of time. Noah could accomplish everything he wanted to with a letter to Sledge, in which he would weave biting rhetoric to rival Sledge's and memorialize his points for later use in motions practice. Before writing that letter, he dialed Shaw's cell phone to ask about the corporate formation papers for Undertow Acquisitions. He knew he would need to produce them and he also wanted to know precisely who was running the company. The phone rang to voicemail and Noah left a message. He was sure that Shaw was off on the water somewhere, having much more fun than he was.

***

The ring of Shaw's phone echoed in the one room apartment across from Noah's office where Shaw sat perched next to the window observing Noah's every move. He was again impressed by how Noah handled Sledge, but some of Sledge's requests had made him uncomfortable – the request for background information concerning the corporate formation of Undertow Acquisitions was especially troubling. Shaw could see Noah rising from his desk and could tell he was about to take his morning coffee break to a nearby café. In the beginning of his surveillance, Shaw had followed Noah on these mid-morning jaunts, just to get a sense of Noah's schedule and what he did throughout the day. But, following Noah all the time, everywhere, would be risky because Noah knew what Shaw looked like and Manchester was a small, quiet town where tailing someone on foot without being seen was difficult to do even once. Shaw staid put, filled his popcorn bowl, and took the time to update his boss.

"Well, we're never going to give them that," was Casimir's response to Shaw's report, "the judge is going to have to rip that information out of my hands because we're not giving it up. You know as well as I do that it's the key to this whole endeavor. Hell, if Noah knows what's in there, he'll quit before he even has a chance to produce it in discovery."

"I know, I know, I'm just telling you what happened on the call. Don't worry, Noah's not getting that information from me. He's a bit of a pit bull, so he's going to keep asking us for it, but we'll keep it from him until it's too late."

"Ok, good, now give me the report from Netwanye. I've been waiting to hear about that all morning."

"Well, those pictures we sent anonymously to the Cape Town Gazette have had the intended effect. The head of finance for Sud-Coast has been completely disgraced and is on his heels, professionally and legally. He tried to deny everything at first, but when it became clear that wouldn't work with the press, his bosses, or the police, he ran. No one has seen him in a month. Whether he surfaces again at this point doesn't really matter for our purposes – he's never going to work for Sud-Coast again."

"Perfect. So where does that put Netwanye in the pecking order?"

"He has been promoted to head of finance at Sud-Coast, just as we predicted – we're set, we can't lose now!"

"Excellent, Duncan! Netwanye will make sure that Sud-Coast pays, the only thing that could mess this up now is Noah, and that means you can't watch him too carefully."

67

"I know boss, will do. Hey, I want to talk to you about what happens to Noah when this is all over. He's a good kid. If he plays by the rules and doesn't cross us or try to go to the Feds or anything after we reveal the whole scheme to him, I don't see any need to kill him and his wife. He's a lot like me when you first found me. I didn't know anything, and I was in trouble, but once you set me straight, I was a great asset to you. I think Noah could be the same way. When the time is right to reveal the plan to him – if he cooperates – I want to keep him alive and make him part of our organization. There's been too much killing over the years, Casimir, we're close to our retirement and it's time to stop."

There was a long silence on the line, then Casimir broke it, "Duncan, I know you like the kid, but it's too dangerous to let him hang around after this is over — he's seen both our faces and has enough documents and information to sink us now. He's married and has a kid coming and there's no way he'll buy into all this and join us – even if he said he wanted to, I wouldn't believe it. Sooner or later, he would go to the feds to protect his family and both of us would be put away for life. Once the case is over, and we get our money, we have to get rid of him and his wife – based on your excellent surveillance of Noah's office and apartment, we already know that he has told her pieces of what he is doing for us, and there's no question that he's told her a lot more than we've been able to listen in on. This is the big one for us. We'll retire off this one and we can't leave any loose ends."

"Boss, I've been loyal to you for many years, but I don't think I can take any more innocent lives. I had no problem feeding those partners to the feds, they were already corrupt when we started working with them. But Noah and his wife, and their future kid, are completely innocent in this and there's no reason we have to slaughter them. Let's just find another lawyer – a corrupt one – to take this on. Then we can cut Noah loose. He hardly knows who we are anyway, so there's no risk – not yet."

"Look, Duncan, I know you have a soft spot for this kid, and you are incredibly valuable to this organization. But there's no way we could find another lawyer on such short notice and be sure, like we are with Noah, that we can control him and that he won't ask too many questions. It's just impossible at this point. This scheme is just too important to us – and not just me and you, I mean my bosses too. I have people to answer to as well, bad people even by our standards, and I can't just pull out of something like this. I'll be dead in a day. Don't let your emotions get the better of you – this is not something we're doing on a whim. This is business – life or death business."

Noah's plight put in stark relief the regret Shaw had about the criminal path he had travelled down – the regrets had been buried deep and not allowed to see the light of day, but were now flooding into the forefront of his mind like a revengeful, neglected child. Suddenly Shaw had no filter. He exploded.

"This whole thing stinks, Casimir, and you know it. I can't just take three innocent lives and destroy them. I will not do it. If we can't work together on this to find some other flunky attorney who will take on the case, and take the fall, then I'm going to have to take matters into my own hands – I'm not going to let three innocent lives get eviscerated so you can make a little more dough and buy another couple properties around the world. It ends here."

Silence on the line again, but this time followed by a comforting tone that strained unnaturally out of Casimir, "Okay, Duncan, okay, you've made your point. I can see that you are passionate about this one, and about this boy and his family, for whatever reason. Look, I don't want to fight you, I want to talk this through with you – we are partners after all, and we've been doing this together for a long time. But I want you to think this through as well. I respect your opinions, but making the drastic move that you suggest at this point puts all of us in danger. Please, just take a couple days to think about it – go out on your boat, get some fresh air, get away from people, and think about what you really want – and then let's meet, and we can make a decision.

Another pause was filled with a grumbled, "okay, boss, let's talk in a few days," and the line went silent as Shaw ended the call abruptly.

***

One of Shaw's first purchases with the money he made smuggling cocaine for Casimir was a yacht. It was a decommissioned Corsair 45, once used by the navy to teach their officers how to sail. The boat had beautiful lines, and an imposing profile. It could be sailed single-handed, and also comfortably fit eight. While it was a large boat, it was also fast and with enough heft and ballast to handle the roughest of seas. He had the hull painted a deep mahogany and had custom crimson sails sewn, making it one of the most unique boats in the islands. Shaw made a tradition of sailing from the Caribbean to Boston each year, by himself, to take stock and assure himself that his sailing skills were still sharp and instincts still tuned. In the summer, he kept his prize moored off West Beach – close enough to the beach and its rocky cove so that he could swim out to the boat on fair days and slip away for hours of sailing around picturesque Great Misery and Bakers and beyond, often going far enough to the east so that he could feel the ocean swells effortlessly lifting the hull and enjoy the natural detachment that came with it. Sometimes he would go away for days at a time and anchor in favorite spots in the evenings and cook himself dinner, and look at the stars and think. That is precisely what he planned to do after his conversation with Casimir because he was angry after the call and blinded with pent up rage. He planned his trip hastily and took little notice of the weather – forecasting a gale in the coming days – or of the rundown pick-up truck with out of state plates parked in the West Beach lot that afternoon.

He took some canned food with him, and something to drink, and swam his gear out to his boat in a dry bag strapped to his shoulder. The frigid water that engulfed his body on the swim cooled his rage, and when he pulled himself onto the boat and toweled off in searing direct sun that warmed and rejuvenated his muscles, he felt at home again and distracted in anticipation of a couple days away. His mind was so focused elsewhere, that he didn't immediately notice some things out of place on the boat. The screw-pin that battened down the forward hatch was loose, and there were wet spots on the deck around the hatch leading to the front of the boat where one could easily climb aboard using the mooring line to hoist up over the rail. The mooring line was also dripping with water, which was unusual on such a hot and sunny day. Shaw didn't notice any of

70

this. Beyond unlocking the door to the cabin and throwing his bag down onto the padded bench in the interior, he conducted no examination of the boat. He wouldn't go into the cabin until he was ready to make dinner in the small galley that evening. After motoring away from the mooring, Shaw raised the mainsail and sailed away into the distance.

***

Coast Guard Report No. 56034

Location: Latitude 42.557, Longitude -70.768 (.5 kilometers due south west of Manchester Harbor, Manchester, MA)

Reporting: Ensign Roberts; Ensign Rodriguez; Commander Flox

Vessel: U.S.C.G. Medium Response Boat, "Perseverance"

Weather: Small craft advisory in effect. Gale warning in effect in preceding 24 hours.

Narrative: On 25 July, 08:15 hours, the above listed crew were on routine patrol returning to Gloucester Station from a patrol to Salem Harbor when an approximately 45 foot sail boat with brown hull and red sails was seen near the rocky coast to the south west of Manchester Harbor. Upon approaching the vessel, it was determined that the vessel had hung up on submerged rocks near the coast. The vessel was also listing slightly to starboard.

At the direction of Commander Flox, Ensign Roberts brought the response boat to within twenty-five meters of the suspect vessel for a closer inspection, but could not come up along-side because of numerous submerged rocks in the area. Commander Flox attempted to raise the crew of the vessel via radio transmission over the usual channels without response. Commander Flox then attempted to raise the crew of the vessel via the response boat's megaphone without response. Commander Flox then radioed for a back-up response boat and ordered that Ensign Rodriguez gear-up and swim to the boat for a well-being check and investigation of the seaworthiness of the vessel.

Ensign Roberts swam to the vessel at 08:32 hours, and was able to climb aboard the aft of the vessel that was situated furthest from the rocks. At about this time, small response boat "Intrepid" arrived on scene with Lieutenant Williams and Ensign Scott on board.

Ensign Roberts entered the cabin of the vessel at 08:37 hours after a search of the cockpit and forward deck revealed no occupants. Ensign Roberts swept the interior of the cabin from approximately 08:37 until 08:50 during which time he found no individuals on board. A duffel bag was found within the cabin of the vessel containing various clothing items, a flashlight, a VHF radio, and a wallet with identification for Duncan Shaw. The stove in the vessel's galley was found to be in the "On" position, and the gas cannister was found to be empty. Ensign Roberts observed a soot mark on the wall behind the camp-stove suggesting that it had run for an extended period of time. A number of items were found on the floor of the cabin including various charts, eating utensils, and flatware. The running lights of the vessel were also found to be in the "On" position. The vessel was neither anchored nor moored at the time of inspection.

Ensign Roberts collected registration information from the interior of the vessel that indicated that the vessel is named "Aggressive Nature," and is registered to Duncan Shaw out of Tortola, British Virgin Islands. Upon exiting the cabin Ensign Roberts observed a small collection of what appeared to be dried blood droplets on the cushion of the starboard side bench in the aft of the cockpit. There was no additional blood on the fiber glass back of the seat and on the outside of the hull opposite this location. Rain and high seas in the area over the past 24 hours likely washed away any additional dried blood on these fiberglass surfaces.

Ensign Roberts was met at the aft of the vessel by the small response boat Intrepid that was able to safely come alongside the vessel because of its smaller size and draft. Ensign Roberts transferred the particulars found within the vessel to the crew of the Intrepid who returned to Gloucester station to provide these materials to law enforcement. Ensign Roberts returned to the Perseverance, and the Perseverance and its crew stayed on site until a tow vessel arrived to remove the subject vessel from the rocks and provide a tow to Beverly Harbor.

This incident is considered suspicious due to the presence of blood in the aft of the vessel, the lack of persons on the vessel, the location of the vessel, as well as the state of the interior of the vessel. A copy of this report has been submitted to the Beverly and Manchester Police Departments with a request to follow up with regard to the abandoned vessel and to ascertain the location of Duncan Shaw. The request to the Beverly and Manchester Police Departments to search for Duncan Shaw includes a request to conduct searches of the islands in the vicinity of the location where the abandoned vessel was found, including Misery Island and Baker's Island.

Duncan Shaw's current status is "missing at sea."

- CHAPTER 11 -

It had been weeks since Noah texted and called Shaw repeatedly asking for the corporate documents related to Undertow Acquisitions but he had received no response at all – not even an acknowledgment that the communications had been received. This was unusual, but he wasn't overly worried. Noah told himself that Casimir and Shaw were busy people, and that this case was likely one of many business ventures they were pursuing and maybe not even the most important.

Noah distracted himself with his work on the case, of which there was plenty. He had recently received Sud-Coast's gargantuan production of documents. They were sent to his office in hard copy, rather than electronically – as was the standard practice – and the two dozen boxes in which the documents arrived occupied most of the floor space in Noah's office. The boxes were accompanied by a letter from Sledge indicating that these were all the relevant documents in Sud-Coast's possession. Before long, loose papers were scattered around the office, many with highlighting or with colored tabs, and Noah's office was divided into the area for the relevant documents and the pile of documents that were of no importance to the case and which Sledge had provided likely only to add more work for his opponent. Noah would often look up from his work to see confused and pitying looks on the faces of passers-by viewing the mayhem in his office, and he considered keeping the blinds drawn at all times so that he could maintain the image of an organized and professionally run firm.

The next communication from Sledge came indirectly and only a few days later on a Friday afternoon and was announced by a loud ping from Noah's computer, announcing that Noah had a new email in his inbox. Noah looked up from a pile of papers with weary eyes and saw that the email was an automatically generated notice from the court that a pleading had been filed in his case. He immediately dropped the thick ledger he was examining and moved to the screen on his desk. He opened the email and two words immediately jumped off the screen – "summary judgment." Noah remembered that Sledge had threatened a motion but didn't expect it so soon as this type of dispositive motion usually came much later in the case. He quickly opened the document and reviewed the pleading and its exhibits by quickly scrolling through them using the click wheel on his computer mouse and skimming the documents' contents as he went. The thrust of the motion was that Undertow Acquisitions was precluded from recovering the entire value of the bonds because the majority of the other owners of Sud-Coast's bonds had offered Sud-Coast a deal to pay off the bonds at a significant discount after Sud-Coast announced its bankruptcy. The deal with the other bond holders was based on the group action provision in Sud-Coast's standard bond purchase agreement that Sledge had mentioned in his first call with Noah. That provision was buried deep in the thick legalese of the agreement and Sud-Coast argued that based on its language, Undertow Acquisitions had to take a lower payout on the bonds, because a majority of the other bond holders had already agreed to do so as a result of the bankruptcy. Noah could feel his heartrate increase as he read through the motion, because none of it seemed unreasonable, or incorrect. Once he had finished a quick first read and thumbed through the exhibits, he knew he was in for a long night trying to figure out how to oppose the motion. He wearily called Alana to cancel their dinner plans, and then made a cup of coffee in the machine he had purchased for his office. He gritted his teeth, bid adieu to the weekend, and dug into the material.

He woke with a start the next morning to find his head laying on a stack of heavily marked up papers on his desk with one side of his face flattened from the pressure of resting on them. When he picked his head up, he could just make out in the reflection on the blank computer screen an impression of pen ink on his check from the document he had used as a pillow. He reached for the coffee he had been sipping, but it had long since gone tepid. Rising to get himself a fresh cup, his final thought of the night shot back into the forefront of his mind.

"We're going to lose this motion," he said to himself.

It was one of the best written and most tightly reasoned pieces of legal writing he had ever read and far better than anything he had come across in law school or working at Markus Stillfield Brice. The argument tied perfectly with the evidence that supported it. The centerpiece of the motion was a discussion of the settlement agreements Sud-Coast had reached with other bond holders who had all accepted the same lower payout that Sud-Coast was asking Undertow to accept. In fact, over ninety percent of other bond holders had accepted this deal and the motion argued that because that threshold had been surpassed, Undertow had no choice but to accept Sud-Coast's offer. The motion even cited another case where the bond holder pressed for full repayment on the bonds, as Undertow was, and then lost on summary judgement and was forced by the court to take an even lower payout than originally offered.

The case was now at a crossroads, and Noah knew he needed to speak with Shaw and perhaps Casimir as well, to relay this news and get their take on next steps given the strength of the motion. He texted and called Shaw again with the urgent request that he please call as soon as possible. Again, he received no immediate response. For the next two days he continued to wait for any communication in response to his repeated requests for a meeting, and spent the time pouring through the relevant law on the issue, trying to find some silver bullet to defeat the motion. He all but neglected Alana, spending only a few hours in bed each night before jumping back into his research. When he still hadn't received a response a week later, he began to get very nervous. His response to the summary judgment motion was due in two weeks and without his client's consent, he couldn't file anything. If he didn't file anything he would surely lose, and also risk a mal-practice suit. On the eighth day of silence he was in a panic. While pacing across his office in the irons of indecision, a new idea occurred to him. Why not go directly to Casimir. He didn't have contact information for Casimir, but he had the next best thing – his address. He could simply drive down the road and get his answer – it was that simple. Buoyed by this thought, Noah hopped into his Audi and tore down the road to the Farms.

When Noah pulled through the gates and down the drive into the pavilion before the grand home, he was surprised to see a similar scene of flurried activity on the grounds. Staff were flitting here and there again, with flowers and furniture and other festive accoutrements. He parked, but with no one to greet him this time he made his own way to the front door and stepped inside. He wasn't exactly sure where to start without a guide and none of the staff members seemed to notice him in their rush, so he continued walking deeper into the immaculate home and entered into a grand ballroom with high ceilings and sweeping views of the beach and ocean at the back of the property and of a low island sitting just about a mile off shore.

"These people sure throw a lot of lavish parties," he thought to himself. Then he saw someone with a clip board who was giving directions to some of the staff. She appeared to wield some level of authority, so he approached her first.

"Excuse me, I'm Noah Ellwood-Walker, I was wondering if Mr. Casimir is in?"

The woman returned a look of confusion, "sorry, who are you looking for?" Her mind was still visibly lost in her responsibilities, so he clarified.

"Mr. Casimir, he owns this place. It's his party you're getting ready for."

Focusing on Noah completely now, she responded directly to his question, "no, I'm sorry, these are preparations for the Cunningham wedding, I'm the wedding planner. This building is owned by the college. They rent it out as an event space."

Noah stumbled a bit when these words registered with him and he slipped into momentary shock.

"Um, wait, how long has the college owned it? They must have just purchased it, right? said Noah, as he started to feel lightheaded with unease.

"I don't know for sure, but I can tell you that I've been doing weddings here for over ten years, so they must have owned it for at least that long."

He managed to say, "oh, thank you," as the wedding planner hurriedly walked away and started pointing across the room and yelling directions at someone concerning the placement of an ice sculpture. Noah stood there for a moment staring out a long bank of windows onto the ocean beyond, as he realized that the whole meeting with Casimir had been a charade. Casimir didn't live there and his wife hadn't been planning a cocktail party. It had all been a farce.

"But why?" thought Noah to himself in a daze now as he walked back toward the entrance, "what could they be hiding?"

On his way back to the front door he peeked into the private study where he had met with Casimir and Shaw, and he saw that the room now had a photo booth in it and a bucket of costumes for that evening's wedding guests to create entertaining pictures. He was dumbstruck and wandered slowly out the front door of the building, wondering what exactly he had gotten himself – and Alana – into.

He found himself back at his desk without remembering how he got there, and staring at his email inbox on his screen he saw three missed calls and two nasty emails from Sledge, demanding his discovery and also that Noah concede the motion.

Noah couldn't face Sledge now, especially with the shock he had just suffered and his realization about his client and the case, so he went upstairs and enlisted Alana to join him on a walk to town. He didn't have the courage to reveal to her yet what he had just uncovered, and explained instead that he just needed to clear his head before getting back to his work on the summary judgment motion. Noah and Alana walked past the many storefronts, and she talked and he listened, trying to focus on anything but the case.

"I just can believe that in a few months we'll be strolling a baby down this sidewalk. Oh, that reminds me, we should finalize our registry and decide on stroller options. Maybe we can do that tonight." mused Alana as they walked slowly down toward the harbor.

It was peaceful just walking and Noah was just beginning to let himself detach for a moment, when something caught his eye. They were just passing a travel agency that had a new display in their window with a model of a Boeing 747 passenger jet with

"South African Airways" emblazoned on the side. He stared at it blankly for a moment before an idea burst from his mind. Sud-Coast's main office was in Cape Town, South Africa – why not go there and settle the case. That way he could avoid the sure loss on the motion for summary judgement, and also recoup something for his client, and at the same time avoid any plausible claim of malpractice. His client was not responding to him, so he had no choice but to take matters into his own hands. By settling, he would get his client at least something, and at the same time get himself out of this case, and end his relationship with his dubious clients and whatever misdeed they were actually pursuing with this litigation.

His mind was made up. He would tell Sledge to convene a settlement conference at Sud-Coast's offices in Cape Town. He would fly there and would not leave until they had struck a deal that would avoid a total defeat, accomplish the best he could for his client, and end the case once and for all.

***

Casimir pulled a handkerchief across his perspiring brow. While he'd made a comfortable living off of his criminal activities, his passion was farming. He took time each year to work side-by-side with his seasonal staff harvesting the vines by hand. Each man and woman working the fields wielded a small curved harvesting knife that made it possible to quickly sever heaping grape bunches from the vines and fill the large tubs used to transport the grapes to the farmhouse. After harvest, the grapes would be crushed and fermented to create a robust pinotage that was popular with the diners at the local restaurants to which it was sold. With the success of his latest scheme, Casimir could retire to winemaking and relished that thought. He wasn't remorseful about making money at the expense of others – many had done the same thing and he was comfortable with his path to wealth. The decision to eliminate Shaw had been a very difficult one for him, though, and it weighed on him and was something he was still coming to terms with. They had worked together for years and he felt responsible for him in a way. But the man had crossed him, and challenged his authority, and put him in danger. Casimir worked in a world of thugs, and to control that raw aggression he had to portray strength, always. Letting Noah

79

off would be the beginning of his own downfall and he could not let that happen. If Shaw was going to take matters into his own hands, the only answer was to eliminate him. It was him or Shaw, and Casimir had every intention of surviving for years to come.

He stood up after bending low to grab a bunch of grapes swollen with a season's worth of growth and held his lower back for a moment looking into the distant hills lit by a setting sun. His final scheme would soon be complete and he could retire to a quieter way of life. In time he would forget about Shaw entirely.

***

Noah boarded a plane that resembled the model he had seen in the travel agent's window. He still had plenty left in his retainer and used some of it to pay for a business class seat so that he could have some space to stretch out and to think. He knew almost nothing about Cape Town except that it was his flight's final destination and that he had a small room reserved. Sledge had been overjoyed to hear that Noah would participate in settlement talks and insisted that the meetings be held at the Admiral Hawlsey Hotel, a grand property in the center of the city. A complimentary champagne in hand, Noah sat back and tried to forget about his predicament. After a short taxi, Noah's flight was lined up for take-off. The press of acceleration pushed Noah into his seat and calmed him and he drifted into a slumber as the aircraft climbed into the clear evening sky.

– CHAPTER 12 –

Asthma and nearsightedness gave Special Agent Eve Rust a bookish demeanor as a child. She lived in the library where she read voraciously and became well known to the librarians who eventually lifted all restrictions on the number of books she could take out at a time. The library later hired her part time to work at the front desk, which gave her the ability to check out her own books – as many books as she could read, as often as she wanted.

Time was Eve's friend. By high school the asthma had resolved and her glasses were replaced with contact lenses. She developed good endurance and joined the cross-country team. She grew long and sinewy, and attracted the attention of boys and enjoyed the excitement of flirtations. She also continued to excel in academics and her combination of talents left her with a bevy of higher education institutions offering scholarships. She decided to stay close to home for college, not wanting to leave the rolling hills of western Massachusetts or move far away from her parents. Hutchins College was conveniently just down the road from her family home, and she got in early, with a spot on the cross-country team. The transition to college was seamless and Eve enjoyed the ability to see her parents as often as she wanted to, but to also have her own space in her dorm. She fit in perfectly with her new team and was a favorite amongst the freshman class in her first year. She had her sights set on a career in investigative journalism after college.

It was the spring of her sophomore year when the tragedy struck. The news reached her via a telephone call from her sobbing mother on a Saturday afternoon just after Eve had returned to her dorm following a successful meet. The crying was so extreme that at first it was hard to get any narrative explanation, but Eve was eventually able to gather that her father had been in a boating accident in the British Virgin Islands, where he travelled for extended periods multiple times a year for his business. He was swimming to the ladder on the back of the boat when someone hit the ignition and the instant vortex from the spinning propeller sucked his legs into the sharp, powerful blades. He was rushed to the hospital, but it was too late. He died amid a team of doctors and nurses who were frantically trying to stem his bleeding and provide enough blood by transfusion to stabilize the patient. He had lost an enormous amount of blood in the initial injury and because the wound was so large and had continued to bleed in transport to the hospital in the ill-equipped ambulance, there was little the team could realistically do to save Eve's father in the end. When the doctors went to notify the next of kin of his death, they found no one waiting in the hospital lobby to claim him. The ambulance drivers had not taken anyone's name in their haste, leaving the authorities few leads with which to ascertain who he had been boating with that day.

They scattered his ashes along the family's favorite hiking trail and a memorial service was held and Eve and her mother grieved with family and friends. It would take time to come to terms with this immeasurable loss – that is what everybody kept telling them. Eve and her mother would take it slow and let time do what it could to heal their deep pain. They tried to return to their daily lives as much as possible while time took its course, but it was difficult to fully begin to grieve with the outstanding questions concerning who had been with her father on the boat that day, and why they had never come forward.

It was two weeks later when Eve answered a call from her mother and for the second time was greeted with a panicked and breathless voice.

"They came out of nowhere; they shoved some paper in my face at the front door and just came in and started going through our things. I don't know what to do. I need your help."

"Mom, what are you talking about, I can't understand you, tell me what is going on. Who is 'they?'"

"The FBI, the FBI is here, please, I need your help."

Eve altered her course immediately and went straight to her car and then directly home. What she saw at her house was like something out of a movie. There were a bevy of vehicles on the street in front of their home in what was normally a quiet neighborhood. The medley of law enforcement automobiles ran the gamut from police cruiser to black SUV. There were even a couple parked on the lawn with a dozen uniformed police officers milling about around them in an ostentatious show of force that turned the small, quiet corner of the world into what resembled a major crime scene.

She went right up to the police line across the walkway to her mother's front door and a uniformed officer approached preparing to shoo her away. Her mother was standing with arms crossed on the porch, and saw her and rushed over.

"This is my daughter! You have to let her through!" her mother pleaded.

Eve pushed past the officer and leaped onto the porch. She hugged her mother and tried to console her the best she could. They waited together in silence as federal agents ransacked her childhood home and watched as a procession of agents carried out boxes of papers and any computer they could find. When the collection was complete, the agents left unceremoniously and Eve escorted her mother into their home to begin to pick up the pieces, again.

One of the first things they found was a thick warrant on the kitchen table. That evening, Eve dove into the dense legal instrument, and learned quickly that the United States government did not think too highly of her father's business dealings. In fact, they thought he and his business partners were completely crooked and that they were making millions off of an alleged Ponzi scheme and hiding the profits in off-shore tax havens in the British Virgin Islands. The warrant also suggested that her father's death was suspicious, that the individuals on the boat that day may have been hired by one or more of her father's illicit business partners. The document also suggested that her father may have been a smaller player in the Ponzi scheme and may have been assassinated to keep his mouth shut. The government did not identify any of the individuals who were with Eve's father that day or the leader of the plot in which her father was implicated who may have ordered his murder.

Eve could not sleep for weeks after the raid. Her father had been slain by an unidentified criminal still apparently on the loose and the authorities were doing nothing about it. She knew her beloved father could not knowingly have been involved in the fraudulent scheme described in the warrant. There had to be some explanation and something had to be done to clear his name and to bring the person responsible to justice. But what could she do – she was just a college student. She first tried calling the local authorities in the British Virgin Islands long distance to see if she could learn anything, but, on each try, the phone was answered by an island constable who professed no knowledge of the incident and promptly put Eve on hold indefinitely. When she called the U.S. Consulate on Tortola she was also put on hold, but only briefly before a young sounding consular officer answered. After exchanging introductions, the consular officer swiftly attempted to placate Eve.

"Ms. Rust, I can assure you that we are doing everything we can to investigate your father's death, but it is an ongoing investigation and I can't comment beyond that."

"You have to give me more than that, please, this was clearly no accident. You need to find the person responsible."

"Thank you, Ms. Rust, we know this is important to you, but the consulate has dozens of situations it deals with daily relating to American citizen issues on the islands. We are doing the best we can with your father's case in cooperation with the local authorities, but that is all I can tell you. Have a nice day."

Eve was shocked at the abruptness with which the call ended and was again without any sense of what to do next. It was the next day before she realized what she had to do. She was walking past the student center on her way to her dorm when, out of habit, she glanced up at a message board on the outside wall of the building where flyers were posted for a variety of student activities. The one that caught her eye was an offer for an all-inclusive spring break trip and in a moment the pieces aligned in her mind like a magnetized puzzle. She told her mother that she just needed to get away and think and have a break from all the stress brought on by her father's death and the raid on their home. She said that she was going to

California to visit friends at school out there for a few days for her spring break, and that night she booked a trip to the British Virgin Islands. The following morning, she packed a small suitcase, went to the bank and withdrew as much cash as the ATM would allow, and made the three-hour drive to Boston to catch her flight out of Logan International Airport. It was difficult to leave her mother alone, and to do so on such short notice and to lie about her destination and the reason for her trip, but her thirst for answers compelled her to go to the place of her father's death and find answers for herself. If her mother knew Eve's plan, she would have never let her go.

After arriving on Tortola, Eve checked into a cheap motel in Road Town with a view of a parking lot and two sickly palm trees where she dropped her things on the tile floor of her room and immediately headed back out into town, bringing the cash she had withdrawn with her. She pushed through crowds of drunk and jubilant spring breakers spilling out of a string of pubs on the ground floor of a block of pastel-colored buildings lining the main road leading to the waterfront. It struck her how different her intentions were than those of the throngs of carefree revelers.

It was early afternoon when she reached the waterfront, and things were busy. The long dock stretching away from the downtown was a frenzy of movement as the early morning charters had just returned and the customers were happily disembarking from their vessels, while the crews were busy cleaning and restocking for the next shift of customers to arrive for the afternoon cruise. Eve removed a laminated picture of her father she had prepared before the trip and started to make her rounds. She knew her father often stayed in Road Town on his trips to the British Virgin Islands and she assumed his boat must have left from this very dock and that someone might recognize him and be able to tell her more – anything in addition to what the authorities were willing to share. She started approaching men on the dock tending to their boats and simply showing them her father's picture and asking if they had seen him before. Eve was completely ignored on her first few attempts, but when she started dangling a twenty-dollar bill next to the photograph the workers started to respond eagerly. But, of the twenty men who examined the photograph on the dock, none could remember her father. When she returned to her motel room, disappointed, there was a note on the door.

"Ms. Rust, please come to the U.S. consulate building on Waterfront Drive this afternoon, at your convenience."

Eve left immediately for the consulate building near Government House on Waterfront Drive. She checked in at the front desk and then waited on a small couch before a floor to ceiling window in the lobby of the 1970s era building in which the consulate was housed. As she was glancing over the covers of a pile of outdated government publications strewn across a coffee table under a tropical frond plant, she was approached by a man in a light grey suit with a lanyard around his neck with an ID card dangling from it.

"Good afternoon, Ms. Rust, I'm consular officer Max Davis, we spoke on the telephone a few days ago, please come with me."

He opened a door behind the reception desk with a key card and showed Eve through it down a short, well-lit hallway with a large window at the end, and into a small office with a number and Mr. Davis' name by the door on a placard. He showed her a chair opposite his desk. After she sat, he politely addressed her.

"Now, Ms. Rust, I really do wish that you had listened to me when we spoke a few days ago. It is not safe down here for a civilian to be doing their own investigations into a potentially suspicious death."

"What do you mean 'potentially?' My father was killed, you can at least admit that. Then you can tell me what you are doing about it."

"Ms. Rust, as I explained, it's an ongoing investigation and I cannot comment on it."

"That is ridiculous. I am family. At least tell me what you've uncovered so far." Eve was irate and now almost yelling at him.

"Look, all I can tell you is what you saw in the warrant. I can't comment on an ongoing investigation. That's the end of it. Sorry. Now please, don't come down here to try to investigate this

86

on your own again. These are dangerous people and you're going to get yourself in real trouble, or worse. Just leave this to the professionals."

As Officer Davis was finishing this remark, a Marine in a full blue dress uniform appeared at the door and Officer Davis explained that the Marine would escort Eve back to her motel room, and then to the air filed where she was booked on a government transport back to Boston.

"Enjoy the free ride," were Officer Davis' parting words, as Eve was escorted out of the office.

Eve knew the government wasn't going to put any further effort into investigating her father's case. On the plane later that evening, battling insomnia again and in a moment of clarity while peering out the window onto the dark sea punctuated by moonlight 30,000 feet below, Eve's future became clear to her. The only way she could leverage the investigative power of the government to pursue her father's killer was to become a part of it. She relished the excitement of the investigation she had conducted thus far, and being a federal investigator was a career similar to her initial ambitions entering school and one that would enthrall her, but importantly also allow her to uncover the information she needed concerning her father's case. She would become an FBI special agent herself, and she would seek out her father's killer, and bring that person to justice.

***

The FBI's Boston field office had never been well known as a financial crimes juggernaut. Special Agent Moody was hell bent on changing that. Eve was one of many new hires with the specific purpose of improving the financial investigation muscle of the Boston office, and the investigation of Markus Stillfield Brice was the first case she worked on in the new financial crimes task force under Agent Moody's direction. She had requested the post specifically because she knew the Boston field office was the office that would have investigated her father's case and would give her the best opportunity to pick up where the FBI had left off years ago.

The Markus Stillfield Brice investigation had unexpectedly fallen into the lap of the new task force. The FBI had received an anonymous tip advising them to "take a look at the cases filed by Markus Stillfield Brice. The firm is manipulating the market with its lawsuits to gain from the demise of its targets."

That was about as good a tip as you could hope for and the financial crimes task force worked day and night running it to ground. Eve was assigned to review the firm's communications with its clients concerning product liability cases. At first it seemed like a monotonous task – the review of thousands of emails, many having nothing to do with the investigation. It was hours of nose to the computer screen, bottomless coffee mug work in her small cubicle that boasted a six-lane highway as its view.

Before long, though, she made a breakthrough. Eve noticed that in the communications between Markus Stillfield Brice and their clients, it was the partners that appeared to be running the client and dictating its actions, like no client actually existed. In these communications, it was the partners that directed cases to be filed and then withdrawn shortly thereafter. This was truly suspicious.

Agent Moody was prone to deep entrenchment in his office behind large, teetering stacks of papers and binders, perpetually at grave risk of falling victim to a paper avalanche. Eve marched into that perilous mountain pass at approximately 9:00 p.m. on a Tuesday night after the team had all taken a break for dinner. Eve cleared her throat when she entered the office and he perked up.

"Yes, Eve, come in, what is it?"

"If you have a minute, Chief, I have something to show you that seemed odd to me."

"Yes, yes, come on in – just let me finish my thought here," and Agent Moody turned to his computer and spent another five minutes putting the finishing touches on a memorandum, while Eve sat in patient silence. Agent Moody had committed his life to the Bureau and the commendations on the wall evidenced that. Along with them were framed pictures showing him shaking hands with various politicians. He kept his office doused with bright light at all hours where he could be reliably found crunching the data to take down titanic financial fraudsters. When he was done typing, Agent Moody turned back to Eve, and with a sweeping gesture, moved an amalgam of papers from the center of his desk.

Eve placed her neatly bound report in the cleared void and proceeded to explain the odd phenomenon she had encountered in the communications. He listened intently, only grunting at times to show that he understood a point she was trying to make or the relevance of a document. Then, as if struck with an important thought, he yelled, "Stop!" and the room fell silent for a split second before he got up, grabbed Eve's presentation, and moved briskly to the door.

"Follow me, please," he instructed.

He was already out the door and walking fast down the hall to the "war room" – the windowless conference room where the core documents for the case were kept and where a majority of the team was often congregated sorting through documentary evidence or discussing the case. Bursting through the door, he caused everyone in the room to stop what they were doing and watch him intently as he attacked a pile of boxes in the corner. He threw most of them out of the way before he got to an overflowing banker's box buried at the bottom of the pile. He slammed it on the table, tore open the top, and took out an overstuffed folder from which he grabbed a handful of papers and spread them on the table. He started moving individual papers around the rest, like he was assembling a puzzle. The gathered junior agents on his team just watched, entranced and hoping to learn from his legendary methods. He stopped suddenly once the sheets were lined up, stood up straight, and exclaimed,

"Okay, folks, we've got ourselves a case here."

– CHAPTER 13 –

The "Short on Law" investigation had been thrilling for Eve. She played a major role in bringing down the partners of Markus Stillfield Brice. She had helped right a significant wrong, and felt fulfilled because of it. Her contributions to the case were also noticed by her superiors, and she had since been assigned to a number of other high-profile investigations being conducted by the financial crimes task force in Boston. All her new cases were busy, and each moment of each day was committed to pursuing justice through one or another of her growing number of assignments. She was thrilled with the fast pace of her work and of the challenges it presented.

Though her assignments pulled her in many directions and kept her working at a furious pace, there remained something buried deep in her mind – a nagging thought about the "Short on Law" investigation. While there was no doubt that the partners of Markus Stillfield Brice had been instrumental in the scheme underlying the case, and that they were guilty of the crimes for which they had been convicted, Eve always felt that there was something bigger behind the scheme – someone. A hidden hand that had directed the conspiracy from the shadows, and had thus far evaded scrutiny. The parallels between her father's case – now a cold case for many years – and the "Short on Law" scheme were also apparent to her and the more she considered the similarities, the more she convinced herself that there was a connection between the two cases. In both cases there was an un-apprehended co-conspirator that may have been the leader and organizer of the whole plot. In both cases, that individual left so small a trail that he or she could not be investigated sufficiently to bring a criminal case, or even be identified. The FBI was not aware of anyone being assassinated as part of the "Short on Law" case, but there was no question that the partners that eventually went to prison for their crimes were under great pressure from an outside entity, and feared that person so much that none of them dared to name him or her and strike a deal for themselves that might have avoided a federal prison sentence. The nature of the crimes – the modus operandi – was also strikingly similar. Both frauds centered on complex financial schemes that surreptitiously stole money from many unsuspecting individuals and funneled it to the members of a small group running the operation. Whoever the unnamed leader of these plots was, he or she was able to isolate him or herself by working only with that small group of co-conspirators at the top of the plot. Whoever that person was, it was someone who was omnipresent and yet leaving little trace. While she didn't yet have any proof, something in Eve's gut told her that the two plots were related by the individual that put both in motion. She had convinced herself that it was that same individual who had killed her father.

This conviction drove Eve to dig deeper into the case and she repeatedly expressed this concern about a hidden individual pulling the strings in the "Short on Law" case to the special agent in charge based on evidence that came to light during the investigation – without mentioning the connection with her father's case, about which she had never spoken to anyone at the FBI after she began working there as a special agent – but the evidence was never enough to catch the attention of Agent Moody. He was focused on gathering enough evidence to allow the United States Attorney's Office to initiate prosecutions, and once he felt like the team had met that threshold and transferred the information to the U.S. Attorney's Office, the investigation slowed. Once the partners were indicted, any calls for further investigation fell completely into the background. After the resounding victory at trial, the team members were promptly given new assignments on other cases and Eve's demands for further inquiry into the "Short on Law" scheme were completely lost in the transition and never acted upon by her superiors.

But Eve did not forget them. The thought that something was missed in the "Short on Law" case – that she had missed something – stuck in Eve's head. It bothered her for months until she finally decided to take action herself. From that moment, whenever she had a break in her work on her other cases, she blocked off time in her schedule, called back the boxes of case documents and evidence from storage, grabbed a large cup of coffee, and went to work sifting through the evidence in search of any clue that would generate a new lead pointing to the true mastermind behind the scheme. She had done this three times over the course of months with nothing to show for her efforts, but was determined to go back to the well once more for a last deep dive into the material before putting the case to bed for good.

One loose end the investigation never tied up were numerous cryptic emails from a numbered email account – "17341@1734.com" – to the partners of Markus Stillfield Brice. Eve and her colleagues had never been able to tie the email account to an individual, but knew whomever sent the emails had significant involvement in the scheme because the contents of the emails contained incriminating directions concerning when to file the fraudulent lawsuits:

"Be ready to file on my signal, we just need to close the deal first."

"The short has been executed – file the suit."

"Time to withdraw, we've made all that we're going to."

When the domain was traced, it bounced off a number of servers around the world before revealing an origin in Eastern Europe. That was essentially a dead end, as that part of the world housed an intricate tangle of criminal syndicates and the FBI generally reserved wading into it for matters of national security. Whoever housed the server was likely an illicit front, one of many in that corner of the world hired to obscure the source of illegal internet activity.

Eve and her colleagues also couldn't shed any light on the origin of the email address from the partners of Markus Stillfield Brice, because they each refused to cooperate with the FBI during the investigation. Even though the evidence against the partners was strong and they all knew they would likely get prison time if found guilty, they didn't once come close to talking. That told Eve and her colleagues that whoever was really in charge of the operation was deeply feared by the partners.

Eve started by reading the text of all the relevant emails again to see if anything had been missed in them, but after three

92

hours of reading and re-reading, nothing new jumped out at her. Then, she looked at the background files that had been prepared on each of the partners and each of the other lawyers at the firm, hoping that there would be some connection to a prior co-worker, a schoolmate, a family member – anything that would direct her down a new path and shed new light on this missing link at the heart of the case. But after thumbing through endless online profiles, college face book pages, and extensive organizational charts showing webs of each individual's close contacts, nothing was clicking. Now six hours had passed and she felt like she was spinning her wheels.

It was time for a break and for more coffee, this time from somewhere other than the office coffee machine. She could already feel the acrid government coffee starting to burn a hole in her stomach lining. She was on auto-pilot as she took the elevator down to the first floor and walked outside just as a commuter rail train whizzed quickly by on the tracks that abutted the FBI field office and the locomotive's horn emanated one long, piercing blast as the powerful machine crossed the road before her. After waiting for the railroad crossing gates to lift, she crossed the road to a local café frequented by weary FBI agents. Her daze continued as she stood in line, passively listening to the conversation of the two customers ahead of her.

"Yeah, it was just annoying because I had prepared for the call all morning and then it got cancelled at the last minute because they clearly didn't check the meeting invite before accepting so didn't see the conflict," said the tall pinstripe suit in front of her.

"That's definitely happened to me before – people just do not check the time zones when accepting meeting invites, so when you are working with people overseas, arranging meetings almost always gets screwed up the first couple times you do it because you're right – people just are not paying attention," replied a tan suit with no tie.

Something struck Eve and she forgot about her coffee and ducked out of the café and quickly back up to her office.

***

93

She cleared the conference room table and again took out the critical emails. She then took a yellow highlighter and highlighted the time stamps of when the emails giving the directions for the illicit scheme were sent. When she had highlighted all the time stamps and laid the communications out on the table in front of her, the documents confirmed the connection she had made in her mind while in line at the café – all the responses to these emails by the partners of Markus Stillfield Brice were from six hours earlier than the time when the email had been sent. This could mean only one thing – that the individual that she believed was leading the criminal plot was pulling the strings from the time zone six hours ahead of Boston's.

Eve went out to the bullpen – the open collection of cubicles occupying the center of the floor where the special agents' desks were tightly packed together like lobster pots stacked for the winter – where a large world map hung on the wall just above the coffee machine. She stopped herself from automatically filling her cup with the government issued sludge, and instead focused on the map and saw quickly that the time zone she was looking for was GT+2, which covered much of Central and Eastern Europe and also large swaths of Africa. It was a step in the right direction, but she was still far from pinpointing a location, or even a hemisphere.

She took her findings back to the conference room and sat to think again. Her eyes wandered back to the documents before her, and she started paging through them one by one again – reading each word. Another two hours passed, and many of her colleagues had left for the day, when she noticed a second overlooked clue. It was in one of the rare exchanges between the thieves where topics other than the procedures of the crime were discussed. In this particular email, the suspected mastermind discussed the seasons:

"Sorry for the slow response – I'm outside of the city on summer holiday – yes, you are cleared to withdraw the case now."

On its own this message was innocuous, but what struck Eve now was the date of the email – January 15. How could the mastermind be on summer break in January? Then it hit her – the suspect was in the southern hemisphere. She raced back to the map,

94

and examined it while this time absent mindedly filling her coffee cup. The southern hemisphere in this time zone meant only one thing – Africa. She had narrowed her search to half a continent – eight sub-Saharan African nations. She had coffee now, but she didn't need the caffeine – she was on the type of adrenaline high you can only get chasing down criminals and she rushed back to the conference room to get more of the same rush.

Back in the room the papers spun through her fingers like a money counter counting hundred-dollar bills seized in a massive drug bust. She could feel she was close to something big now. First, she looked at the FBI's schedule of international internet outages, pulled from a database kept by the Central Intelligence Agency and made available to the intelligence community. She tried to disqualify certain of the countries on her list by seeing if emails were sent during time periods when that country's internet was down, but none of the emails were sent during those periods so it was a dead end. Next, she pulled out her laptop and examined all the attachments to the emails the FBI had seized pursuant to search warrants to see if the metadata on any of them contained some fragment that would suggest a single sub-Saharan African country, but the eye-watering review of lines and lines of data in spreadsheets revealed nothing she didn't already know. She had hit another roadblock and felt she was losing momentum. She could feel the fatigue coming on. It was 3 A.M.

She walked out of the conference room and to the windows of the bullpen that faced the highway and stared mindlessly for a few moments at the solitary cars zipping by, wondering where they were all headed. Then she thought about on how many occasions suspects being investigated by the FBI's Boston field office must have actually driven past the office on the highway, blissfully unaware of a coming indictment. She suddenly became aware of a ravenous hunger and reviewed her very limited options which were a choice between the vending machine, and the vending machine. At the machine, she chose an energy bar after weighing the unenviable options, and dug into her pocket for change. She was disappointed to pull out only British pounds left over from a recent trip to London on assignment for a different case, and plumbed her pocket again hoping to unearth some American currency when a final thought struck her.

   In some of the emails there were large numbers referenced that she and her colleagues assumed were payments related to the scheme, but they could never prove that because they never found the end accounts into which the money was deposited. They didn't need that information to get the indictments and convictions against the partners, so they never pursued it further. The odd thing about the amounts was that they were not in round numbers, but were instead always a string of seemingly random numbers. That was unusual for a periodic payment for services, even between criminals. But a new explanation had just occurred to her – what if those numbers were a conversion from a foreign currency? The exchange rate could easily turn a round number like 10,000 into a jumbled mess of random digits. She rushed back to her conference room, and again dug through the pile of emails and found two examples of these numbers within the messages. Using an internet search, she was able to find the exchange rate to dollars for the currency of each of the countries within the time zone in sub-Saharan Africa at the time the emails were sent. She plugged each into a spreadsheet that would automatically calculate the value in dollars based on the exchange rates once the numbers from the emails were also inputted. She typed the subject payment amounts as fast as her fingers could move and as fast as she was done the result was clear. While the Ghanaian Cedi and Nigerian Naira were both close, only one currency made both numbers she tested round – the South African Rand. She was at once elated and exhausted. It was 4:30 A.M. on Saturday, and she could hardly keep her eyes open. She took all the relevant papers, put them in a large folder and brought it out to her desk in the bullpen. She then went back to the conference room, packed up the rest of the material, and shut the lights and headed home to catch a couple hours of sleep before having to report to a stake out later that morning. She would write up a full report in the coming days and get it to Agent Moody as quickly as possible. She just hoped it would be enough to re-open the investigation, and give her a chance to pursue the true mastermind behind the scheme.

– CHAPTER 14 –

Noah awoke to the sound of a woman's voice and realized that he had fallen asleep with his headphones on in the comfortable business class seat, and a pre-recorded message was playing on the small screen before him. He looked around and saw that flight attendants were waking all the passengers in preparation for the aircraft's arrival, and he realized the voice he was hearing was a welcome message describing the plane's destination. While he took a moment to wake up, he listened passively to the beautifully accented voice.

"Cape Town is nestled between the tumultuous South Atlantic Ocean and the foot hills of Table Mountain – a flat topped rock face towering over the "Mother City," as Cape Town is known. Cape Town was settled by the East India Company in the seventeenth century and is one of South Africa's three capitals, along with Pretoria and Bloemfontein. It was also South Africa's largest city for decades before Johannesburg took over that title. Cape Town is still recognized as South Africa's cultural hub and boasts beautiful suburbs, a national park skirting Table Mountain, botanical gardens, and delicious restaurants with gorgeous sea views. Each year, hundreds of thousands of tourists are drawn here from all corners of the globe to taste Cape Town's exquisite cuisine, to experience the local culture, and to view the exotic locales that are only a short drive from the city center. Cape Town is also home to South Africa's Houses of Parliament, which are flanked by the pristine Company Gardens boasting rare tropical flowering plants that surround the parliamentary building that houses South Africa's governing body. Perched just up the hill from Parliament is The Admiral Hawlsey Hotel, a beautiful sprawling property, with sweeping views of the harbor and ..."

Noah lifted off the head phones at the mention of the Admiral Hawlsey Hotel. It was the location where the settlement talks were to take place, and its mention reminded him of where he was and the task at hand. His flight landed late in the evening and he called Alana to tell her he had made it and she wished him good luck on the following day's conference. Noah hadn't yet relayed to her his experience trying to find Casimir and his realization that he had been misled by his mysterious client and that he was now unsure about the real purpose of the litigation. With a baby on the way, he didn't want to worry her any more than was necessary and concluded that the best thing for him to do was deal with this situation quickly, and be done with it for good. He was confident that he would be out of this case soon through settlement and he would then tell her the whole story over dinner once he returned home. She would be furious that he had kept her in the dark regarding his revelations about the case, and his new concerns about his client, but he hoped that ending the litigation and being through with whatever his client was up to would allow him to provide a silver lining when he explained the whole situation to her – a happy ending he could tell her that would assuage her anger and lead to a discussion of what they would do next.

He hailed a taxi after collecting his baggage from a carousel, and enjoyed the ride into Cape Town on a raised highway from which he could observe the shimmering magnificence of the city at night. He crashed onto his bed the moment he entered his room in a small hotel on Roeland Street near the Admiral Hawlsey for a few more hours sleep before the next day's main event.

His settlement strategy was very simple – his first offer would be for about half the amount due on the bonds at their par value – $50 million. He knew that would be rejected, but hoped that it might prompt Sud-Coast and Sledge to come up from the paltry $2.5 million they had originally offered. Noah knew he had to get out of the lawsuit today, so he was willing to go as low as $2.5 million, but still felt it was his obligation to get as much out of the settlement as possible.

He rose early the following day to a view of the glimmering sunlit sea in the distance outside his hotel room window, and traipsed down to the cafe on the ground floor of his hotel. There were a handful of young locals quietly occupying low tables in the café typing away on the laptops sitting before them. Noah approached the counter and considered the menu written in bright pastels in a swirling font on a large blackboard above the front counter.

"What can I get for you this morning?" asked the young woman behind the counter who had a collection of intricately braided hair, flowing down her back.

"I need some strong, dark coffee please, and, well, what do you recommend for a first timer to South Africa?"

"Lekker! Welcome to Cape Town. Well, I'd have to recommend the Protea Special – bacon, egg, and cheese on thick rye toast and a half-grilled pomegranate muffin."

"That sounds perfect."

"Doesn't it! I'll bring it to you. Please, take a seat and relax."

That was a welcoming thought to Noah, and he found an unoccupied booth with a view of the busy street outside through the large glass storefront window. He was extremely relieved with the thought of the lawsuit ending. With a settlement inked, he could sever ties with his client and move on from this representation. There was still a small part of him that was disappointed that this case was coming to a close. It was by far the biggest case he had ever been in charge of, and now it was going to be over before it really even got started. There had been no depositions, no expert reports, and no trial. He hadn't even gotten the chance to respond to the motion for summary judgement. The litigator in him wanted to keep going at all costs, to fight Sledge on every point of law, and take the case to trial. But the summary judgment motion was strong, and even if Noah's case survived the motion, he would have a difficult time winning at trial given the facts set forth in the motion. He would have other cases. His career was still young, and he would have other opportunities to show his litigation chops and be the winning trial attorney he had dreamt of. Unfortunately, a retreat to settlement was his best strategic move in this case.

He returned to his room, showered and dressed, and descended to Roeland street for the short walk up the hill to the Admiral Hawlsey on an unseasonably hot morning. It was less than a quarter mile to the gates of the grand hotel, but Noah's brow was sopped with sweat by the time he reached the entrance. Inside, the air was frigid thanks to a powerful air conditioning system cranked to maximum power, and Noah stood just inside for a moment enjoying the relief it provided. He watched a flurry of activity as porters, maids, the concierge, and various other members of the hotel staff flitted here and there, each eager to serve the large volumes of guests that patronized the hotel. Just listening to the varied languages used by the staff and guests circling around him was striking, and he enjoyed a spectrum of tongues from Afrikaans, to English, French, and Xhosa with its characteristic click syllables.

Noah next set about finding the room where the conference was to take place and climbed a grand staircase in the middle of the entrance rotunda in search of it. The activity upstairs was slightly less and Noah circulated the floor looking for the "Treaty Room," the aptly named space reserved for the conference. The walls on the floor were hung with oversized portraits of past leaders of the country and other notables, and he was admiring one of the massive portraits when he felt a tap on his shoulder and turned quickly to see a man wearing a navy-blue suit, white shirt and dark tie. The man's eager eyes fixated on Noah.

"You must come with me quickly," the man exclaimed in an urgent tone as he extended one arm behind Noah and extended the other in the direction they were to travel. Noah was reluctant to move, as he did not know the man or where he was taking him, so he resisted and stood in place.

"Come, come, please, this way," said the man, even more urgently.

"For what," replied Noah, "who are you?"

"For the case. Please, come with me."

Now Noah understood. This man was leading him to the location of the settlement conference, so he went along at the man's direction. They passed numerous conference room entrances and then turned down a side corridor, and then down another into a hallway lined with guest room doors. Noah was surprised to be led away from the group of conference rooms but thought that perhaps the Treaty Room was in another part of the hotel and that this man was saving him the trouble of locating it himself. Without warning, the man diverted Noah into one of the guestroom doors, quickly following and closing the door behind them.

The room was small and dark, but was opulently adorned with expensive fixtures. The man beckoned Noah to a chair at a small desk. Noah had no idea what he was doing in this room, but the man clearly knew about the settlement talks and so Noah figured he'd at least hear what he had to say. Noah's eyes settled on the man, who sat down opposite him and who was now smiling calmly, as if relieved.

"I am Netwanye," the man said grandly, "have they told you about me?"

Noah didn't know what to say, so he answered honestly.

"No, I don't know who you are and no one has told me about you. Can you please tell me why you've brought me here – the settlement conference is supposed to start very soon, and I don't want to be late."

"I understand completely. I'm sorry this is all coming as a surprise to you, but you must listen to me. You are not meant to settle this case. We have a guaranteed way to win it."

Noah was now thoroughly confused and frustrated. He looked the man up and down while searching for the appropriate response and in the process, he noticed something on the man's lapel. It was a blue pin that said "Sud-Coast." Now all was clear to him – the man had mistaken Noah for one of the many lawyers for Sud-Coast also in the hotel that day. He wanted to discuss Sud-Coast's settlement prospects, but Noah could not do that with this man. The ethical rules prevented him from discussing the case with any Sud-Coast employee unless Sud-Coast's lawyers were present. Noah knew he needed to immediately end the conversation and leave. While rising from the chair, he started to explain that he did not represent Sud-Coast, and that the man should go to Sud-Coast's lawyers if he wanted to discuss the case. But the man was quickly out of his seat and to the door behind Noah to block him. The quickness of this move made Noah even more uneasy and convinced him that he needed to get out of the room immediately. Noah put his hands on the man's shoulders and tried to push past him, but the man's next words stopped him dead in his tracks.

"Please, stop, listen to me, Casimir does not want this case settled!"

Noah's hands instantly dropped from Netwanye's shoulders and he stood there with a confused look, trying to figure out how this man could possibly know that name. To this point in the litigation, he had not disclosed that name to anyone. Technically, Casimir wasn't even his client – his client was Undertow Acquisitions.

"How do you know that name?" asked Noah dumbfoundedly.

"Please, we don't have time for questions now – you're correct that the conference is about to begin and you should not be late. All you need to know is that I am the head of finance for Sud-Coast and you are not to settle this case. We're close to a massive payout and all you need to do is keep the case going a bit longer. Settling now will destroy any chance of that. If you settle, we lose everything, and Casimir will not be happy."

Noah was livid now with his own confusion.

"How do you know Casimir? How do you know what he wants out of this case?"

"My god, did he not tell you? We are all working together, Casimir, you and I. I can guarantee that Sud-Coast pays the full price on the bonds because I am in charge of the company's finances. By filing your lawsuit, you have given me the perfect excuse to hand millions over to you and we will all split the profits. It's simple. We can't lose."

Noah had never fainted, but now he felt like he was going to. He had tunnel vision and everything in the room became blurry except for Netwanye's grinning face.

"I can explain more later, but we must go now. Please know that the directions from Casimir are to not settle this case. You must keep this case going so that we can get the payout that I will provide. I don't know why you came, but you are here, so you must attend the conference today so you do not arouse suspicion, but you must not settle this case. You have no authority to do so. All will be explained to you later, but now there is no time to waste. Let's get this meeting over with. Come with me."

As if in the haze of a dream, Noah rose with Netwanye and followed him from the room back into the halls of the hotel. A cold sweat poured down his back as he remained hopelessly stunned by the circumstances. When they reached the doors of the Treaty Room, Noah looked to his side and saw that Netwanye had disappeared at some point along the way – gone as quickly as he had interrupted Noah's morning and completely blown apart his world.

Noah was alone and lost. Then Sledge strolled in, as if on cue.

"Hello, you must be Noah Walker, good morning!" he approached gregariously and shook Noah's hand but when he got a look at Noah's face he laughed and exclaimed,

"Wow, you look a little green around the gills. Was there something in the water this morning?"

Noah, still in a daze, managed a weak defensive remark.

"Ah, yes, just a bit of a slow start this morning with the jet lag."

"No worries, we have coffee for you, bud, and plenty of other treats. They've put out a great spread for us here, and even have some local fruits and juices and stuff like that. They do a great job at the Admiral Hawlsey. Help yourself. We're all set up in there, but take your time, we're in no rush."

Noah glanced over Sledge's shoulder through the open door to the conference room and saw Netwanye already sitting with coffee and breakfast before him, smiling and joking with some colleagues. Noah was still completely in a daze and stared silently into the room forgetting Sledge's presence.

"Well, I'll see you in a minute, no rush though."

Sledge moved away and left Noah before the ample spread of food. He was not hungry but his mouth was arid, so he reached for a cup of black coffee and steadied himself for a moment. His situation was impossible.

He had just been informed for the first time that he was abetting a financial fraud. The fraud he was apparently helping to commit was being perpetrated by the person who hired him together with a representative of his opponent. He could not report the crime. His obligations of confidentiality to his client kept him from telling Sledge or anyone else about it. And he certainly couldn't go to the police – he was in a foreign country and he had no knowledge concerning the laws and customs of South Africa, much less how the police might handle this debacle. For all he knew he might be treated as a co-conspirator. And what if this Netwanye character had connections to law enforcement? By reporting on him, Noah might find himself arrested and in jail by the afternoon.

He stared out a large window at the tropical gardens surrounding the property. A gardener in a blue jumpsuit was walking from one plot to the next with trimming shears, making sure all the flowers and other plants on the grounds of the hotel were immaculately shaped for presentation to the guests. In that moment he longed to trade places with the gardener.

Noah had resigned himself to the conclusion that he could not settle the case today. Whatever his client was up to, he had no authority to settle the matter. In fact, he had been given explicit instructions to do the opposite. He would scuttle the conference and then determine whether there was any truth in what Netwanye had revealed to him. And then he would figure out how to get himself out of this representation once and for all.

***

Sledge made the first presentation during the settlement conference and explained that Noah and his client had no chance of prevailing in this case, but even if they won there was no way they would get a dime out of Sud-Coast, because the company would fight tooth and nail before they parted with even a cent in satisfaction of a judgment. Sledge then delved into the impossible procedural hurdles Noah and his client would face trying to enforce a judgment against Sud-Coast in any of the dozen African nations in which the company operated. Noah started to come to his senses during the presentation and as he listened to it, he realized he had heard it all before and that Sledge was performing for his clients. The act was having its intended effect as the representatives from Sud-Coast in attendance beamed throughout the entire show, at times even making whispered comments to each other while outwardly smiling. At one point, Noah even caught Netwanye winking at him slyly making Noah feel even more grotesque at his involvement in the sordid affair. Sledge closed his presentation by making the same offer to settle for $2.5 million that he had made before.

It was Noah's turn. His strategy as of ten minutes ago was to capitulate quickly and take the rest of the afternoon to enjoy being rid of this case. That was now out of the question, and instead he stood and unleashed a stream of consciousness rant touting Sud-

Coast's obligations under the contract, the inequities of the group action provision, and the likelihood that a jury would plainly see the abject unfairness of the provision and hand Undertow Acquisitions a resounding victory. He had close to no factual or legal support for what he was spouting and as he spoke, he could see a tempest brewing in Sledge. After an exhausting fifteen-minute diatribe, Noah stopped abruptly and sat down leaving the room in shocked silence. Sledge had prepared his clients for a quick resolution, and now it was clear they were not going to get one. All the faces in the room portrayed blank stares of surprise.

Sledge looked like he was about to explode and quickly called for an intermission in the proceedings and beckoned Noah out into the hallway.

"What in the hell are you doing in there! You told me you were ready to settle and now I get this speech about the strengths of your case. What is going on here?"

Sledge was standing only inches away from Noah as he continued yelling at him, and Noah had to wipe spit from his brow halfway through Sledge's lecture. Sledge then stopped abruptly to catch his breath. His chest was heaving and his brow was soaked in exasperation. But Sledge's aggression on top of the curve ball he had just been thrown by Netwanye had so frustrated Noah that he didn't care anymore about the displeasure of Sledge or his clients – he just wanted to get out of the hotel and fast. He fired back.

"Sorry, but I can't dictate what my client wants to do. You know as well as I do that the client is in control, not the lawyer, and my client decided to reject your offer. There's no use getting angry at me, there's nothing I can do about it and you know that. Stop your grandstanding. I appreciate all you've done to host this conference, but it's over."

Sledge continued to stand there with an incredulous look on his face. Noah stared back at him in defiance. Netwanye came out of the conference room and approached Sledge from behind, and whispered something in his ear. The fuming attorney was disarmed immediately, as if nothing had happened. A smile crept across Sledge's face as he half turned to Netwanye and said, "ok, understood," before turning back to Noah and continuing in a lighter tone.

"Your conduct here was unprofessional, Noah, but you're a young lawyer and at the whim of your client, so I understand. If this ever happens again, I'll seek sanctions from the court."

He turned and walked away. Netwanye smiled and winked at Noah again, before following Sledge back to the group of Sud-Coast executives.

***

Noah walked straight out of the hotel and toward Long Street, the commercial thoroughfare that ran down the hill toward the harbor. He walked all the way down Long Street past the restaurants, bars, and shops, with his jacket over his shoulder and his shirt sleeves rolled up – immediately hot again upon exiting the coolness of the Admiral Hawlsey. At the bottom of the street he turned around and headed back up, moving against the throngs of tourists patronizing one of the most popular areas of the city, and wandering aimlessly in the throes of panic and anger. He was somehow a criminal again without doing anything but trying to practice law honestly. How had this happened? What was he missing? What was he doing wrong?

"How could I have been so stupid!" he exclaimed to himself while continuing up the street, a growing sop of perspiration collecting on his forehead.

He finally settled on what looked like a dark, forgotten hole of an establishment and slinked in and took a center seat at the vacant mid-day bar. He ordered a beer and stared at the dark wall of alcohol before him and enjoyed for a moment the cool air provided by the ceiling fan overhead while the bartender began unprompted to spin his own life's tail of coming to Cape Town for "only a few weeks after college," but then never leaving.

A hand touched Noah's shoulder and it startled him and he turned to see Netwanye sitting next to him. Another larger man had also taken the seat on the other side of Noah at the bar.

"Get him another," said Netwanye, "and two more for my friend and I."

The large man on the other side of Noah made a kind of grunt in acknowledgement of receiving the drink before downing it in one gulp and beckoning for another. Netwanye took a sip and then focused on Noah again.

106

"You did good in there Noah, you did good. Sledge is a great attorney, he's relentless, but he's a jerk too. That's what makes him so good. But you stood up to him. Casimir will be proud of you."

Noah had so many questions bouncing around his brain he didn't know where to begin.

"What is going on here, Netwanye? How long have you been involved and how do you or whoever you are working for think we are going to get out of this case. Sud-Coast – your employer – has a very strong case and they're going to win their motion for summary judgment. Settlement was the only chance to get something out of this case, but that chance is gone now. I don't know what kind of scheme you're running, but any prayer you had of making any money on this case just evaporated up there in that conference room. There's no way Sledge will back down from that motion now and he's going to win it and the case will be over."

Noah downed his beer and motioned to the bartender for another.

"He's fiery, isn't he Solomon," said Netwanye to the man sitting on the other side of Noah, "Noah, calm down, man. It will all be taken care of, trust me. Sledge cannot make a move without my permission – I pull the strings here – I control the purse. Sledge will do what I say."

"But where the hell is Shaw – I haven't heard from him in weeks. And I've no clue what Casimir thinks he's doing – I went to his house last week and it wasn't even his house. It was some event space he rented. What is going on here Netwanye? I'm not going to be jerked around like this and pulled into some scheme I have nothing to do with!"

"Noah, calm down, calm down. And lower your voice, please. There are ears everywhere in Cape Town – we wouldn't want others coming in on our little plan, would we? Casimir is a very complicated person, and he works in mysterious ways, but he is fair and just. I promise. There is a plan, and all will be explained to you soon."

"And how's that, Netwanye? You clearly don't have all the answers I need. 'Casimir is very complicated,' is not going to cut it for me. I'm going to need more information from someone soon."

"I know, I know, Noah, and that brings me to my next point which will please you. You will be able to ask all the questions you want of Casimir soon because I am taking you to him today."

"Today, what do you mean, he's here?"

"Well yes and no, not in Cape Town, but out in the country a bit. Not a long drive, you just need to come with my friend and I and we will take you."

One look at the friend was all Noah needed to tell him that he did not want to be going anywhere with him without some form of backup.

"There's no way I'm getting in a car with you two to go anywhere without some more information about what the hell is going on here. Where is Shaw, for instance, and why hasn't he been returning my calls? And I want to know exactly what kind of criminal scheme you all are running. Now!"

Netwanye turned calmly to his beer and took a long sip and smiled silently. With his frustration through the roof now, Noah rose and threw some crumpled bills on the bar and turned to leave. A strong hand on his shoulder stopped him in his tracks and another equally strong grip around his opposite upper arm kept him from moving any further. Netwanye stood up fluidly and moved between Noah and the doorway. The bartender had mysteriously disappeared from the barroom.

"Noah, please, do not be hasty. Solomon here will not let you go anywhere, trust me. He was a star player on South Africa's rugby team back in his hay day and he has not lost a step. I think he's even stronger now. There is nothing mere mortals like you or me could do against him. I just don't want you to get hurt. Now, have a seat. Let's get one more beer and then we can go talk to Casimir."

Noah was guided back to his seat and Solomon reached behind the bar for three more beers.

"Drink up," said Netwanye, "don't worry, we will have a pleasant drive out to the country and everything will be explained to you soon."

– CHAPTER 15 –

Netwanye grew up destitute. His life was typical of many children in the townships surrounding Cape Town. His parents each worked two jobs, and this left Netwanye and his siblings to fend for themselves for large stretches of the day and night. They cooked for each other and watched after each other as their parents toiled for hours on end to make enough to provide the basic necessities for a family of seven. Netwanye benefitted from the sacrifices of his three older siblings who took much of their own time outside of school to care for him and the youngest and to tend to the house while their parents were working. Though he was the second youngest, this attentive care by his older siblings allowed Netwanye to have the time to be the first of the children to get a job and take some of the financial burden off of his parents. He was hired by a neighbor to help scour the township for discarded cardboard that they loaded onto a dolly Netwanye pulled around the rutted streets. Once the dolly was full, they took it to a recycling center where they were paid for the discarded material, with Netwanye getting a quarter of whatever they received. The money went directly back to his family.

Netwanye was a natural athlete and with the added strength in his legs and arms from pulling an overloaded cart around the damaged streets of the township for hours on end, he became a standout on the soccer field. He dominated the various school leagues to such an extent that he gained the attention of a local professional club that brought him on for a trial period, and after observing his skill signed him to a youth contract when he was only fourteen. It was not very much money and had no guarantees, but he had supreme confidence in himself and his abilities. Nothing could stop him from rising to the top of the professional game and earning enough to take his family out of the township.

With each month at Real Cape Town, young Netwanye's profile rose. And not just at the club, but also within his neighborhood. It was hard to miss the sky-blue track suit he wore and the new shoes he was given by the club. He took to strutting around the township in this brightly colored outfit with supreme confidence and was not shy about telling people what team he was playing for and how he planned to be a superstar in the future. While he was still making a meager wage, he made himself look like he was making big money and all sorts came out of the woodwork seeking a handout. All of a sudden he had third and fourth cousins he had never heard of, and scores of township residents were remembering favors they had done for him in the past and were now seeking their favor in return. When Netwanye tried to tell them he had no money to give, he was met with surprised and disapproving stares.

One night, the family's home – a shack made of corrugated metal – was robbed while they were out, and completely ransacked by thieves clearly looking for money. Nothing of value was taken – they didn't have anything to take – but it started a trend. Two weeks later, Netwanye's father was mugged – he had no money, and got a black eye and broken nose for that transgression. A week after that, Netwanye's older brother was chased down the street by local thugs, but managed to escape.

Many of Real Cape Town's games were played in the evenings, and this meant that Netwanye had to make his way back home at night, riding the train and then walking the last mile from the station. Always alone in the dark that was broken only occasionally by a makeshift street light. The many alleyways of the township provided ample cover for thieves. It all happened very quickly. Netwanye was within sight of his family's home one night when one bandit leapt out of an alleyway in front of him.

"Hey, what you got?"

Netwanye knew what this was immediately and turned to run in the opposition direction but it was too late. Two other bandits had come up behind him already. Surrounded, but physically bigger than each of his attackers, Netwanye decided to push his way through and run. He tried, but the moment he did, a knife opened in one of the bandits' hand and was brandished just inches from Netwanye's stomach.

Netwanye had some money for them, but it wasn't enough – they were expecting the big score that the fleecing of a professional

110

athlete promised. A beating was not sufficient retribution this time. The pain came only later because Netwanye was overtaken with shock when it happened. After the shot rang out, he could remember the group running away and a steady stream of red flowing out of his leg, but nothing else.

He woke in a charity hospital the next morning. After coming out of anesthesia he was encouraged to see that his leg was still intact, but when the doctors told him his soccer playing career was over because the bone had to be completely reconstructed, he was inconsolable. He didn't speak to anyone for a week. When he was released from the hospital he was confined to a wheelchair and spent his solemn days sitting at home, alone and depressed. One week later he found himself back in the hospital after drinking an entire bottle of liquor.

It was in the hospital for the second time that Netwanye met the priest. A former athlete himself, the priest also lost his career to a tragic injury. The priest read scripture to Netwanye that calmed him as he laid in his bed, day after day, looking at the windowless walls and obsessing over the life he had lost. Over hours of conversation, deep into the night on many occasions, a bond formed between them and the priest was able to convince Netwanye that life was still worth living. After leaving the hospital a second time, Netwanye focused all his effort on his education. He was near the top of his class by the time he graduated secondary school, and earned a prestigious scholarship to a private college, where economics grasped his attention. After college he undertook graduate studies at a prestigious university in London before returning to Cape Town to be near his family and with the aim to do good for his community while doing well for himself.

He took a job with Sud-Coast because it was a huge company with many opportunities. They started him within the firm's consulting group where he provided analysis and advice to various of the company's businesses in South Africa and other African nations. He spent weeks on end hopping from one metropolis to another providing business advice and living mostly out of hotels. His frugal mindset was still present form his upbringing in the township and prompted his collection of a wide variety of soaps and lotions from the myriad hotels in which he stayed. He was eventually moved back to Sud-Coast's operations group in Cape Town, to his relief, where he met everyone in the company. Netwanye charmed them with stories of his soccer days and was quickly recognized as a rising star within the company due to the quality of his work.

Next, he was given his dream job as an executive in charge of Sud-Coast's charities. He dove into the project with idealistic fervor, but upon digging into the charities' financial records he soon found what appeared to be an accounting mistake whereby significant monies were being directed away from one of the charities and into expense accounts for executives. It was an obvious oversight, some error done in haste years ago that had never been remedied. Netwanye instructed his staff to make the accounting change that would direct the money back to the charity. But as he continued to dig, he was troubled by what he found. The anomaly he found was not an outlier – for each of Sud-Coast's charities there was a mechanism by which money was diverted clandestinely to general expense accounts used by Sud-Coast executives. With all the charities being affected he knew this wasn't just negligent accounting and that something nefarious was going on. He thought carefully about his next step. Fixing the accounting so that the charities kept the money was a priority for him, but pursuing fraud investigations within the company was not. He had his staff quietly make the change that would stop the diversion of money, but took no further action to highlight what was an apparent fraud.

Then came an unexpected call from Sud-Coast's head of finance.

"Netwanye, hello, this is Klousman. I haven't had a chance to reach out since you were elevated, but wanted to welcome you to the executive level. Do you have time to meet me this afternoon in my office?"

This was odd because Klousman had never shown an interest in Netwanye before and wasn't known as a welcoming person. Netwanye had no reason to rebuff this outreach, however, so he happily agreed.

"I appreciate your coming on short notice, I know we're all busy here at Sud-Coast, and especially me, but I wanted to welcome you and all that. I figured it was expected, you being new and all."

It was an odd introduction, but Netwanye graciously thanked the man for the opportunity nonetheless, and then got up to leave explaining that he didn't want to take any more of Klousman's time.

"Wait, wait. Hold on a second. There's one more thing," Klousman continued, "we've noticed you've made some changes to the finances for Sud-Coast's charities here in South Africa. We need you to change those back. Have a good day." And Klousman put his head down dismissing Netwanye in favor of other work. Netwanye stood there, surprised.

"Well, Sir, my apologies, but that money was being improperly diverted to executive expense accounts. That was clearly a mistake, so I diverted it back. Now it can be used by our charities as intended.

"It was appropriately allocated, you should not have made the change without asking permission, please change it back today. Thank you," said Klousman calmly, without lifting his head. Then he made a backhanded motion as if to shoo Netwanye out of his office.

Netwanye was shocked into stiff silence for a moment before reacting without thinking, "it is not going to the right place, you are mistaken, and it would be illegal to direct it back into yours and the other executives' expense accounts, Sir, and I will not do it."

Klousman's head snapped up abruptly and he leered at Netwanye.

"Where that money goes is not your concern. Your job is to run those charities with the money we give you and not to ask questions. If you ever threaten legal action against me and the other executives again, we will make sure you are thrown in prison yourself – for many, many years. You will receive a special bonus for your good work, so don't worry. We are not leaving you behind. But if you ever speak to anyone outside this room about our conversation you will find yourself in a hole for the rest of your life.

113

You know this company's connections and you know we can do it. Now, good day to you!" Klousman depressed a button on his desk and his secretary immediately entered and ushered a dumbfounded Netwanye out of the room. He left the office in a daze and went straight home.

Netwanye woke up in a cold sweat that evening with a gut-wrenching dread that he had gotten himself into something that he could never escape. The people that were threatening him were some of the most powerful in the country and he knew they had connections with the government and law enforcement and that it would take them no more than an afternoon to arrange his arrest and to frame him as a criminal. He would be locked away and forgotten.

He rose from bed and gazed out his window onto the dark hills of Table Mountain visible from his high-rise apartment building. He knew there was no way out of this company, at least not now – if he quit, they would surely go after him, and if he stayed and tried to report the fraud somehow, he would suffer the same fate. He had no other option but to fight fire with fire. He would continue with the company and do his bosses' bidding and appear as the perfect employee, but underneath it all he would search for a way to siphon that money away from Sud-Coast and back to those who needed and deserved it.

– CHAPTER 16 –

Netwanye stood with Noah outside the bar on Long Street while Solomon went to get the car. Moments later, a large, black Mercedes sedan pulled up and Netwanye ushered Noah into the back passenger side door facing the busy sidewalk before walking around the car and getting in on the opposite side and taking the seat next to Noah. Solomon accelerated away from the curb and they weaved through traffic aggressively, with Solomon relying heavily on the horn to warn other vehicles to keep out of their way. He was far from the only motorist with this strategy, as the Mercedes joined a chorus of honks and accelerations making up the symphony of Cape Town traffic. The noise of the congestion only reached them as distant emanations in the sound proofed luxury vehicle that stood out amid the slow-moving flow of cheap and damaged automobiles like a thoroughbred amongst pack horses. Noah gazed searchingly out the window while Netwanye tapped with purpose on his oversized cell phone, like nothing out of the ordinary had happened that day. They climbed a narrow highway on-ramp too quickly, pushing Noah into the passenger-side door as if he was in a centrifuge, before the car took off toward the country. They easily weaved around the other, less powerful vehicles. Slipping past the townships that flanked the highway on the outskirts of Cape Town, Noah observed a group of children playing soccer on the grass median between the three-lane thoroughfares. The only prerequisite to take part in that game was having the nerve to dodge traffic on the way to the field – to take your life in your own hands, just for a chance to play the beautiful game. Netwanye saw Noah watching the children.

"Some of those kids will make it, and some of them will not – it's a shame people aren't doing more for them." Netwanye commented.

They continued east. As the distance between them and the city grew, the shoulders of the highway opened up to expansive views of a dry, hilly region dotted with rocky outcroppings seemingly forever in the distance. The scent of eucalyptus leaves accented the air. They had slipped into a different world, entirely removed from the hustle of Cape Town and the surrounding neighborhoods. The eerie silence in the car persisted, punctuated only by Netwanye's continued tapping on his smart phone and his making a handful of calls. Each conversation was carried on in his native language of Xhosa, and his speech was punctuated by clicks and rolls of his tongue. Noah listened passively, but could make no sense of what Newtanye was saying. The view outside was beautiful but Noah could not enjoy it as his mind remained grasped in the terror of his kidnapping and the unknowns of his circumstances. His mind swirled with dozens of questions. His world was upside down again and he had once again lost control not only of that afternoon, but the rest of his and Alana's life. Their future was now in even more jeopardy than it had been when he boarded the flight to Cape Town less than twenty-four hours earlier. He ran every possible scenario through his head, and each ended in imprisonment, or worse. His simply disappearing now seemed like a real possibility as he had no idea who Casimir actually was or what he was capable of. Either way, he could see only a bleak future for Alana and their child. It was infuriating and heartbreaking at the same time. After an hour and a half of worry, his mind was exhausted with the stress of his predicament. The fatigue was exacerbated by the extreme jetlag he was starting to feel and the alcohol he had consumed earlier at the bar. He eventually gave in and nodded off into the plush headrest behind him.

He was abruptly jolted back to the present when the car took a sharp turn down a long driveway of white gravel. Upon opening his eyes and seeing the road, Noah was momentarily transported back to his first trip down the long driveway in the Farms when he first met Casimir. Instead of trees, they were flanked now by rows of grape vines that ticked by like nature's library stacks as the car approached a massive, white Cape Dutch style farmhouse topped with a thatched roof and with tall shutters painted a dark green and crowned in the center with a decorative gable. As they pulled into a wide courtyard, Noah observed a receiving line standing at the front of the building. Then Casimir's hefty frame came into focus at the end of the line, where he stood with arms crossed and a beaming smile.

The car stopped, and Netwanye hopped out and shook everyone's hand vigorously, his wide smile matching the intensity of Casimir's. When he reached Casimir, he greeted and hugged him. Noah couldn't clearly make out their conversation as he was still in the car and they were a distance away, but caught Casimir's loud exhortation after the two embraced.

"Great rewards are just around the corner for us!"

Casimir beckoned for Netwanye to continue into the grand front entrance of the house then briefly greeted Solomon with a nod, before the henchman followed Netwanye through the front entrance.

It was Noah's turn. As the car had entered the compound and drove up to the house, Noah decided that lashing out would do him no good. There was no way he could force his way out of the situation, at least as long as Solomon was lurking nearby. He would do his best to keep calm and listen and collect information in the hope of acting on it later to protect himself and his family. If Noah wanted to get through this, and get out alive, he would need to play by Casimir's rules for a bit longer. He reluctantly eased out of the cavernous backseat of the car and moved cautiously toward Casimir. The large man stepped forward to meet him and embraced him as vigorously as he had Netwanye.

"Noah, you made it! I am so very glad to see you and welcome you to my farm. Please come this way, I've so much to tell you."

Casimir ushered him to the building's entrance and directed him to follow Netwanye and Solomon through the house to a back patio. The interior was beautifully adorned and Noah found himself wondering whether Casimir actually owned this property or whether it too was merely on loan. He passed through a set of French doors onto an expansive patio extending from the back of the farmhouse. On one end of it was a small farm table set for three. Netwanye and Solomon were already seated and Noah had no choice but to join them. He had not been seated more than a moment before uniformed servants silently arrived and served each of the men wine and then small plates with assorted cheeses, breads, and olives. Then Casimir made a grand entrance from the house.

117

"Welcome, welcome, now please eat and drink. We will all talk business later, but for now, you must enjoy yourselves and the bounty of my farm."

Casimir withdrew back to the farmhouse as quickly as he had appeared. Then a line of servants again emerged from the farmhouse with large platters of grilled meats and local vegetables that were placed on the table before the three guests. They ate and drank mostly in silence, focusing on the delicious feast before them, and accompanied only by the sounds of chewing and drinking and of Netwanye's suggestion between guzzles of wine to Noah that,

"You've got to try the springbok and the warthog, and don't forget the king clip – it's a delicious white fish found only in South Africa."

Noah was famished – he had not eaten since breakfast. The heat of the day had relented as the sun fell behind a rocky hilltop in the distance and the sky displayed brush strokes of pink and orange. The wine and heaping portions helped ease Noah's temperament as he watched the sky change by the minute. The servants returned with blankets and cigars and a fire pit was lit on the other side of the patio and the three men moved to plush arm chairs set around the large blaze.

Casimir returned, lumbering onto the patio in corduroys, an olive-green flannel shirt and heavy field jacket. He was holding a cigar of his own that was already half gone and seemed small in the man's enormous hands.

"I can see that everything was to your satisfaction," he exclaimed proudly while standing at Noah's shoulder, "now, if you don't mind, I'd like to join you and we can smoke and talk a little business on this beautiful evening. Solomon, Mila has just arrived and requires your help inside."

Solomon rose to his feet and strode into the farmhouse that was now warmly lit inside. Casimir sat in Solomon's seat by the firepit and took a long drag on the fine hand rolled cigar. Noah had not smoked a cigar in years, but somehow the infusion of nicotine in his veins did nothing to calm his reaction to Casimir's reappearance.

118

His heart started pounding again as Casimir sat down next to him. Noah's psyche braced for his long-awaited confrontation with his enigmatic employer. He was wide awake and alert once again.

"Noah, thank you for coming here, and again for not settling this little case of ours this morning. I know this is all coming at you quickly, and it is probably quite shocking for you and so I appreciate your poise at this dynamic moment in our venture."

"Like I had a choice with Solomon's iron grip around my arm," thought Noah to himself as he listened, but he stayed silent as Casimir continued.

"I understand that Netwanye has filled you in on some details. You must know, Noah, that it was not my intention to involve you in all this. My intention was to isolate you – to protect you. But, now that Shaw has double crossed us, we had no choice but to bring you into the fold. I am sorry about that, but have no fear. We all stand to benefit greatly from this case."

Noah's heart rate jumped again at Casimir's mention of Shaw. The synapses in his brain were firing like pistons on overdrive now. He had endless questions to ask and wanted more than anything to interrupt Casimir and ask them all. It was everything he could do to hold his tongue and keep to his plan. He reminded himself of the vice grip Solomon had put on his arm earlier, and told himself he needed to continue to listen and wait.

"Let me start at the beginning and give you some background. It will make everything clearer. This is not the first time we have worked together, Noah, just the first time you were aware of our collaboration. You may remember Markus Stillfield Brice."

"How could I forget?" thought Noah, "it was where I got arrested and then interrogated by the FBI." Noah now hung on each word.

"I was responsible for their rise, and their downfall. I devised the scheme that the partners of your old firm put into play. What an elegant fraud it was. We were all making out well, but then your former bosses got greedy. They starting skimming profits before giving me my share. I caught them in the act and, well, we all know

119

how they paid for it. I was the one who leaked the scheme to the FBI, anonymously of course, and because it was their names on all the emails directing when to short the stocks and it was the partners themselves who filed the lawsuits, they were the ones that found themselves in the cross-hairs. I was blissfully in the shadows and far off the FBI's radar – they have no idea who I am.

"The plot Netwanye and I are putting into play promises to be even more lucrative. Shaw was a part of our plan too – he helped devise it, but just like the partners in your old firm he got greedy and put himself before you, Netwanye, and I. He threatened to go to the authorities if he wasn't given a larger cut of the proceeds. That's why he stopped communicating with you, Noah. He held up all the information he could to try to get the better of me and put us all at risk. It was because of him and his refusal to cooperate that you had to come to Cape Town. You were in the dark and did the only thing you could. I understand and forgive you for that, and thank you again for your quick action this morning. Netwanye was highly complementary of your abilities. And please don't worry about Shaw. He will not be meddling in our plans any longer, I assure you."

Noah was getting more panicked by the second, but he had to know more. He took a large gulp of wine and kept is mouth shut and focused on Casimir's continuing narrative.

"You already know most of the rest. I bought the bonds that Sud-Coast refuses to pay and you sued them for me. They have refused to pay up to this point, but we expected that. It's why we have Netwanye. As the new head of finance for Sud-Coast, all he has to do is authorize payment on the bonds and we get our money. The lawsuit and the bad publicity it's brought are the perfect excuse for Netwanye's decision to pay out.

"Netwanye is a modern day Robinhood. When he found out his bosses were stealing money from the company and its charities – charities meant to help the townships where Netwanye grew up – he made it his mission to find a way to get that money back to those who deserved it. Netwanye's brother is a hand on my farm and when

I learned of Netwanye's troubles at Sud-Coast, I was happy to provide assistance in a way that benefitted us both.

"The final piece of the puzzle was your lawsuit, Noah. With that, we have given Netwanye the perfect excuse to fully pay on the bonds – no one is going to go digging into the amicable resolution of a lawsuit where thousands are filed each year."

The servants had just brought out another tray of freshly opened wine bottles and Casimir paused as he helped himself to another hefty pour. The tension in Noah was now overflowing and he could not contain himself any longer.

"You're kidding yourself if you think no one is going to look into this. You're planning to take tens of millions out of a struggling foreign company and bring it to the United States – you can try to cover with a lawsuit all you want, but it won't keep the SEC or the FBI from investigating – they are going to want to know what really happened here and aren't afraid to ask questions. The first question they are going to ask is who is behind this vulture fund based in the United States that is syphoning money from a troubled company in Africa. I will not be a part of this. I am your lawyer, but will not abet a fraud. I am out!"

Casimir took a long drink and then smiled and looked out over the dark vineyards barely visible against the inky sky. There was a sweetness in the air from the grapes releasing their aroma into a cooling breeze that had kicked up with sunset.

"Well, Noah, you had better hope they don't. You ask an excellent question, and you are the answer. Did you really think that I would put my name on the lynchpin of this whole scheme? The director of Undertow Acquisitions will certainly be at the center of any investigation, and that is why it was important to make you the owner and founder of Undertow."

"What do you mean? I was never involved in the founding of Undertow. You and Shaw brought that to me. It was already founded when I took the case," Noah retorted. His hands were now shaking with anger.

"Noah, please, don't be naïve. With all the information we already had on you, it was easy to start a company in your name."

"But what information – what do you mean, I hardly know you."

"Noah, take your time, have some wine, please, we are all in this together now, I will tell you everything. We had all the information we needed from your old firm. I took all the employee files before the firm went under. With that, it was easy to start a company in your name – I could have done it ten times over. You really should have been more forceful is asking for the corporate documentation for Undertow because it would have shown you that there's only one person officially in charge of the company – you. To anyone looking in from the outside, the Feds for instance, you are the one running Undertow and this whole scheme.

"You couldn't have known this, of course. We used a P.O. Box for all mail related to Undertow Acquisitions so that none of it made it to your doorstep. But telling that story to the Feds won't help you either, especially considering that the P.O. Box is in Manchester, just down the road from your apartment."

As Casimir spoke, the servants came with a new beverage course – a deep purple dessert wine filled to the brim of new glasses placed before each of them. Noah was so engaged in Casimir's narrative he didn't notice. As another wave of anger struck him, he reached for the new glass and took a deep drink. Like a sprinter on the starting block he then shot to his feet intending to launch another tirade at Casimir, but an odd feeling coursed through his legs. They could not support him and he fell hard back into his seat.

The sedative that had been mixed with Noah's wine was not a deadly one, but it was fast acting and had already taken the strength out of Noah's limbs. His body now felt numb, but his mind was still keenly focused and exploding with anger. He could hear Netwanye chuckling to himself. Casimir sat back in his seat with a grin on his face.

"Noah, please do not over exert yourself. The sedative works quickly. Your body will be quite numb for an hour or so. No quick movements – we wouldn't want you to injure yourself. Now, please listen to me. I am not angry with you. Quite the opposite – you showed excellent judgment when you listened to Netwanye this morning. Trust me, if you had not, we would be having a very different conversation. The next steps for you are very simple. You leave here tonight under Solomon's care."

Casimir looked beyond Noah's shoulder and Noah turned his head to see that Solomon had made his way quietly back to the patio and was standing behind Noah's chair. He already had Noah's bag in his hand.

"He will escort you to the airport just in time for your flight back to the States. You will challenge that motion for summary judgment. You know as well as I do that the judge will take months to decide it and during that time Netwanye will organize payment from Sud-Coast so that the case will be over before the judge has a chance to rule on the motion.

"Casimir, I will never…" began Noah again, but Casimir interrupted him.

"And one more thing, and I know I don't have to say it because I trust you Noah, but I have learned that it is important to be very clear with my business partners. I will not tolerate any insubordination. That doesn't just mean you should not steal from me, like your old bosses. You are also not to go to the authorities. Don't go to the Feds Noah – they will not help you, and Solomon here can do much worse than breaking your arm – believe me. Noah, your wife and your unborn child will both thank you dearly for your cooperation – you do not want to do anything that could jeopardize their future, or their safety."

Another sickening pang of fear struck Noah as Casimir mentioned Alana and their child. How did he know about either? Casimir could read the fear on Noah's face.

"Oh, you didn't realize we had eyes on you. Yes, we've been watching you and yours and will continue to do so every step of the way from here. Please, for your sake and for the sake of your family, do not make a misstep. Do not test me."

123

Noah's head was spinning, and he didn't notice that Solomon was already in the process of easily lifting him to his feet. Solomon proceeded to guide him off the patio and around the side of the house – supporting him all the way as Noah's legs were still almost useless. Noah's eyes were sensitive to the bright lights at the entry of the grand home. He could not make out the Range Rover that was waiting in the courtyard at the front of the building until Solomon was in the process of securing Noah in the back left passenger seat. Solomon engaged the internal locking mechanism in the vehicle's door that would make it impossible for Noah to open the door from the inside, and then walked around the vehicle and took the seat next to him. Noah could barely make out his suitcase in the space between them. He realized that they must have broken into his hotel room and collected his things, likely after rifling through them first. This infuriated him. They had completely ripped open his life and were planning to completely control it now. Noah was not going to let this happen. His heart raced and his blood flow increased, pushing the toxin to the organs that would clean it from his system and bringing clarity to his mind again, allowing him to think and plan his next move.

The ride was silent, and dark, with only the odd traffic light punctuating the darkness outside Noah's window. The SUV whipped past the townships and the earthy smell of open fire cooking penetrated the vehicle. Soon after, the lights of Cape Town illuminated the night sky. As the Range Rover pulled up to the international terminal at Cape Town International Airport, Solomon put his hand into his jacket pocket and Noah momentarily braced for whatever weapon he was about to pull out, but then saw that Solomon was holding an envelope. He saw Noah's apprehension and chuckled to himself before handing the envelope to Noah and beckoning for him to open it. Inside was a first-class ticket to Boston's Logan International Airport and a wad of hundred-dollar bills.

"Less than 10,000, don't worry," said Solomon in a thick accent almost impossible to comprehend, referring to the amount over which you must declare currency when you are carrying it on an international flight.

124

"Don't forget what the boss said – we'll be watching you," continued Solomon as he pointed to the door indicating that Noah should get out. Noah took his bag from the space between the seats and eased out of the car, taking a moment to test his legs. Whatever he had been given at the farmhouse had almost completely worn off, and he was able to walk into the airport terminal. While Solomon wasn't following him, he was certain that Casimir had someone else on him now, watching his every move. Perhaps there would also be someone on the plane. Noah was very conservative in his movement – he bought some water and a couple magazines for the flight and then went straight to his gate. He consciously avoided eye contact with anyone and simply watched the jet traffic outside the terminal window until it was his turn to board. He texted Alana when he got on the plane to let her know he was safe and that he had caught an earlier flight and would be home sooner than expected. Just before the plane took off, he also texted an old friend from law school about catching up – nothing that would raise any suspicions.

– CHAPTER 17 –

Joshua had not heard from Noah in years – since shortly after law school – so he was surprised to receive a text, and even more so by its content, which could only be described as cryptic:

"Hey man, I'm back from a business trip tomorrow, can you grab me from the airport and bring a fire talker? I land at 4:30 pm. South African Airlines flight 145. Thanks!"

Joshua stared at it for a while without being able to make any sense of it. He eventually concluded that it was mistakenly sent to him and put it out of his mind. It was early in the afternoon the next day while he was taking his husky for a walk up the steep sidewalk on Monument Street in the Boston neighborhood of Charlestown toward the park that surrounds the Bunker Hill Monument, when a long-forgotten memory jostled free and tumbled into his conscious and the meaning of the text became immediately clear.

Joshua took out his phone and sent Noah a quick text in reply – "I'll be there in my black Toyota Camry" – and hoped Noah would be able to receive it while he was in the air. Then he turned around and leaped down the steep stair case leading to the Monument. Wilder resisted at first, sensing that the walk was ending sooner than usual, but after turning and digging in his front paws momentarily, he gave in and the two of them jogged back home together. Joshua left the husky in the care of his girlfriend with the excuse that he had forgotten something in his office that he needed in order to finish writing a motion due the following Monday.

"I just need to pull a few documents and may need to do a bit of research in the firm's library. It might take me a few hours. Sorry about dropping this on you last minute. We can grab a nice dinner in the Navy Yard tonight when I get back. Then movie night – your choice," he said as he headed toward the door of their apartment.

"Don't forget to grab ice cream on the way home then, and I can guarantee a chick flick tonight."

"You're on," Joshua had no choice as he closed the door behind him.

On the way to his car, he stopped at the convenience store on the corner. He moved quickly to the back of the cramped space and reached high onto a wall of colored glass liquor bottles and pulled down a handle of Jack Daniels. At the front of the store, he placed the bottle of whiskey on the counter.

"This, and I'm going to need a phone. Do you have any prepaids?" said Joshua to the stooped older man behind the counter with a fully grey mustache and tousled hair.

"Young man, you don't seem like the type that would need a burner phone. What do you need this for?" asked the man in passing as he turned and opened a low case behind the counter using a key on a chain attached to his blue jeans. He pulled out a clear plastic package containing a simple looking cellular phone.

"Yeah, I know how it looks, but it's nothing. I'm just grabbing it for a friend who's coming into town from abroad."

Joshua paid with cash and left quickly without collecting his change. His car was parked nearby and he was soon on the highway headed for the airport. The last time he thought about Noah was when he read about the charges against the partners of Markus Stillfield Brice in the papers. He had followed the coverage of the arrests and the trial like everyone else, but had never gotten a first-hand account from Noah. He had thought of reaching out to him, but he had never picked up the phone. He was never sure how to broach the subject, so had perpetually put it off.

After arrival at the terminal, he sat for a few moments before being told by a state trooper to move along and wait in the cell phone lot. The trooper wasn't convinced by Joshua's attempt to explain that his friend did not have a cell phone, and so Joshua looped around once more. He had told Noah what his car looked like, but wasn't sure Noah would be able to pick it out in the crush of people and vehicles at the international terminal. When he came around to the terminal a second time, he was waiting for two minutes before he saw the same trooper eye him, scowl, and start making a beeline toward him. As he reached for his keys to start his engine and loop around again, the passenger door popped open.

"Hey man, did you get my fire water?" Noah said with a smile, as he jumped into the seat and threw his bag into the back. Before Joshua could even answer Noah flashed him a note that read:

"I might be bugged and followed. Please go quickly!"

Joshua was stunned, but managed a response through the confused look on his face,

"Uh, yeah, got it."

"Okay, great!" continued Noah with all the enthusiasm he could muster, "do you have time for a quick game over at the club before I head home?"

Surprised again, Joshua went with the flow and reciprocated,

"Sure, yeah, I'm still a member, let's do it."

Noah started a conversation about the weather and the Red Sox to fill the time during the short ride to the squash club they had both joined during law school to exercise between classes. Once there, Noah left his bag in the car and they both walked silently to the club. It was mostly empty and after some perfunctory remarks to the receptionist at the front desk, the two headed back toward the locker room where Noah was relieved to see that they still provided clothes to play in so that he could ditch the ones he was wearing that still smelled like Casimir's fire pit and Noah feared could potentially contain a listening device planted on him during his visit to Casimir's farm. They both changed and on the way-out of the locker room, Noah suggested they stop at the sauna quickly before they played. After closing the door to the 190-degree wood paneled room, Joshua turned to Noah,

"Okay, what the fuck is going on here?"

***

Noah confessed his troubles to Joshua and apologized for dragging him into them. To Noah's surprise, Joshua was actually

128

excited to be involved. After discussing Noah's hectic last few months, the conversation turned to reminiscing about law school and Joshua's current work as a public interest lawyer helping political refugees to get asylum in the United States. Joshua was happy doing good every day, and Noah thought that perhaps he could take up similar work in the future if he ever got himself out of this mess. Then they talked about the clinic where they met in law school and where they represented prisoners trying to get paroled. They discussed in particular one client who had been a gang member and before being incarcerated had been in charge of getting burner phones for his compatriots – disposable cell phones that could not be traced to any one individual because they were prepaid and bought off the shelf at convenience stores and thus had no names associated with them.

"It was a complete shot in the dark – I really wasn't sure you'd remember what our client used to call those phones," said Noah.

"How could I forget – his scheme was brilliant, using the term 'fire talker' to refer to the phones and then delivering them in a bag with whiskey – 'fire water.' That way the police could never get him on a phone tap talking about burner phones because 'fire talker' sounded so much like 'fire water,' and he could always claim it was the whiskey he was talking about. And, of course, their system matched that story perfectly because the first thing his compatriots took out of the bag was the whiskey, just in case the police were watching."

"Yeah, it worked great until the police started asking themselves why this gang was drinking so much whiskey and decided to look into it. But I knew the ploy would work perfectly for me for the first time and that if anyone was bugging me, they would have no idea what I was talking about when I said 'fire talker.' If anyone is watching me today, they will see that when I leave the club, I'll be carrying a handle of whiskey and assume that I mis-typed 'fire talker' and meant 'fire water.'"

"This whole thing is completely nuts – just unbelievable. But thanks for thinking of me – I'm really happy to help," said Joshua.

"I know, I almost can't believe it myself."

The two played a couple perfunctory games of squash to keep up the ruse before cutting out early and leaving the club for the short drive to Manchester where Noah had more pressing business. For the rest of their visit, the conversation only touched briefly on Noah's current plight as neither wanted to belabor a subject fraught with peril. Focusing on the fast-moving squash ball pinging around the enclosed court at over 100 miles per hour let Noah's mind be momentarily free of the pressure cooker environment he had experienced for the last couple days. The squash match and the phone he clandestinely received from Joshua was the catalyst for Noah's first step out of his criminal entanglement with Casimir and Netwanye. He was nervous at the uncertainty he faced ahead, but was sure that the plan he devised was the only chance to get him and Alana and their child to safety.

– CHAPTER 18 –

Whenever possible, FBI agents prefer to conduct surveillance while on the move, whether it's following a target who is walking through the city to meet a contact, or one who is driving down the highway on his way to making his next sale of illicit goods. In this way, agents can protect themselves by blending into the background by how they are dressed or what they drive. Agents can keep as much distance between them and the target as they are comfortable and always have the ability to abort if counter-surveillance is detected or any situation becomes too hot. Getting injured or worse doing surveillance would never be worth it – the aim of surveillance is to collect a piece or two of the puzzle at a time, but almost never to completely solve the investigation, or even apprehend the culprit.

Sometimes more static surveillance is necessary and a stakeout is conducted. Stakeouts can be monotonous affairs, but at the same time are fraught with danger. Often, the participants sit in a car in a dangerous neighborhood and watch for long periods of time for something that might happen, or might not. There's action sometimes, but more often the agents sit in silence, and simply observe and record. At the same time, they're exposed – out in the open. What they are doing is no secret to anyone paying attention. It doesn't take much to notice an unfamiliar car with unfamiliar people sitting inside for hours, especially for a criminal on the lookout. There are many blind spots in a car, and a savvy target, if inclined, can easily get the drop on two weary FBI agents losing focus toward the end of a shift. And the food doesn't help. Just about the only food available to agents working an overnight stakeout is fast food. A constant coffee drip is necessary to keep agents' eyes peeled after grazing on burgers and fries from the closest fast-food joint, delivered most often by a fresh graduate of the Academy getting some of his or her first undercover experience. The odor of the cuisine typically hangs in the air the entire evening, working its way into the fibers of the agents' undercover attire.

Eve was just coming off a stakeout and was looking forward to a shower, a smoothie, and some much-needed sleep before turning back to the research she had done on the "Short on Law" investigation two nights earlier. She was walking through the parking lot at the Boston field office eager to change out of her stakeout disguise of a dark grey hoodie, black baseball cap, dark jeans, and work boots, when her work phone began to buzz with a call from a number she did not recognize. This is not unusual for FBI agents who are constantly on the move and regularly get calls from law enforcement officials from various locations, and so she picked up, eager to learn what the call was about and hoping it wasn't a telemarketer.

"Special Agent Rust," she said.

"Hi, um, I'm Noah Walker. You interrogated me in the Markus Stillfield Brice case a couple years ago. I'd like to talk."

Eve paused, and had to think for a moment. She was surprised to be contacted about the "Short on Law" case given her recent revelation about the potential leader behind the scheme.

"Um," said Eve, as she tried to remember the name.

"I was the one who went to the same law school as your boss, Agent, what was his name?"

"Oh yes, now I remember you. Please, go ahead."

There was another pause on the line, as Noah thought through his response.

"Um, yeah, I'd really rather do this in person, if that's okay."

FBI agents are very cautious when sources ask for in-person meetings, because it can sometimes be hard to protect their own safety. Eve balanced this concern at lightning speed when she heard Noah's request and her reaction came like a reflex because she had been in this situation with other informants many times before.

"Okay, we can discuss that, but can you tell me a little more about what's going on?"

Another pause.

132

"Sorry, my mind is a bit foggy – I'm dealing with some serious jetlag – just got back from a very short trip to South Africa. I've learned some information about who directed the partners' scheme in that case. It's something I need to share. Please, can we just pick a place to meet. I'm afraid for my family's safety."

The mention of South Africa caused alarm bells to go off in Eve's mind, as the conversation turned quickly from a run of the mill informant call to an urgent situation. Her excitement was hard to contain. She was now closer than ever to the mastermind behind the whole scheme – the individual behind the "Short on Law" case and the person responsible for her father's death. Her emotions were kicked into high gear by a combination of adrenaline and anger and she could feel her heart race and the pressure of blood pulsing through her body increase in an instant. Switching gears immediately, she stopped listening and started giving directions.

"Okay Noah, I remember you and you have my attention now. I think it's important to get you in as soon as possible. I don't want to scare you, but these are serious people and we don't want you or your family getting hurt."

"You're telling me," responded Noah, relieved that she seemed to be taking his call seriously, "just tell me what to do."

"Okay, we should meet tomorrow, if possible. Do you know 'The Downstairs' lounge, in Cambridge?"

"I know it."

"Okay, good, I'd like you to meet me there at noon tomorrow."

"Not a problem."

"Great, and Noah – do you own a navy-blue Red Sox cap and a plain white t-shirt by chance?"

"Sure, I think so."

"Good, please wear those, with dark jeans, and brown dress shoes. And obviously, don't tell anyone about our meeting – and I wouldn't discuss what happened in South Africa with anyone yet either, at least until we have a chance to talk."

"I'm on board. Thank you. See you tomorrow."

Evelyn hung up – her heart was racing and she couldn't believe that Noah had called only days after her own investigation had turned up a new lead in the case. Her mind was already itemizing each preparation necessary before her rendezvous with Noah the following day. It would be a long night, but that was not a problem. She was close to something very big.

- CHAPTER 19 -

Noah was purposely vague when discussing the details of his trip with Alana that evening and he didn't even get close to his unplanned excursion to the wine region outside Cape Town. Had it been a sightseeing trip, it would have been a beautiful escape from the day-to-day grind of the case, but it had been far from a relaxing spin through the country. He focused instead on the frustrations of a failed settlement conference – not unusual in litigation, especially in the early stages – and lamented not having the time to explore such a beautiful country on a very short trip. She comforted him and encouraged him and thanked him for working so hard on the case to support them and their future child. He felt uncomfortable not telling her the whole truth about his trip and about the case and the potential danger they were both in, but at the same time he felt it was his responsibility to keep her safe and not to worry her unnecessarily. He told himself that telling her would put her in more danger because then she too would have the information that he knew Casimir would kill to keep from being exposed. Noah was also sure that telling her would cause immediate and incredible stress, and he did not want to do anything to risk the pregnancy. He had a plan and he felt he could get them out of this. Then he would tell her after it was all over. Noah was thoroughly exhausted when he arrived home with his mind and body suspended in time somewhere over the Atlantic trying to catch up to the time zone he was now inhabiting. They had dinner and watched a movie and Noah mostly listed to Alana talk, unable to focus for too long on any one thought. Despite his exhaustion, however, he could not sleep. He laid in bed that evening with his mind singularly focused on the events of the next day.

Noah had told Alana that he needed to go to the city to meet with a number of vendors about next steps in the litigation given the failure of the settlement conference and that he would be out for most of the afternoon. He suggested she spend her day at the beach, or the park – thinking she would be safer in the company of many other people. She didn't notice that he was toting a gym bag, which would have been unusual because he did not belong to a gym and had no reason for a change. He was dressed normally for business that morning in a button-down shirt and slacks. On the way to Cambridge, he stopped at a state park trail head and changed his clothes in the car. He knew the small parking lot would be empty at that time on a weekday and also chose the spot because the lot was so small that he would easily spot anyone following him. The parking lot at the trail head was elevated from the two-lane road that led to it and Noah had backed his car into a spot that gave him a view of both the entrance to the lot and the road leading to and from it. After he had changed, he sat there watching the entrance and the road beyond to confirm he was alone. After twenty minutes, he was satisfied and turned over his key in the ignition and sped out of the gravel parking lot kicking up dirt and stone on the way to the most important meeting of his life. The drive to the city was fast and a ball of unease began growing in the pit of his stomach as he approached the meeting location. After parking in a garage, Noah made his way to the bar, very conscious now of his surroundings. He hadn't noticed anyone following him that morning, but he also had no experience looking for tails so could not be sure.

The interior of the bar was dark and it took a moment for his eyes to adjust from the bright daylight outside. When they did, he saw that it was almost empty. To his right when he entered was a bar that ran the length of the long and narrow room and to his left was a succession of booths that lined the opposite wall. There was a single man sitting at the end of the bar furthest from Noah. As he started easing his way into the space, not sure exactly what to do next, Noah noticed that the man was wearing a baseball cap similar to his and upon closer inspection was also wearing a white t-shirt and jeans – all matching those Noah had been told to wear. An odd coincidence, he thought. Then it dawned on him that it must be some sort of signal. He made his way to the end of the room and sat next to the man who had what looked like a gin and tonic in front of him. He continued staring straight down at his drink when Noah arrived and made no acknowledgement of him. There was silence for a moment, then Noah felt compelled to fill it.

"Hi, I'm supposed to meet someone here, I'm not sure if you're him, my name is …"

136

"The bathroom's in the back," interjected Noah's doppelganger.

"Uh, no, I was actually just saying that..." continued Noah, thinking that the man must have misheard him.

"The bathroom's in the back, just over there," continued the man, pointing now, but oddly still not looking up from his drink, "that's where you need to go."

Silence again. Noah went to speak, but the man interjected for a last time and whispered an order that only the two of them could hear.

"Go now!"

Noah felt the urgency and got up quickly and did as the man directed, continuing to the end of the bar and around an even darker corner to a hallway with signs for men's and women's rooms on opposite sides and an exit door with a half-operating exit sign above it between them at the end of the corridor. He made for the men's room and was reaching for the handle on the door when the exit door next to it eased open – another man poked his head in from outside.

"Noah Walker?"

"Yes."

"Good. Come with me."

The two exited through the back of the bar, and the man proceeded to move quickly through a labyrinth of alleyways. Noah did his best to follow closely, and quickly lost his bearings with the multitude of turns. Then the man stopped suddenly and they stood still and silent for a moment in an eerie standoff before a black SUV pulled up out of nowhere and the back door closest to Noah opened. The man ushered Noah into the car, and then he saw Special Agent Rust's smiling face. The door closed and the SUV accelerated down the alley and onto a main street.

"Sorry for the theatrics," Eve smiled confidently, "but we can't be too careful, and besides, these operations guys get a kick out of ex-filtrations, right?"

"You got that right," retorted the driver, flashing a thumbs up, as he took a corner at speed.

"You may have noticed that the man in the bar was wearing the same thing as you and perhaps also that he was approximately your height and build – that's no mistake," explained Eve, "If someone follows you into the bar, they will see you sitting there, pondering life for a while with a quiet drink. Don't worry, they wouldn't dare approach you and blow their own cover, but our little ruse buys us some time to talk. We still need to be efficient, though – anyone tailing you won't believe that you can sit in the bar drinking for hours and then get into your car and drive away. So, let's get right to it. What did you learn on your trip to Cape Town and how does it tie into the case against your old bosses?"

Noah had been ready to spill his guts since landing in Boston the day before. He took a deep breath, and launched into the ordeal he had been living for the past months. The SUV continued on a circuitous route through the city, as Noah told all. Eve interjected every so often with a probing question or to direct Noah where she wanted him to take the narrative. Noah finished his account with a description of his experience at Casimir's farm and when done, he paused for a minute to take a breath after recollecting his last few harrowing days. The car fell silent as Eve finished the notes she was dutifully taking. Her heart pounded out of her chest with the excitement of finally catching a huge break in her father's case. She finally had a name. Roth Casimir. She wrote it down and underlined it forcefully three times.

Noah could feel the rumble of the powerful engine as the vehicle sat at a stop light in the middle of a crowded street and he absentmindedly watched the people outside. To Noah, the crowds walking down the shop lined street – wearing sunglasses, carrying colorful bags, and eating and drinking outside – felt like a dream he had once been a part of.

"Okay, let's head back to the rendezvous." Eve broke the silence and the driver took a quick left turn and Noah realized that they were somehow already close to the bar. "Noah, this next part is going to be the hardest for you because I'm going to need to take all

138

this back to headquarters and meet with my bosses and sort out a plan here. Your only job for the time being is to keep your head down and wait for my call. Do you still have your burner phone?"

Noah was distraught. "Wait, you're cutting me loose? Alana and I are in danger. There's no telling what these people are capable of. We need some support today, right now." His heart was pounding and he could feel the panic in his own voice.

"Noah, I know this is stressful for you, trust me, but as long as they think you are following their rules, you will be fine. Remember, if everything you've told me is true, they still need to get their money and they can't do that without you. You're essential to them until the plan is complete – it's only after that you become expendable. And trust me, if we put an agent on you now, you'd be in even more danger, because they might notice. As far as they know, you're following directions – let's keep it that way. Now, do you still have your burner?"

The word "expendable" rang in Noah's ears as he slid the burner phone out of his pocket and held it up to Eve. "I've still got the phone," he said feebly.

"Good, I will call you on it – sometime in the evening while you're home so it won't arouse suspicion. If you're not in a good place to pick it up, just don't answer and I'll call back. You need to carry on with your life for the next couple days as if we never met." Eve placed her hand on Noah's trying to make him feel that she was on his side and had his back.

"I know that won't be easy, but it's essential to your and Alana's safety. Get to work on that opposition to the motion for summary judgment. Just try to get lost in your work, and I will be back to you with a plan before you know it. You did really good here. You did the right thing. We won't let anything happen to you."

"Okay, will do," was all Noah could manage. They pulled up to a spot near the back entrance to the bar that was obscured from view by a large, tattered awning above and a line of dumpsters.

"Now, when you go in, go straight to the bathroom and our man will meet you there. Then go back to the bar, pay the bill, and leave. Don't worry, he's been drinking soda water and lime, so it shouldn't be a hefty tab."

Noah reached for the handle, but Eve grabbed his hand.

"Stop, hold on a second." She reached for her radio, "are we clear?"

"Clear," a crackled voice answered.

"Okay, go now." She released his hand and Noah went swiftly from the car to the back door of the bar and then to the door of the bathroom. The agent from the bar entered a second later.

"You have a tail – second booth from the door, leather coat and glasses. Do not look at him when you leave. Just pay, go back to your car, and drive home. Good luck."

The agent spoke quickly while removing his white t-shirt to reveal a red t-shirt underneath and flipping his cap inside out to reveal a Yankees symbol. Then he was out the door in a flash and Noah was left to fend for himself. He entered the bar room almost in a trance with the multitude of instructions running through his head. Keeping his head down, he walked back to the chair the agent had occupied. He sat for a moment before flagging the bartender for his bill, doing his best not to raise his head while doing so as he was terrified that the bartender would recognize that a new face occupied the seat and make some remark that would blow his cover. The bartender glided to the register and then to Noah, slipping the bill into an empty glass and sliding it before him. Noah paid quickly with cash, then got up slowly, turned, and made the long walk down the room toward the front door – eyes forward all the way until he was blinded by the sunlight outside. When his eyes recovered, he couldn't help but look around to observe his surroundings. The sidewalk was empty. He moved directly to the garage, collected his car, and was on the highway again before regaining full consciousness. He found himself looking in the rear-view mirror often as he drove back to Manchester.

"Hey babe, welcome back. Why did you change?" was Alana's first observation when he arrived home.

140

Noah's mind had been so preoccupied during the ride that he forgot to change back into his work clothes.

"And where have you been?" continued Alana.

"Um, yeah, I forgot to tell you, but I met some law school friends for a beer at an outdoor beer garden on the way home and so brought a change of clothes," responded Noah, with the first excuse he could come up with in the moment.

"Well, I'm glad you're home. You look tired. Can you take some time today to rest?"

"I wish I could, but this deadline is crushing me."

Hoping to avoid any further questioning he hugged her tight and then moved quickly to his office under the guise of working on the opposition to the motion for summary judgment and told her it would be a late night and to not wait up.

Once in this office, he tried to work, but he couldn't. Completely distracted, he looked at his phone every two minutes to see if he had missed a call. Every pedestrian that passed by his office's picture window was a new tail keeping tabs on his every move.

***

Throughout her conversation with Noah, Eve had kept close track of everything he said on a small pad as she was trained to do. Good investigative work means recording the things you learn and putting them in reports so others can use the information as well. After dropping him back at the bar, she went straight to the office to write up her report. It would later be forwarded to her boss with an urgent request for a meeting in which she would ask for the opportunity to take the lead of a reopening of the investigation. She couldn't write fast enough. After keying the last word in her report, she picked up her head after what felt like an hour of nonstop typing, took a lap around the hive of cubicles that occupied the floor, then reviewed the report once more before shooting it off to her boss with an urgent meeting request. It was late in the afternoon by the time she hit "send." Special Agent Moody was unlikely to have the time to read the report and respond that afternoon so Eve went home to catch up on sleep. Tomorrow would be another long and busy day.

***

After an hour of staring into space, Noah was finally able to disassociate from his concerns enough to work on the opposition to the summary judgement motion. The hurdle he had to get over was the language of the group action provision that essentially required Undertow Acquisitions to take a lower payout on the bonds because the majority of the other bondholders had already agreed to take the lower payout. Typically, contractual language is thick with legalese and reads like a foreign language, but the group action provision was eminently simple and Noah had trouble thinking of a single creative argument to counter the clarity of the provision. Undeterred, he attempted to jog his brain by first digging into a stack of dictionaries, examining the minutia of each definition for each term in the clause, and looking for some possible ambiguity. He found none. Next, he read and re-read the entire agreement to see if anything in the rest of the long contract affected the meaning of any of the terms in the group action provision. That too was a dead end. He was frustrated, and got up to clear his head.

It was late and dark outside – a front had moved through bringing a driving, frigid rain. He looked out his picture window onto a black street and pondered for a moment why streets look darker in the rain. A solitary car passed by and he watched the tail lights ooze an oily blood red light onto the slick pavement as it drove away from him. He turned back to his desk and picked up the remote for a small outdated flatscreen television he had installed on the wall of his office after it had been left in the corner by the previous tenant. A replay of that afternoon's Red Sox game was on and he watched a half inning before leaving it on in the background and turning to his work again. He spent another hour buried in the dense text of the bond purchase agreement but when he came up for air, he still had nothing.

The baseball game was over and in its place was a late-night televised megachurch sermon. Noah glanced up to see a well-coiffed preacher clad in an expensive looking suit strutting back and forth on

142

a stage, microphone in hand, speaking to hundreds in attendance. Noah's mind was completely numb from reading the bond purchase agreement over and over again, and it was a welcome respite to blankly listen to the sermon.

"It is all there in the text, it is all there in the text, my friends, my children, the Lord has written it out for you, and all you need to do is heed his warnings. Heed his warnings in the text and it will guide you to righteousness."

The preacher paused every few phrases to let the audience express their approval in sweeping applause.

"It is all in the text, but it is not a simple text, and that is why I am here today, and every week to interpret that text, to make sense of that text where there may be any uncertainty in the meaning of it. I am here to be your guide."

The camera panned to the crowd. All walks of life were represented. Noah was struck at the size of the crowd and the stadium seating from which they watched the spectacle.

"My duty before the Lord, my children, is to interpret the words in the bible to give them meaning for you, so you can apply them in the way they were meant to be applied. That is my calling. Blessed be to the Lord."

As the applause swelled up again, a thought hit Noah like a ton of bricks. He suddenly knew how he would challenge the motion for summary judgment and at the same time help the FBI capture Netwanye and then Casimir and save himself and Alana in the process.

***

Eve was up at 5 A.M., as usual, but it was easier than normal to shake off her drowsiness, as she was immediately electrified when she remembered what the day held. She showered, changed, and ate a spartan breakfast of coffee and two hard-boiled eggs. After receiving the email from Special Agent Moody late the night before she almost couldn't sleep. He had read her report and was very interested in hearing more about what she had found and wanted to

143

meet with her first thing this morning to discuss next steps in the investigation. She was picking up her gun and extra clip and loading them into the holsters around her waist when her phoned dinged with the arrival of a text message. She looked down to see a blocked number, but the text told her everything she needed to know.

"I need to talk this morning as soon as possible. I know how we are going to catch the two we talked about yesterday."

Eve instantly knew she needed to collect this information before heading into the office because she did not want to walk into the meeting with her boss without information Noah had that might change her analysis. The timing was tight, so she decided that she would collect Noah on the way. They could discuss on the way to the office and sort it all out together at headquarters. She immediately called Noah's burner phone.

"Noah, good morning. Thanks for your text. I want your new information, but it's safer to do this in person, and I may have some more questions for you. I'd like to pick you up, if that's okay.

"Sure," replied Noah, "but is that safe?"

"Well, I'm not going to come to your house because we know from yesterday that you are being followed, so we're going to have to do another covert pickup. What I need you to do is take the number 425 bus from a couple blocks west of your office on the corner of Park Street and Main Street, do you know the spot?"

"Yes, but how did you know about that bus?"

"We do this for a living, Noah, we always have contingencies in place. Now, we want to know if you have a tail, so try to keep track of the people who get on the bus after you do. Ride the bus to the Salem train station and get off there. I want you to pay close attention to who gets off the bus with you at Salem. If it's anyone that got on the bus after you did, you should abort. Get a coffee, walk around for a while and then go home and call me tonight. If not, take the stairs to the third floor of the parking garage and you will see me in a silver jeep – got it?"

"Yeah, I think so."

"Okay, good. Go now so you don't miss the bus. If you're quick enough, no tail in the world will be able to catch up with you. See you in a bit. Good luck."

She hung up the phone, put her gun and extra ammunition into their holsters and rushed out of her apartment and to her vehicle, driven by pure excitement.

***

Noah could feel a pit in his stomach when they approached the FBI field office in Chelsea. It was the first time he had seen it since his arrest years before, and fear and unease were still burned into his subconscious from the experience. It was surreal to be sitting next to one of the agents that interrogated him, but now on the right side of the investigation. He felt even more uneasy when Eve asked him to wait downstairs while she had an initial conversation with her boss and the guard showed Noah to the same room where he had been interrogated years before.

"Would you mind leaving the door open?" asked Noah, as the guard was leaving.

"Yeah, no problem," said the guard, oblivious to Noah's harrowing past experience.

As he sat and waited, Noah could feel the hairs on his neck stand up. He stared at the sound proofed wall opposite him. Noah could not hear anything in the vicinity of the room even though the door was open. Then faint footsteps in the distant hallway, the kind made by black combat boots. They got progressively louder before reaching the threshold of the door.

"They're ready for you," said the guard who had brought him down, "come with me."

Noah followed the guard to an elevator bank down the hall, and they travelled six flights up where Eve was waiting for them when the elevator doors opened.

"I'll take it from here," she said to the guard. Then to Noah, "follow me."

145

They walked silently down another corridor, through a cubicle filled room and then toward one of the corner offices. Eve knocked on the door and a voice told them to enter. Noah saw a man sitting behind a messy desk stacked high with binders and other papers – he was directed to an empty seat and Eve sat next to him.

"Noah, you may remember Special Agent Moody, the agent in charge of this investigation. Now, please, tell him what you told me on the ride down here."

- CHAPTER 20 -

A court will always listen to an expert witness or a witness with special knowledge concerning the matter at issue, and what Noah had realized that evening while watching the television preacher was that he needed someone from Sud-Coast to testify concerning the meaning of the group action provision – it was the only way to convince a judge that the provision meant something different than its clear language. Netwanye was the obvious candidate for this task – he was in charge of the department within Sud-Coast that issued the bonds and thus ultimately responsible for the bond purchase agreement itself. Testimony from him that the provision meant something different than it seemed would certainly be enough to muddy the waters sufficiently for any judge to punt and let the jury decide at trial what the term meant. If Noah could get Netwanye to testify, he could kill two birds with one stone – Netwanye's testimony would lead to a denial of the motion for summary judgment, which would prolong the case as Casimir had directed, but also would bring Netwanye to the United States and within the jurisdiction of federal law enforcement. That was crucial because it would give the FBI an opportunity to arrest him. Noah correctly anticipated that the FBI would want to get their hands on Netwanye and interrogate and pressure him to turn against Casimir. Once a cooperating witness, Netwanye would be invaluable to the collection of evidence necessary to extradite and later convict Casimir.

When he presented the plan to Eve and Agent Moody, Noah wasn't entirely sure how to prompt Netwanye to change sides and if it could even be done – Noah wasn't a special agent at the FBI, after all, and didn't know the nuts and bolts of pressuring a potential informant to cooperate. The two seasoned agents were ready to fill in the gaps.

"Netwanye has a lot to lose," explained Agent Moody, "South Africa does not take embezzlement lightly and has particularly draconian minimum sentences for that crime. They also have a prison system that's known to be brutal. The prospect of

147

years behind bars in his country if he doesn't cooperate will be a huge incentive for Netwanye."

"Information we've collected from the intelligence community also suggests that Netwanye does not really have any sort of political connections in South Africa, and certainly doesn't have the type of political clout that would keep him out of jail if his activity to defraud Sud-Coast came to light. All things considered, we think Netwanye can be easily turned," continued Eve.

Netwanye and Casimir did not have a law degree between them, so had no idea what it would take to beat the summary judgment motion. Eve, Agent Moody, and Noah all agreed that if Noah could paint Netwanye's testimony as the key to prolonging the case, which in reality it was, he could do as Casimir had directed and still get himself out from under his thumb. Netwanye was now the key to Noah's salvation, and with the FBI's blessing Noah would attempt to lure Netwanye to the United States so that Noah could set himself and Alana free from Casimir's grasp. Six months ago, Noah would have shuddered at the thought of walking this tightrope, but having gone through what felt like numerous gauntlets already, he felt almost at ease picking up the phone to put this plan into action.

Noah had been given a number to call if he needed to get in touch, and he dialed the number into his cell phone while sitting at his desk in his office mid-morning as the sun light, unobstructed by any clouds in the sky, streamed into his quiet and still office space. The phone rang once before going to an answering service where a polite female voice with a British accent instructed Noah to please leave his name, a short message, and his telephone number. He did that, only explaining that he was hoping to have a quick discussion about the Sud-Coast case. He was amazed at the speed of the response. He immediately got a text on his personal cell phone that someone would be with him shortly. He wasn't sure exactly what that meant, so he kept his phone near him as he continued to work through some ancillary outstanding issues in the case. About five minutes later, a man with the build of a running back appeared at the door to Noah's office. Noah didn't notice him until he paused for a moment in the doorway to tap something into his phone, then turned the handle and entered. The man was dressed in Bermuda shorts, a golf shirt, and dark sunglasses – no one would have given him a second look as that outfit was common on the sidewalks of Manchester. He stepped up to Noah's desk, as if he knew exactly where he was going, and reached into his pocket and pulled out a cell phone. He handed it to Noah without a word. At first glance, it looked like a normal smart phone – it was entirely black, with a screen that comprised one side, and a brushed metal backing on the other side – but it was heavier than a regular phone and upon closer inspection Noah noticed that it was slightly thicker and boxier too, and that there was no branding on it.

"This will let you talk to the boss securely. It's encrypted so no one will be able to listen in. He will call in 15 minutes."

The man got up, and was out the door as quickly as he had arrived. Noah was shocked at how closely he was being watched, and he panicked for a moment thinking that they must have seen him yesterday when he met with Agent Rust and realized what he was doing. Fears for the safety of Alana and his unborn child shot through his body. But then his mind was oddly calmed by the macabre thought that they would have already killed him if they knew what he was up to. It would have been easy for the man who had just been in his office to have lured Noah away from his storefront window and then shot him, if he had wanted to. It struck Noah that the man must have been armed and that there was likely an armed man watching him at all times. Now more than ever he felt a need to put an end to this engagement. He was emboldened by his anger brought on by their encroachment in every aspect of his life.

The phone finally rang. He snatched at it.

"Hello, Casimir?" asked Noah.

"No, no, it's me, Netwanye. Casimir is busy. How can I help you?"

"Netwanye, we have a problem with this motion. Sledge did a good job with it – too good – and there's no easy way around the language in the bond purchase agreement. The language of the contract clearly states that because the other bond holders have taken

149

a lower payout, Undertow Acquisitions must as well. No judge is going to side with us based on the language of the contract alone."

Netwanye thought for a moment. "No worries, Noah, we will simply tell Sledge to withdraw the motion. He has to do what I say, remember, and then we will be in the clear, and I can arrange payment."

Noah had anticipated this parry and responded immediately. "That would be far too suspicious, Netwanye. First, Sledge will blow a gasket because, as it stands, this motion wins the case for Sud-Coast. But he's not even your biggest problem. If you purposefully withdraw the motion, alarm bells will go off in your company because it will be clear you are rolling over and just giving away money. There will certainly be investigations, and it might even attract the attention of the press. The spotlight will be directly on you, and that's the last thing Casimir wants. Our only chance of beating the motion and not attracting attention is to have someone from Sud-Coast's finance department testify that the clause means something different than it appears. If you gave that testimony, we would easily beat the motion, extend the case, and pave the way for payment in the face of a seemingly legitimate lawsuit. What do you say?" Noah held his breath waiting for a reply knowing that if Netwanye didn't agree he was out of options.

"Noah, your idea is interesting, but I have a question – does it matter that I helped draft that part of the bond purchase agreement? One of my first projects with the company was working on the standard bond purchase agreement language that has been used since, including in the agreement in our case," asked Netwanye.

Noah couldn't believe his luck. Because Netwanye had actually helped draft the provision, a judge would have no choice but to believe his testimony concerning its meaning – the testimony would be the silver bullet needed to defeat the summary judgment motion. Noah now had every reason to push for Netwanye to testify at the hearing in Boston.

"That's perfect, Netwayne, well done. Your testimony will convince the Judge that the provision is vague enough to push the issue to trial. That will provide the perfect cover to end the case on our terms with a settlement because it will look like you and Sud-Coast are being reasonable and avoiding the considerable risks of a trial. And because you helped draft the agreement, you are the perfect candidate to testify – it has to be you."

The line was silent again while the head of finance for Sud-Coast digested this.

"Okay, but if I come to testify, then it's going to look like I'm cooperating with the opposition, right? How can that be the right solution here, Noah? My cooperation will put me on the radar just as much as if I told Sledge to withdraw the whole case."

"You don't need to worry about that," Noah had anticipated this question too, "all you're going to need to do is play dumb, and do a bit of travelling. I am going to ask the court to compel you to be at the hearing through a subpoena. That way it won't look like you testified willingly. In fact, to the outside world it will look like you resisted." Noah's blood was pumping furiously now as he waited again for Netwanye's answer.

"I like it, Noah, I like it, but what do you mean by my doing a 'bit of travelling?'"

"Well, you will have to come to the United States before the hearing so I can serve you with the subpoena, because a subpoena won't work if you're sitting in South Africa. All you have to do is come up with some excuse to travel here and I will have a process server waiting with the papers. Once you're served, you'll have no choice but to attend the hearing, and that will get around any accusation that you assisted the opposition."

"Casimir was right, you are sharp – it's so good to have you on our team. And I already have the perfect excuse to come to the U.S. Bafana Bafana, the South African national soccer team, are playing an exhibition in the United States. Now I have an excuse to go watch the game – maybe even Casimir will pay for my ticket! All my colleagues know that I am a massive fan, so it will not seem at all out of the ordinary if I decide to take a bit of a vacation to go see the team play. I will go out to Casimir's farm tonight and will run this all by him and will let you know what he decides."

151

It was only a few hours later that Noah got a text on his encrypted phone:

"We are a go."

***

Outside the stadium located just south of Boston, Netwanye was completely caught up in the excitement and anticipation of the match. He reveled at the chance to see the South African team play on the international stage and to enjoy the pageantry of an international competition. After meeting beforehand for a tailgate in the parking lot surrounding the stadium, Netwanye and his friends started the short walk toward the entrance jubilant and detached from the outside world. They were surrounded by throngs of similarly eager fans, exuberant at the prospect of seeing the "beautiful game" played at its highest level, and marched toward the entrance to the stadium to the sound of vuvuzelas – the plastic horns ubiquitous at South African soccer matches that emit a low-pitched drone that is deafening when the sound-makers are played in a chorus. As Netwanye's group came upon the gates, none of them noticed an individual in jeans, a t-shirt, and sunglasses approach from the shadow of the gate where they were to enter the stadium. When Netwanye stepped up to the gate and rooted in his shirt pocket for his ticket, the man quickly stepped in front of him and in the same motion reached into his back pocket and pulled out a stapled document that he shoved into Netwanye's hands.

"You've been served," was the man's summary statement. While Netwanye stood there putting on a bewildered look as he examined the papers, the man snapped a picture of him with his cell phone, and then was gone into the crowd as quickly as he had appeared.

- CHAPTER 21 -

Three days later Noah got a terse voicemail from Sledge,

"This is Sledge from the Sud-Coast case. We need to talk – as soon as possible – regarding the reckless and entirely improper subpoena you have served on my client. Please call me."

Noah had been anticipating the communication and readied for the most pivotal part of the plan. He emailed Sledge asking for a call in the early evening the following day in the hopes that Sledge would be fatigued from his day's work and have less energy to resist the critical argument Noah knew he had to win to keep his plan in motion. Sledge consented. Though he felt he gained a slight advantage on the timing, Noah nevertheless girded for a venomous onslaught from his opponent. Sledge delivered.

"What in the hell makes you think that you can go around chasing a representative of my client with a process server at a personal event and serve him with a subpoena without contacting me first? I am Netwanye's attorney, God dammit, and you owe me at least the courtesy of telling me when any employee of Sud-Coast is going to get a subpoena."

"Sledge, I'm perfectly within my rights to serve a subpoena on someone who I want at the hearing. You know as well as I do that I have no obligation to provide you with any notice," replied Noah with his prepared response.

"That is not how it's done Noah. But, in any event, I called to tell you we are going to challenge the subpoena. There's no way we're bringing Netwanye to that hearing. Netwanye is back in Cape Town and he's staying there. There's no way that someone so important to Sud-Coast's operations should have to take the time to fly half-way around the world again in a week for a hearing on this frivolous case."

"Sledge, you're wrong again." retorted Noah, "You filed the motion, not me, and you know as well as I do that the judge is not going to look kindly on the head of finance for Sud-Coast refusing the testify concerning the company's own summary judgment motion where it directly implicates his department's work. You're welcome to try, but the only outcome will be that the judge will realize that you are trying to hide something and will believe my side of the story instead of yours. In fact, be my guest – challenge the subpoena. I'll be able to make some great arguments off of that blunder. I can't wait."

Noah stopped and held his breath while his heart beat out of his chest. He obviously needed Netwanye at the hearing, but he also had to make sure that Sledge didn't challenge the subpoena because that process was so long that they'd still be fighting over it well after the time for the hearing had come and gone. And as long as they were fighting about the subpoena, Netwanye would not be obligated to appear. Selling Sledge on his bluff was Noah's only chance at winning the motion. Noah could hear Sledge breathing through the receiver, then Sledge finally broke the silence.

"Fine Noah – have it your way. We're bringing Netwanye to the hearing, he is going to testify, and it will only strengthen my case. I'll see you in court."

The receiver slammed down on the other end of the line, but Noah took no notice as a broad grin stretched across his face. The trap was set and Netwanye was walking right into it.

***

The night before the hearing, anyone watching the back door of the federal courthouse in Boston would have seen a small contingent of quickly moving people dressed in jeans and dark jackets enter under cover of darkness. This contingent of FBI agents gathered in the United States Marshal's office in the basement of the courthouse to review plans of the building and of the courtroom where a hearing on a summary judgment motion in the matter of *Undertow Acquisitions v. Sud-Coast and Company* would take place the following day. They took turns speaking, and pointing to various areas on the map where agents should be stationed, while each handled a fresh cup of coffee in preparation for the long night of planning ahead. After gathering in the building's security office that included a wall of video screens showing the feeds from all of the

154

dozens of security cameras placed around the building and property, the group then moved to the halls of the courthouse upstairs. The interior of the courthouse was dark and deathly silent at this late hour, with the only sound being the chorus of footfalls created by tactical boots on the freshly buffed marble floors and the echo reverberating in the cavernous building. The team spent the next hours blocking out locations and movements for undercover agents to take the following day so that they could be fully prepared for Netwanye's apprehension. They prepared for any eventuality, including the possibility that Netwanye would have a security detail with him. In that circumstance, they would announce their presence, swoop in quickly, and take Netwanye into their custody before his security detail had time to lift a finger, much less grab for a hidden firearm. By just after midnight, the team of agents had satisfied themselves that their multiple contingency plans covered all the likely scenarios for the following day, and they all went back to their homes to get a few hours rest before the next day's events.

***

Noah arrived on the day of the hearing ready for battle. The briefing on the motion for summary judgment was extensive and he carried behind him a roller bag the size of a small suitcase packed full of documents and binders. He felt like a litigator walking through the entrance to the courthouse in a grey pinstriped suit, crisp white shirt, and light blue tie. He flashed his bar card showing that he had been admitted to practice law at the entrance to the building so that he did not have to stand in the long security line – like legal royalty – and then continued directly to the courtroom with a singular purpose. Outside the courtroom he saw Sledge standing with Netwanye and he did his best to avoid eye contact. That wasn't a problem with Sledge, who pivoted his back to Noah the moment he saw him, but Netwanye was a different story. When he saw Noah, he made right for him, leaving Sledge dumfounded. Noah tried to turn around and retreat to a set of benches by the doors to the next courtroom down the hall, but it was no use, Netwanye moved quickly and Noah could not escape an interaction. Sledge hurriedly caught up with his client just as Netwanye reached Noah. Noah was extremely fearful of what Netwanye would do or say. He was on the

155

precipice of finally putting into motion the plan that might deliver him from Casimir's grip, and Casimir's main henchman was unwittingly about to ruin any chance Noah had at getting himself and his family to safety. Running through his head were the dozen and a half ways Netwanye could completely destroy Noah's plan – and the rest of Noah's and Alana's life – in this moment. Netwanye extended an eager hand and Noah had no choice but to accept the handshake, play his part, and hope for the best.

"Nice seeing you again Mr. Walker. Last time I saw you, you pulled out of our settlement at the last minute and now you have forced me to travel across the Atlantic to appear in court. I'm starting to think that you don't like me." said Netwanye with a grin.

"Um, no," staggered Noah, "of course not. Nothing personal – just doing my job."

"Well, it's nice to be wanted, but please, in the future, let me watch my Bafana Bafana in peace, okay?" Netwanye chuckled. Noah laughed nervously, but thought that Netwanye was having way too much fun with this situation. He put his arm around Noah, continuing to laugh at his own joke.

"Okay, that's enough Mr. Ndlovu," intervened Sledge. He grabbed Netwanye by the upper arm and ushered him back to their corner outside the courtroom.

The hearing was to be presided over by Judge Hilary Lynden, a veteran of the bench who was known for her exceeding intelligence. Noah was thrilled at having this judge, because he felt that with Netwanye's testimony he would have the better of the arguments. With such an adept judge he had a very good chance to prevail.

"All rise," was the directive of the court officer as Judge Lynden entered the courtroom. She admonished everyone to be seated and immediately jumped to business.

"This is *Undertow Acquisitions v. Sud-Coast and Company*, and I have a motion for summary judgment before me that is fully briefed and I understand that there will be at least one witness today, is that right counsel?"

"Yes, your Honor," Noah responded quickly.

"Very good Mr. Walker, you may call your first witness."

Noah announced Netwanye and the Sud-Coast head of finance strode easily to the witness stand, obviously enjoying his experience. Noah wondered if he was already counting the money in his head. Netwanye was issued the oath and promised to tell the truth, the whole truth, and nothing but the truth.

Noah jumped into his questioning, starting with Netwanye's background, his education, and his rise through the ranks at Sud-Coast. While not the most exciting line of questioning, it was necessary to lay the foundation for Noah's later questions about Netwanye's knowledge of the bond purchase agreement and group action provision. He was enjoying being on his feet in the court room again and liberally asked questions to extend the experience. He also hoped that if he could extend these mundane questions long enough, he might lull Sledge into a stupor and be able to later catch him off-guard with eviscerating questions about the group action provision. It wasn't long, though, until Judge Lynden grew tired of the background herself, and asked Noah to get to the point.

"Okay, Mr. Walker, I understand Mr. Ndlovu is well qualified. And I don't expect that Mr. Sledge will be making any objection given Mr. Ndlovu's long tenure and extensive experience at Sud-Coast. Please, move to the substance of his testimony."

"Yes, your honor," continued Noah, "Now, Mr. Ndlovu, can you tell me who drafted the bond purchase agreement at issue in this case?"

"Yes, of course, it was the finance department within Sud-Coast that drafted the agreement, along with some assistance from our legal department, so it would have been a number of individuals from our Cape Town office."

"And that's the office that you work in, correct?" Continued Noah.

"Yes"

No reaction from Sledge. His face was stuck in the passive focus of someone who had done this hundreds of times as he sat at his table, picking at the side of a binder with his pen.

"And did you work in that office at the time of the drafting of the agreement?"

"Yes, of course I did."

Sledge stopped picking at this answer. He was now paying attention.

"Did you draft any of this agreement, Mr. Ndlovu?"

"Yes."

"Are you aware of the group action provision within this agreement?"

"Yes, I am."

The testimony now had Sledge's full attention and Sledge was halfway out of his seat, like a sprinter ready to burst off the mark.

"Did you draft the group action provision in this agreement?"

"Objection!" yelled Sledge, who was gripping the sides of his table now, "your Honor, he is getting into evidence concerning the drafting of the contract, which is completely outside the scope of the motion or this inquiry."

Sledge was caught off guard, and grasping at straws. This was clearly relevant testimony, but he knew this area of inquiry could hurt his case.

"This is clearly relevant, your Honor," retorted Noah, "this clause is at the heart of the defendant's motion."

"I agree with you counsel, the objection is overruled. Mr. Walker, you may continue." Judge Lynden ruled.

With the objection overruled, Noah was free to question Netwanye at will about the provisions in the bond purchase agreement. The rest was academic. Noah ably led Netwanye through

158

an explanation of the group action provision and how the finance and legal departments at Sud-Coast had always recognized it to be flexible in its approach and had on many occasions let other bond holders out of the clause's strict language. Sledge continued to object feebly throughout, but Judge Lynden let the entirety of Netwanye's damaging testimony into the record. Once Noah had finished his questions, Sledge sat as still as a statute at his table. The color had run out of his face, and he didn't answer the first time the judged asked if he had any questions.

"Counsel, I'll ask it again, do you have any questions for the witness? Otherwise, let's please not use any more of this man's time," prodded Judge Lynden, now irritated that Sledge was not paying attention after she listened to each of Sledge's objections during Noah's examination.

"Um, yes your Honor, I may have a few, but may we approach first," answered Sledge, asking that he and Noah be allowed to address the judge privately at the bench so that Netwanye could not hear their conversation.

"Yes, but this better be quick," replied Judge Lynden.

Noah and Sledge both walked up to the front of the courtroom and the judge joined them at the side of the bench away from the witness and turned on recorded white noise in the courtroom that prevented the witness from hearing what they were discussing.

"Now, what is this all about, my patience has about run out with you Mr. Sledge," said Judge Lynden, now clearly exacerbated.

"Your Honor," replied Sledge, "I would like your permission to treat Mr. Netwanye as a hostile witness in my questioning. He is clearly working at odds with his company's best interests and we should be allowed to aggressively question him."

Noah reacted quickly, "your Honor, Sud-Coast did not even object to my subpoenaing Mr. Netwanye today, they brought him willingly, and now they're accusing him of working against the company. Those two positions cannot be squared."

159

"That's a very good point, Mr. Walker," replied Judge Lynden. Noah breathed a sigh of relief to himself. "Mr. Sledge, you had every opportunity to speak with the witness about his involvement in drafting the agreement before deciding whether to make him available to willingly testify. Did you do that?" asked the judge.

There was another long pause before Sledge answered.

"Well, no, your Honor, we didn't."

"Well, then I can't help you Mr. Sledge, you should have done your homework. Where you didn't object to the witness's presence here today, there's no way I will let you treat him as hostile. If you have some areas of the witness's testimony you'd like to get into on re-direct that's fine, but I will allow no leading or aggressive questions."

The white noise was turned off as the two lawyers returned to their respective tables and Judge Lynden asked Sledge again if he had any further questions.

"No, your Honor," was his answer and Netwanye's testimony was complete.

Noah then made a perfunctory argument that Netwanye's testimony cast doubt on the meaning of the group action provision and that the meaning of the provision would need to be left for the jury to decide at trial. He was telling the judge something she already knew and while she told the parties that she would take the matter under advisement, Noah was already sure of what the judge's final ruling on the motion would be.

Netwanye was feeling triumphant after the testimony and displayed a broad smile in stark contrast to the outrage on Sledge's face. He was so close to exacting his own revenge on Sud-Coast and recovering the money Sud-Coast had been stealing from community programs in the townships of South Africa and being able to redistribute it to where it belonged that he couldn't hide his jubilation. Sledge manhandled Netwanye out of the courtroom, but not before Netwanye clandestinely slid a note onto Noah's counsel

160

table on the way out. Noah did not dare read it until his opponents were through the courtroom doors.

"Let's meet tonight before my flight – I'll call you," the note read.

Noah knew Netwanye wouldn't even get as far as the entry to the courthouse.

- CHAPTER 22 -

By the time the hearing ended, the hallway outside Judge Lynden's courtroom was bustling with litigants from all walks of life from the CEO of a corporate giant leading a phalanx of clean-shaven corporate lawyers, to the asylum seeker, hoping for a chance to spend the rest of his life free from the threat of persecution through the efforts of his pro bono attorney. The increased foot traffic gave the cohort of undercover FBI agents ample opportunity to conceal themselves in plain sight using normal clothing and articles – a newspaper, a cup of coffee, a legal brief – to blend into the mosaic of customers at the courthouse that morning.

As a buoyant Netwanye left the courtroom, the agents leapt to action from out of their covert positions as if a switch had been flipped. Like a choreographed dance, they all moved at once, each to their assigned objectives. The agent dressed in khakis and a button-down shirt sipping coffee by the courtroom door set down his drink and pivoted quickly to put himself directly in front of the exiting procession. By boxing in the group, the agent delayed their progress out of the courtroom and gave the other agents a chance to move in. The man in jeans and a polo shirt idly examining the court schedule on the opposite wall moved to the right flank and blocked Netwanye's progress, while a woman in a suit dropped her newspaper and moved to the left flank preventing Sledge from advancing any further. Netwanye did have a security detail of two that trailed him on the way out of the courtroom, but additional agents in suits who had been observing the hearing moved in behind Netwanye and Sledge the moment they passed through the courtroom doors separating the security detail from Netwanye. The Marshals in the courtroom helped the agents to physically restrain the security guards so that the arrests occurring outside of the courtroom could proceed without incident. Noah was trailing behind Netwanye's group and an agent sidled up to him as well, but with a lighter touch – they were all on the same team now.

With the group leaving the courtroom stopped and secured, Eve emerged swiftly from a side door in the hallway with Special

Agent Moody and approached the mob of now confused litigants. She flashed her badge, and then got to the particulars with the steady confidence of an agent that had done this all before and knew exactly what she was doing.

"Mr. Netwanye, I'm Special Agent Rust, with the FBI. You are under arrest."

She stepped up to Netwanye and in the same motion took out a pair of handcuffs and secured his hands behind him.

"This is an outrage," yelled an incredulous Sledge from behind an agent twice his size, "my client has been compelled to be here by the court, he is a foreign citizen with rights and protections, this is entrapment, this is an ambush." The list of civil liberty violations went on and Sledge continued to waive a pointed index finger at the federal agents, but it didn't stop Eve from escorting a shocked Netwanye from the threshold of the courtroom. Netwanye's exuberant smile was gone now and replaced with a shocked countenance and grey affect as he silently allowed himself to be led away. The agents also rounded up his security detail, and Sledge too, and they were all escorted down to the basement of the courthouse amidst a crowd of gaping mouths and blank stares from the lawyers and other individuals patronizing the courthouse that day. In the basement, the Marshalls had holding rooms for the criminal defendants that were brought to the courthouse each day for hearings and other proceedings, and Eve arrived there with her quarry a few moments later.

Netwanye's two guards were put in a holding cell on their own and their cell phones were taken away from them, so they could not communicate with the outside world. Sledge was put into an interrogation room – a slight upgrade from the hard benches of the holding cells, but by no means a comfortable place to pass the time. His communication devices were also taken away from him. It was a risk taking Netwanye's attorney into custody, even if only for a short time, because the FBI had no reason to believe he was involved in the scheme. It was a bending of the rules, but one deemed necessary by Special Agent Moody to control the flow of information concerning Netwanye's arrest until the FBI had a chance to turn him and get the information necessary to take down Casimir. When released later, Sledge would be told that he had been temporarily put in protective custody so that the FBI could assess any threat posed to him through their interrogation of Netwanye.

Netwanye was placed into a brightly lit interview room by himself, with a table, two chairs on opposite sides, and a large one-way mirror on the wall. Noah stood eagerly on the other side of the mirror. His possible salvation was now sitting only feet away, and it was all he could do to keep himself from rushing into that room and wringing Netwanye's neck to force him to cooperate. Noah was praying now that the FBI's expertise could be used to quickly nudge Netwanye to their side, and free Noah and his family from Casimir's grip for the rest of their lives. All Noah could do now was be patient. He just hoped the FBI could deliver.

After letting Netwanye stew for a few minutes by himself, Eve entered and got to work. Given the circumstances, she had authority to move beyond the normal confines of FBI interrogation procedure and planned to gather the information she could without providing the Miranda warning. Without first giving that warning, neither she nor anyone else could ever use the information gathered in the interrogation against Netwanye in court. That was a risk the agents were willing to take as Eve and Special Agent Moody wanted to be able to have a free and open conversation and to not give Netwanye the option of stopping the questioning by asking for a lawyer. The FBI would still be able to use anything Netwanye told them against Casimir, but the ultimate goal was to convince Netwanye that there was no other option for him but to work with the FBI as a confidential informant.

"Mr. Netwanye, welcome to the U.S. Marshal's office." Said Eve, nonchalantly, as she entered the interview room. She sat down opposite Netwanye at the small table with her hands folded in front of her. She looked him directly in the eyes and continued.

"I'd like to have a conversation with you about Roth Casimir."

Netwanye's face took on a sickly pallor at the mention of Casimir, and his eyes stared blankly ahead for a moment before his face turned downward with his eyes trained directly on the brushed aluminum tabletop before him. He brought his hands up to the table and clasped them before resting them in front of him. He was entirely still for a moment in this hunched position, and Eve began to think that the mention of Casimir was all she was going to need to break him. Her mind was switching gear to itemizing the types of information they could immediately use from Netwanye when the prisoner seemed to come back to life before her eyes. He took a deep breath and exhaled loudly before picking up his head and refocusing on Eve. An indignant smug came across his face and he took his arms off the tabletop and crossed them on his chest. He leaned back in his chair and addressed Eve with confidence.

"I don't know who you are talking about. I don't know why I am here. Please release me, I have done nothing wrong."

"Look, Mr. Netwanye, I can understand that you are confused about what's happening here. But the truth is that we know much more about your scheme to steal from Sud-Coast than you think. We know you're working with Casimir and others on the scheme, and we know you're close to completing the conspiracy and making yourself rich. Sorry to say, that's all over now."

"Madame, I thank you for your concern and I know you are just doing your job. However, there is simply nothing I can tell you. I don't know this 'Casimir,' character you are speaking of. You must have gotten some bad information. I don't know who told you these things, but you have the wrong person. You should do a better job checking your sources before plucking innocent people out of courtrooms."

The color in Netwanye's face was coming back and a smile was beginning to appear again as he started to gain confidence in his own lies. Eve could tell that he had decided to dig in his heels and that this was going to be more of a fight than she thought. She and Agent Moody had hoped that naming Casimir immediately would shock Netwanye into quick submission, but Netwanye had chosen the stubborn route that many criminals do. When someone has been living their deceit for years and telling themselves that they are doing it for the right reasons, it can be extremely difficult to accept that their conduct was wrong. Netwanye was either living a delusion, or had decided to gamble that Eve did not have as much information as she let on. Eve did not have time to delve into Netwanye's psyche to determine which one it was – she had a criminal mastermind in her sights and it was time to take the gloves off and get Netwanye's cooperation. But first she had to check in on another critical part of the operation.

She excused herself and stepped outside the interrogation room, after explaining to Netwanye that she was happy to lay out everything the FBI had on him and would be back to discuss that information shortly. Closing the door behind her, she immediately whipped out her cell phone and hit a speed-dial preset.

"Yup," was the concise answer on the other end of the line.

"We have a bit of a situation here. Developing our confidential informant may take a bit longer than expected. Where do we stand in the Southern Suburbs?" asked Eve.

"We are good skipper. He took a drive down to Cape Point with a lady friend today, and we had to keep our distance so didn't have eyes on him the whole time, but picked him up again on his way out of the park headed back to the Stellenbosch region. They swung through Cape Town for an early dinner before proceeding back to his farm in the wine region. He's about five kilometers from his home compound now. We're in good shape – take your time."

Eve hung up the phone and moved briskly to the door next to the one she had just exited and entered to find Noah and Special Agent Moody sitting in chairs facing the one-way mirror and watching Netwanye's every move. Agent Moody turned to her while Noah stayed transfixed on the view, still absorbing the experience of being on the other side of the interrogation. Netwanye continued to fiddle with his hands in the small room, and from time to time he would look up at the mirror. Not yet used to the unfamiliar experience of being invisible, Noah would avert his stare each time Netwanye did so.

"Well, he's digging in, but at least we know that he's going to push back. Time to move to the next step in our interrogation

166

plan," said Agent Moody, with a matter-of-fact tone – he had been through this hundreds of times before and a suspect's resistance was no surprise to him. It was only one step in the process of getting Netwanye's cooperation.

"No question about that," replied Eve, "I'll take him through what we know and see if he bites."

Eve left the observation room on her way back to Netwanye, but before she entered the room, she checked her phone again and saw a text from the field agent.

"Target has arrived at home. All is quiet."

Time was still on her side and she calmly entered the interrogation room again with confidence. Netwanye sat there stoically, with an expression suggesting annoyance at having been detained for so long already. Eve sat and kept a stern expression on her face as she stared directly at Netwanye again prepared to dazzle him with the vast extent of the information the FBI already knew about his and Casimir's plot. With both hands on the table before her, she launched into a detailed explanation of the plot to extract a huge sum of money from Sud-Coast under cover of a lawsuit. She took Netwanye carefully through every step of the plot, using the information Noah had provided to her and Agent Moody and focusing on the parts that made Netwanye especially culpable in the conspiracy, and making sure to highlight that Netwanye himself was the public face of the scheme. He had been the person at Sud-Coast overseeing the case on the company's behalf. If the FBI exposed a fraud, Netwanye would be the person who was held responsible. He was an obvious scapegoat if Casimir was not brought to justice. Did Netwanye really think that Casimir would come to his rescue if Netwanye was indicted, convicted, and imprisoned in South Africa?

"Let me be clear, when we prosecute this case, we will be prosecuting you as the true leader of the scheme, unless we get some more information concerning Casimir's involvement. You are the one with the authority at Sud-Coast necessary to make sure the company will pay, and any jury in the world will believe that you were the one pulling the strings. It will be a quick guilty verdict and a long stretch in a dark hole for you."

Netwanye's state of mind was revealed by his face that became more deathly pale with each successive explanation given by Eve. Perspiration was collecting on Netwanye's brow as the lecture continued. But, when Eve finished, Netwanye made no grand adoption of her narrative or even so much as moved. Eve had seen this before, as it's not uncommon after a subject feels the shock of being caught in the act and realizes they're already behind closed doors with no way out. Eve tried to rouse him.

"Listen, Netwanye, all we really want here is Casimir. He's the one we're really after, and we're willing to deal with you to make that happen. Trust me, the last thing we want to do is turn you over to the South African police. We lose control over your fate the second that we do that. If you are convicted of this crime in your home country you will spend decades in a horrible prison. We want to protect you from all that – all you have to do is cooperate."

Eve let her last comment hang in the ensuing silence as she continued to sit and stare at him. The silence was broken by a loud ping emanating from her pocket as her phone received another text. She looked down quickly and saw that it was from the field agent.

"Call me. He's on the move."

Urgency now pulsed through Eve's veins as she rose to her feet. She put her phone in her pocket, crossed her arms, and stared directly at Netwanye.

"Think about it, Netwanye. It's your life we're talking about here. No one else in your organization is going to lift a finger to help you. If you don't cooperate, you'll be thrown under the bus, and then into a cell where you'll be forgotten forever."

She left the room and hit speed dial as soon as the door shut behind her.

"We have a situation here," said the voice urgently on the other side of the phone, "we thought he was down for the night, but there is now movement in the house and we are seeing the staging of luggage in the portico on the front of the house."

168

"Can you see who is getting ready to leave? Could it just be his woman going?" inquired Eve.

"Hard to say. Our views of the compound are obscured, but from what we can see, it looks like the whole house is getting ready to move – and fast."

"Okay, stay on them. We're going to have to hurry it along here. It's probably time to ring up our South African counterparts too, in case he tries to run. I'll check back soon, but text me if they start moving away from the compound."

"Roger that."

Eve moved to the side room door and entered hastily and explained the situation to Special Agent Moody and Noah. She didn't miss a beat as she turned to face Noah and explained the solution she had already devised.

"Noah, we don't normally do this but we are crunched now because we don't know where Casimir is headed. If we lose him and he makes it to a country that has no extradition agreement with the United States we might not get another shot at him. We also can't pick him up without cooperation from Netwanye because we're not sure we can prosecute him without the evidence Netwanye can provide. If we can't prosecute, there's no point in arresting him and then having to release him. If you're willing, we think your participation here might make all the difference."

"What were you thinking?"

"Well, our original plan didn't include revealing you to Netwanye, because it would expose you to greater risk if Netwanye ultimately decided not to cooperate and then told Casimir about what you'd done. Now our only shot at Casimir might be to tell Netwanye that you're already cooperating. Knowing that he's not the only one turning on Casimir might give Netwanye the final push he needs. Listen, I know it's a huge risk – if he balks, then you're exposed and vulnerable as we might not be able to prosecute Casimir at all. But, without your participation, we'll almost certainly miss Casimir altogether, and there's no telling when he'll surface again and the extent of further damage that he will be able to cause."

It didn't take Noah more than a second to make his decision. He had already made it when he decided to assist the FBI initially – he had to put an end to the havoc Casimir had wreaked on his life once and for all. The lives of Alana and his child depended on it. He did not want to be looking over his shoulder for the rest of his life.

"I'm in," responded Noah.

Before he knew it, Eve was ushering him out the door and to the threshold of the interrogation room.

"Wait here," she said as she entered alone closing the door behind her.

"Netwanye, I have one more thing to show you before you tell me your decision."

She stood and ceremoniously opened the door to reveal Noah standing in the doorway.

"Hello, Netwanye, long time, no see," said Noah, through a wry smile, "come on now, you know what Casimir is capable of – it's time to join the good guys."

Netwanye's visage stayed unchanged for what seemed like an eternity. He glared at Noah and the room and the hallway outside became completely silent. Then Netwanye's scowl turned slowly into a smile so wide it revealed his teeth.

"My friend," said Netwanye, "how can I be of help?"

- CHAPTER 23 -

The small interrogation room saw a flurry of activity from a revolving cast of law enforcement officers in the moments after Netwanye's capitulation. Eve immediately called the U.S. Attorney's Office to arrange for the paperwork that would allow for Netwanye to enjoy immunity from prosecution by the United States in exchange for his cooperation in the investigation. The non-prosecution agreement also included a provision that the United States would not extradite Netwanye to South Africa and also that the United States would work with the South African authorities to ensure that Netwanye would not be prosecuted in his home country when he returned. Netwanye was also offered witness protection and resettlement in the United States, but he refused. He wanted freedom to live his life where he pleased.

Sledge was freed from his temporary confinement and came out of the room on fire, like a bull out of the chute laboring with every muscle to toss the rider on its back. He demanded to see his client but was quickly informed that Netwanye had been assigned a public defender and that neither Netwanye, his new lawyer, nor anyone from the FBI was at liberty to share any information with Sledge. This only led to more yelled demands from Sledge but one of the FBI agents promptly showed Sledge the door with the help of a couple U.S. Marshals, over Sledge's continued loud and obnoxious objections.

Assistant United States Attorney Schoenheight quickly arrived from his office on the third floor of the courthouse exuding energy and excitement about getting a deal done with Netwanye so they could continue to pursue the bigger fish in the scheme. He immediately went to work with Netwanye's new attorney on the proffer – essentially a contract laying out exactly what Netwanye would provide to the FBI and U.S. Attorney in exchange for the leniency of the United States government. The tireless group of attorneys and law enforcement officers were very close to a final version of the proffer, when Eve heard another ping on her phone. It was from a remote drone outside Casimir's compound that had been

171

set to patrol the rear of the property from high above. Because the FBI had very limited resources in the region and could only commit a small team to Casimir's case on short notice, the two assigned field agents employed a small drone to watch the back of the property while they staked out the front. The drone was able to hover high above the property out of earshot of the occupants and was equipped with an array of cutting-edge sensors and high-definition cameras including an infrared camera to allow it to see in the dark. The ping had been sent automatically from the drone when it detected movement on the back of the property and still pictures of activity were sent simultaneously to Eve and the field agents. A moment later Eve got another call from the field agent and stepped out of the room.

"We've got movement in the back – did you see the images? It looks like two individuals moving toward a vehicle," said the field agent in rapid fire stream of consciousness.

"Yes, saw them," replied Eve, "I don't know why it didn't pick them up earlier, maybe they have a tunnel or something. What's our ability to follow them? We're very close to a deal here."

"Well, we're going to have to choose – it's just two of us in a car out front – if we go around back, we lose coverage of the front. We don't know who's back there. Could be Casimir, could be someone else – he has a pretty big staff. His luggage is still piled out front. It could be a diversion. Just very hard to tell at this point. What do you want to do?"

The line went silent as Eve considered the options. Losing Casimir at this point – now that she had come so far and was so close to apprehending him once and for all – was not something that she could allow. The stakes had never been higher for her personally nor for the financial crimes task force – they were close to catching the biggest criminal of the unit's history and she was just steps away from finally bringing her father's killer to justice.

"Wait, hold on," interrupted the field agent who was following the feed from the drone's camera on a screen, "okay, the two suspects out back are moving off the compound. I repeat, they just got in the vehicle and they're moving away from the compound. What do you want to do here?"

"Go get them, and stay on them – it's got to be Casimir, we can't afford to lose him now."

"Roger that."

The line cut out as the field agent exploded to action like a spring under immense pressure. He yanked his vehicle into gear, spun the wheel aggressively, and tore out from behind the stand of trees giving him and his partner cover from those in the compound. The spinning tires sprayed a plume of dusk and rock as the agents began speeding down the road to intercept the vehicle fleeing the rear of the property.

Eve rushed back to the interview room to provide any final assistance she could to get the deal done quickly. As she entered the room, she saw Netwanye rise and shake hands with Special Agency Moody with both men displaying wide smiles on their faces. The public defender was already shaking hands with Schoenheight, and Noah was watching everything from the corner of the room, looking relieved. She knew the deal had just been struck and she whipped out her cell phone once more and called the field agent and gave a simple instruction.

"The deal's done. Take him."

***

The FBI had set its drone to tail the car from a distance, and using the drone's geolocation information, the second field agent riding in the front passenger side of the chase vehicle was able to give directions to where they should intercept the fleeing car. The video was not clear enough to make out the vehicle's make and model, but it was a light color, and clearly some sort of sports car – and it was moving fast.

"He's about to intersect the M12 from the north. If he takes it, we can follow him pretty easily on that."

"Roger."

"Okay, yeah, he took the M12 headed east toward downtown Stellenbosch, so if you keep straight you will intercept the M12 too and we can tail him with cover from the traffic. Push it – he's gunning it on the highway, the drone's not going to keep up."

"Roger that."

Both agents were pushed back in their seats as the lead agent pressed all the way down on the accelerator. The second agent took the drone off target and set it to auto pilot so that it could return to circle the vineyard to keep an eye on the activity there.

"That's got to be him," said the second field agent, as they sped east down the four-lane highway toward Stellenbosch's quiet town center. They could now see that the car was a white Maserati, capable of speeds far in excess of the vehicle the field agents were driving. The lead agent asked everything he could of the small engine in their Volkswagen Polo to inch it closer to the Maserati so as not to lose contact with the suspect who was comfortably travelling at excessive speed down the highway.

"Let's get the South African national police on the line. If we're going to try to take him, we might need some backup and better equipment," instructed the lead agent. The second agent phoned their contact at the South African national police. They had already briefed them about the possibility of making an arrest in Stellenbosch, but hadn't yet given all the details. The FBI was taking no chances that a leak might tip off Casimir and send him jet setting to some non-extradition country.

"Yes, hello lieutenant, just checking in on the thing we discussed earlier. We are trailing the target just outside of downtown Stellenbosch approaching from the west. We anticipate stopping him soon. Will let you know the location before we make the stop so that your officers can be on scene. Be advised that the suspect is driving in a white Maserati. We're probably going to need something fast to catch him if he tries to run. A little extra fire power wouldn't hurt either, if you can spare it."

"Received and confirmed," was the response in a thick Afrikaans accent over the radio, "we have resources ready that

174

satisfy those requirements and are prepared to assist when necessary."

The Maserati slowed slightly as it approached the town and dipped off the highway with a sharp turn onto an exit ramp that it maneuvered with ease. The lead agent had to turn evasively to make the exit and almost lost control as the agents were jolted violently to the left as their car careened down the ramp. They reached the bottom of the ramp just in time to see the Maserati accelerate through an intersection. The lead agent gunned the engine again and sped through a red light and onto a downtown thoroughfare narrowly avoiding a collision with vehicles crossing the intersection. The Maserati was up to top speed again and took another sharp right. The agent had no choice but to follow suit, spinning his tires on the slightly damp pavement and generating fierce honks from other vehicles on the road. The clamor raised by the other motorists gave the driver of the Maserati confirmation that he was indeed being followed.

The speed of the pursuit increased exponentially as the driver of the Maserati put the vehicle into high gear. The Maserati ably navigated tight corners at speed with a chassis that was designed specifically for that purpose in its effort to elude its pursuers. The agents necessarily took the turns tighter than the sports car they were pursuing, cutting too close to a corner shop on one turn and sideswiping a display of wood carved giraffes with their fishtailing vehicle, sending the goods clattering across the street and the pedestrians admiring them leaping to safety.

"Okay, call the national police back, we're in full pursuit now," said the lead agent as he put the chase vehicle into gear and flipped on the blue lights and siren.

The second agent pulled out his phone again and called their contact and passed on word and then took out a walkie talkie from the glove box and tuned it to the local police band and started calling out their position so that support could catch up.

"Headed east down Dorp St. Now left on Neething St., headed north. Now right on Victoria, headed east again."

175

The wheels of the two dueling automobiles squealed in tandem through the mostly vacant roads of downtown Stellenbosch. The agents' siren was now joined by two others from national police vehicles also with their lights ablaze.

"He's headed out of town," yelled the agent in the passenger seat into the walkie-talkie gripped in his right hand as the driver struggled to keep pace with the superior machine in front of them, "if he makes it to the highway, we're going to lose him – he's just too fast in that thing."

"Don't worry," crackled a response from the national police over the radio, "we've got it covered."

"Okay, I hope so."

The Maserati made the highway and headed east out of Stellenbosch toward the hills that encircle the region and was off like a rocket opening up the throttle to full power the moment the vehicle's wheels touched highway pavement. The lead agent put his foot down all the way again, but it was no use. The Maserati was already disappearing into the distance.

"Shit," exclaimed the lead agent. The second agent depressed the transmit button on his walkie-talkie and reported, "we've lost contact – suspect heading east on the R310 toward Franschhoek at high speed."

As the high-pitched buzz of the Maserati engine faded away, things became calm again as the agents continued driving in silence, aimlessly now. Then suddenly a new sound filled the air. A series of low-pitched thuds emanated from far in the distance. With each second, they became more pronounced until the sound of the supersonic blades of a military helicopter thumped against the chests of the agents and shook the ground around the agents' car. It buzzed the collection of police vehicles in a show of overwhelming power before it took off after the Maserati.

"Told you bro!" boasted one of the South African officers over the radio. The chase was back on. Each of the law enforcement vehicles was shoved into gear again as they tore down the highway in the direction they had seen the Maserati disappear.

The updates from the helicopter pilot were made with characteristic military precision and came across the radio in calm, unemotional bursts.

"Subject vehicle is still eastbound on the R310."

"Now turning onto the R45, still eastbound."

"Now approaching Franschhoek."

"Now southbound on the R45."

The agents continued their pursuit via the turn-by-turn directions provided by the helicopter pilot, surreally guided on a high-speed chase by an omniscient voice from above. Then a final transmission emanated from the radio.

"Suspect has deviated from main road. Suspect turned onto private drive at R45 hairpin turn, 2.3 kilometers outside town center. View of property is obscured by vegetation. Will standby in area to await further instructions."

***

While the rest of the congregation of lawyers and law enforcement officers in the basement of the federal courthouse in Boston were now loose and kidding with each other over a job well done and trying to determine where they would go for a drink to celebrate the achievement, Eve remained removed from the group victory lap and still on alert awaiting an update from her team in the field. It finally came when her cell phone buzzed to life again with a call from the lead agent informing her of their position outside the entrance to a private ranch property in the hills of the Stellenbosch region.

"We have a few options here, skipper" continued the lead agent, "we could stake out here and wait, but I think that's the wrong move – he clearly knows he's being followed and the longer we wait, the better chance he has to disappear forever."

"Agree completely, what other options are you seeing on the ground? Can we go into the compound?" asked Eve, so eager now to continue the chase and get Casimir in custody.

177

"We were all hoping you would say that. We're here with the national police. These guys are eager to get in there and show what they can do. They even called in a military helo to assist and they've told us there's more heavy artillery on the way. We're locked and loaded, skipper, just give us the word."

"Excellent," replied Eve, with no hesitation about the next move, "you have the green light to take the compound."

***

The two FBI agents caucused with the national police regarding how to breach the compound. The video feed from the drone showed that things had quieted down considerably at the wine farm since the Maserati sped away from the property, so they were almost certain that it was Casimir that had fled. The U.S. Consulate in Cape Town had also detailed a team of two auxiliary agents to watch the wine farm. They had been made available on an emergency basis given the urgency that now attached to this case, and would inform the lead agents if anything noteworthy took place at the wine farm.

For the agents and national police at the compound, it was now just a question of how to go in and get Casimir. They decided that the national police should take the lead because they had jurisdiction over the arrest, and they had many more resources to bear. As that decision was being made, a special operations team from the national police was arriving in two armored personnel carriers. Painted jet black, the armored vehicles were large, heavy, and loud. Everything flowed seamlessly following their arrival. Camouflage clad officers with automatic weapons at the ready assembled into two columns behind the armored vehicles. The senior officer barked a series of commands in Afrikaans, and the engines of the armored vehicles rumbled to life and began to lead the heavily armed units down the narrow gravel driveway. The FBI agents followed in their vehicle, as did other local police who had joined the chase, creating a long column of law enforcement advancing on their target.

The driveway was hemmed in on either side by thick bushy vegetation, making the narrow road the perfect terrain for an ambush. The tension in the special operators was palpable as each scanned the roadway and strained to see through the vegetation surrounding them. They were given the order to release the safety on their weapons to be ready for action whenever it came their way. After one hundred meters of apprehension, the driveway opened up onto a small grassy clearing. The vehicles pulled up in formation and the troops took cover positions behind them as everyone surveyed the scene.

Atop a hill another hundred meters in the distance was a small farmhouse that looked completely deserted. Everything remained still, and silent. The top hatch of one of the armored vehicles then popped open and the senior officer stuck out his head. The lead FBI agent followed suit and opened his door and stepped out.

"What's going on here? I thought we were going to have a welcome reception – my boys were ready for some action," said the officer.

"I don't know. Maybe they didn't stop at the house. Maybe they continued on foot into the hills. Let's take a team and ..."

The agent's response was interrupted by the SNAP SNAP of bullets flying over-head. He ducked instinctively back into the driver's seat of his vehicle just before a stream of bullets threw up a firework show of sparks off the front end of one of the armored vehicles. The officer ducked back into his vehicle as well. The troops took cover behind the armored vehicles, and at the same time the regular cruisers without armor protection lurched into gear abruptly and reversed to positions behind the special operators.

"Well, there's your welcome," chuckled the lead agent into his walkie-talkie, "can you see where it's coming from?"

"Yeah, we saw muzzle blasts from the second-floor window on the right side," replied the officer.

As he finished his transmission, another stream of automatic fire emanated from the same window causing more fireworks to erupt on the front of the other armored vehicle.

179

"Don't worry, we've got a solution for this," the officer said calmly, after the stream of fire abated again.

"What were you thinking?" asked the lead agent.

The officer didn't respond. Instead, the agents heard a series of loud clicks from one of the armored vehicles as a panel opened on the front. Suddenly a loud fizz sounded and in a burst of white smoke a rocket fired from the vehicle at supersonic speed headed for the house. It danced in the air while honing in on its target before impacting with a direct hit on the second-floor window. The shockwave from the large explosion jolted the FBI agents' vehicle before a shower of debris audibly fell on the roof of the car. When the smoke cleared from the blast, the upper right quarter of the house was gone.

"What the fuck was that," yelled the lead agent into the walkie-talkie gripped tightly in his hand.

"Hey bro, we don't tolerate getting shot at down here in South Africa. We're not going to need to worry about that machine-gun fire any more. Let's take a look and see what we got."

The radio cut out and a moment later the armored vehicles started lumbering forward toward the smoldering house. The troops and the regular vehicles followed suit. As they approached the building, there were fires burning on the second floor and no visible movement inside. The collected law enforcement officers stood there before the building for a moment in awe of the military might they had unleashed.

"Well, headquarters is not going to be happy about this one. They wanted to take this guy alive," exclaimed the lead agent.

"Yeah, they're gonna be pissed, but at least he didn't escape," concurred the second agent.

The officer walked up to the agents and embraced them.

"Good battle – got our man. Don't worry – we had no other option here. We were under fire – we couldn't risk losing any of our own. That's the truth and it's how I'll write it up in my report. All

180

will be good." He strode away toward the house to inspect the wreckage.

The agents followed him in. Flames had spread from the top floor to the rest of the house, making it unsafe to go inside. It was abundantly clear that no one could have survived the strike. Then, one of the special operators that had approached the house in an advance group yelled urgently from behind the building. They all followed quickly around the house to find the Maserati parked behind the burning structure on a small patio. It was empty and collecting grey ash on its roof from the fire.

***

The terrain was rocky and uneven and covered in thick fynbos – a thorny bush endemic to the area. It would have been hard to navigate even in the middle of the day. He dared not turn on a flashlight because it would certainly betray his position. He could tell from the stars that he was moving northwest, and knew that all he needed to do was keep under cover until he reached Franschhoek. After hailing a cab, he would be invisible to anyone following him. He would collect money from his stash house in Rondebosch, and clothes, and a passport, and in a few hours he would be gone forever.

The explosion told him that his companion was gone – she had covered his escape with her life and he would always remember her for that. It would take the police hours to sort through the debris of the mayhem they caused, only after which would they realize that he was not there. By that time, he would be long gone.

The lights of Franschhoek appeared on the horizon. He would be there soon. The thick brush began to clear as he approached a field of grass that reflected the moonlight on its glossy blades that lightly swayed in the breeze. On the other side of the field he could see a farmhouse, and on the other side of that was a country road. His path to freedom.

Stepping into the open field he immediately felt relief from the sharp nettled vegetation that had ripped at his legs since his escape from the farmhouse. He had no cover in the field and was exposed so he picked up his pace. His breathing grew heavier as his lumbering frame trudged forward and it covered up the series of subtle thuds emanating from the horizon. By the time he became aware of the incessant thumping, it was too late. The helicopter emerged from behind the tree line like a giant buzzing insect. The tips of the powerful rotor blades on the gargantuan machine glowed in an otherworldly green ellipse of static electricity and their downdraft beat down the line of trees marking the perimeter of the field. The man made a break for the tree line as the helicopter came into sight, but was soon tracked down by the thundering craft that made a graceful loop and positioned itself between him and the edge of the field. When he tried once more to dart under the chopper and into obscurity in the twisted vegetation, a short burst of machine gun fire from the nose of the bird at the man's feet stopped Casimir's escape once and for all.

- CHAPTER 24 -

Noah emerged from the U.S. Marshal's office at twilight. Passing thundershowers had just blanketed the area with cold rain and he could smell the heat of the day emanating from the parking lot. Huge popcorn shaped clouds glowing a fluorescent pink against a dimming blue night sky came into view as he stepped outside and he starred at them blankly, letting his mind attempt to process the events that had just transpired and their likely effect on his and his young family's life. The last hours were a complete blur in his mind and all he could think about now was Alana. All he wanted was to be next to her and to hold her. He would tell her everything that evening. He knew she would be angry at him for not telling her of the danger they were in, but he hoped she would realize that he was only trying to protect her and their unborn child. He hoped she would forgive him for the mistake of taking on Casimir as a client, and for shielding her from the stresses of that decision until he was sure that he had delivered her from the perils of working against him. On his way home he bought a large assortment of flowers he could not afford and also stopped at a pizza spot in Manchester and ordered Alana's favorite. She was expecting him to be home later, and a story of surprise shown on her face when he walked through the door. Noah took Alana in his arms and hugged her tightly and kissed her.

"I have had an incredible day – I can't wait to tell you all about it, but how are you feeling? How is the baby? Did you have a good day?"

"I'm so happy to see you home early, and thank you for getting dinner – it smells amazing and the flowers are beautiful. You didn't have to do that – you're so thoughtful. I had a good day, just a little nauseous earlier in the day. I think the baby is doing well. Is everything all right with the Sud-Coast case – did something happen today?

"Well, yes, it was a big day for the case, and actually a lot has been happening in the last few weeks that just resolved today. I can't wait to tell you about it, but let's get ourselves set for dinner and I can tell you the whole story."

She changed and Noah set a formal table with candlelight and they sat down to their feast of dough and cheese and she listened as he told her every detail, starting with what happened at the U.S. District Court hours earlier in the day and then expanding his narrative to cover the last weeks and months of their lives and the secret anguish he had been living through. She listened intently – deeply confused at first, then worried for Noah and herself, then finally furious at him for keeping her completely in the dark concerning the danger they were both in.

"How could you have not consulted with me before going to the FBI? That decision could have gotten us both killed! I thought you had trust in me – we need to be able to trust each other in this relationship. I could have handled that information just as well as you and could have helped you make the decision. That was our decision – not just yours. We have a child coming, Noah, and we need to be able to communicate with each other. That's the only way this is going to work. If we're in danger, I need to know about it."

"I know. I'm sorry. I was just trying to protect you. I was terrified and didn't want to put you in fear when I didn't need to. I panicked. I'm sorry. You're right. You should have been part of the decision. It won't happen again."

"Well, are we still in danger here? What if Casimir escapes, won't he come after us? What if he is released before trial? What if he's not convicted. I worked for a criminal defense lawyer, Noah, I know there are dozens of ways a crook can get out of a lawsuit – I helped do it more than once. How can we be sure the government can protect us?"

"I know you're scared, and I'm sorry I didn't bring you in on all of this before, but the case against Casimir is strong – very strong – and the special agent in charge is laser focused on getting a conviction that will put Casimir away for decades. There's no way they are going to release him before trial either – he's too much of a flight risk with all his resources and international connections. There's always a chance that something could go wrong with the

184

prosecution but that's very unlikely given the government's track record in these types of cases. Either way, we are in a much better place on the side of the FBI, rather than as expendable pawns in Casimir's criminal scheme. I hope you can understand my motivation and I hope you believe me when I tell you that I wanted to tell you everything before, but I didn't want to worry you. I didn't want you to know the danger you were in. I didn't want it to affect the baby."

"This is completely insane. You should have told me."

"I know. I'm sorry. I'm so sorry for all of this."

"I know you are. Thank you for taking care of us. Thank you for getting us out of this mess."

They held each other closely and she asked him to tell her the whole story again from the beginning so she could make sure she didn't miss anything. After hours of discussing the Sud-Coast case, their conversation drifted to a discussion of the future and about where they would go after the whole thing was finally over. They couldn't stay in Manchester – they wouldn't be able to afford it. They would miss it, of course, but a fresh start would be good for them and their new child. A new city, in a different part of the country. Noah would call Sledge the following day to withdraw the lawsuit. The rest was up to the FBI.

***

Eve's night had just begun with Netwanye's deal and Casimir's capture. After the congratulations were over, she drove back to the FBI field office, took the elevator to the sixth floor, dispensed a cup of coffee, and got to work preparing the necessary paperwork for Casimir's extradition from South Africa to the United States. She would leave the next day on a chartered flight to personally oversee the extradition. After Casimir was repatriated, Eve would work with Netwanye and Schoenheight to collect every shred of information Netwanye could provide to bury Casimir. They would get warrants and gather additional evidence of Casimir's crimes and the evidence would be organized into a succinct package to be presented at trial. Casimir would hire lawyers immediately and then the months long dance of a criminal prosecution would begin. His counsel would do everything they could to get the case dismissed by challenging every piece of evidence that Eve collected for the U.S. Attorney to use at trial to put Casimir away for good.

The mountain of work Eve faced did not deter her in the least. She could see the light at the end of the tunnel and felt that the most difficult parts of the investigation were already over. They had turned their witness and arrested their suspect and now they just had to connect the dots for the prosecutors to get a conviction. Though they were closer than ever to putting Casimir away, Eve wasn't even close to letting up. The familiar and unwavering drive to redeem her father could not be quieted. Her father had been a good man and she knew in her heart that he had been forced into the illegal life that eventually led to his death. By apprehending Casimir, she was putting closure on the memory of her father and the pain of being robbed of the time she lost with him. Casimir was the villain that dragged her father into a wretched life of crime and tore him from his family and robbed him of his life. By putting Casimir away, Eve would be able to finally put closure on the pain she suffered over her father's murder. She was sure that she was also saving other fathers or mothers and keeping other families from being ripped apart in the future. Eve's eyes began to water as she thought of her father. Tears rolled down her face, and she wept silently and alone under the stark fluorescent lights of the office. Then she refocused, grabbed her coffee, and settled in for another long night.

- CHAPTER 25 -

When new criminal cases are filed in federal court, each is assigned a federal judge to oversee the case. At the U.S. District Court for the District of Massachusetts, the cases were assigned randomly using a bingo ball cage that had been used for this purpose for over a century. The cage resided in a cabinet in the chief clerk's office and it was brought out each afternoon for the clerk to assign new cases while nursing a cup of Earl Grey tea. It had a base of dark mahogany and a steel cage that had collected rust at the intersection of its metal wires over the years. But the bingo cage was manufactured with care at a time when all things were made to last and continued to provide reliable service to the clerk of the federal court in Boston. Each of the wooden balls inside was adorned with a different judge's name, and while the individual wood spheres themselves had been changed out over the years as judges came and went, the device itself was still sturdy enough to last for decades to come.

There was no need to employ this method when assigning *United States v. Roth Casimir* to Judge Halderman. Because he was familiar with the facts and circumstances of the related earlier case against the former partners of Markus Stillfield Brice, the case was automatically assigned to him by the head clerk after it reached the clerk's desk as one in a large pile filed each day in the district court.

On the day of Casimir's arraignment, the participants for each of the cases scheduled for that morning before Judge Halderman sat on the wooden benches in the gallery of his cavernous courtroom that was painted a stark white and adorned with arched wood accents and detailed with a red and grey stenciled pattern inspired by the king protea flower. The benches were carved from hardwood and finished with a light stain, and while appearing elegant they quickly became uncomfortable to anyone sitting on them for long periods of time. Two of the eager litigants occupying the benches that morning were Casimir and his attorney, Guy Rickworth, a veteran from a massive law firm. Rickworth was perfectly type cast for the role of high-priced litigator with neatly parted hair, a clean-shaven face, a lanky figure, and an exquisitely tailored dark pin-stripe suit. He was a former federal prosecutor – common amongst white-collar defense attorneys – and was longtime friends with Schoenheight, his opponent that morning. They had overlapped in law school, and worked in the U.S. Attorney's Office together, before Rickworth decided to cash in on the riches that awaited in the corporate world while Schoenheight remained committed to the cause of justice. They had not spoken for some time, and so before the hearing they caught up in the hallway. Schoenheight was kidded for the long sideburns he had let grow out; Rickworth caught some grief for the four-hundred-dollar pair of shoes he was wearing. Their ribbing was interrupted by the bailiff's announcement that court was coming to order, and they both rushed back to the courtroom to their designated positions on opposite sides of the aisle. As Judge Halderman strode into the courtroom with purpose, all in attendance dutifully rose, and the session was brought to order.

"Okay, everyone may be seated. It looks like we're here for an arrangement today, is that right counsel?" remarked Judge Halderman.

"Yes, your Honor, Guy Rickworth for the defendant."

"Very good, and I see Mr. Schoenheight at counsel table, good morning."

"Good morning, your Honor." reciprocated Schoenheight.

"Okay, Mr. Rickworth, is your client waiving the formal reading of the charges against him?"

"Yes, your Honor, I have explained the indictment to my client and he understands and we do not need the charges read out in court today." replied Rickworth.

"Okay, thank you. Now before we get started, I want to make sure I'm understanding the provenance of this case. It appears that I previously oversaw a related case. Mr. Schoenheight, perhaps you can enlighten me?"

"Yes, your Honor, happy to do that. In addition to the allegations underlying this case, the government alleges that the defendant, Roth Casimir, oversaw the conduct of the defendants in another case you presided over a couple years ago concerning securities fraud by partners of the law firm Markus Stillfield Brice. Thus, we see these cases as related, your Honor."

"Very good, thank you. Mr. Rickworth, how does your client plead?"

"Not guilty, your Honor."

"Okay, thank you, that is noted for the record. Mr. Rickworth, do you expect to be filing a motion to suppress in this case?

"Most certainly, your Honor."

"Okay, have my clerk set a date and we can get this case going. If there's nothing further you are all dismissed. We will reconvene in fifteen minutes for the other cases on the docket today."

"All rise," cried the bailiff as the judge stood from his plush chair and retired to his chambers.

Schoenheight grabbed Rickworth just outside the door for a quick parley. They walked over to the railing of the balcony opposite the courtroom door looking over the atrium on the backside of the courthouse. Light streamed in through the massive window on that side of the building that faced Boston Harbor and they both looked out on two tug boats pulling a massive tanker into the harbor as they spoke.

"Hey, what are the chances we can do a deal on this one? We've got one very convincing witness and I'm sure there's something Mr. Casimir can provide us given the circles he seems to have travelled in."

"No chance," replied Rickworth, "at least not right now."

He walked away from his old friend in the abrupt manner adopted by many lawyers after years of law practice already lost in

189

the next issue he had to address that day on another of his many cases. Schoenheight took no offense as he had done it himself on many occasions. He returned to his office to prepare for the next phase of this case and the dozens of other cases he oversaw.

***

Rickworth's motion to suppress on Casimir's behalf was inevitable. Motions to suppress are filed to exclude evidence from trial that the government needs to prove its case. To be successful, the motion must show that law enforcement acquired the evidence underlying the government's charges in violation of the United States Constitution and its prohibitions against unreasonable search and seizure. Motions to suppress are often filed, but success is far from guaranteed. Rickworth's motion to suppress challenged every piece of evidence the government relied upon. It was fifty pages long with dozens of exhibits and hundreds of cases cited. At the hearing, Rickworth came ready to argue each point at length. He strutted into the courtroom confidently in a grey pinstripe suit on the day of the hearing, trailed by a young associate in high heels precariously hauling two heavy roller cases behind her. While the associate laboriously heaved the tomes contained within onto the counsel table, Rickworth paced at the front of the courtroom in deep thought, running every argument and its counter argument through his head.

Schoenheight, by comparison, travelled light. He arrived on his own with his worn leather briefcase that displayed numerous scratches and scrapes acquired from being set down, thrown down, and stuffed under tables on countless occasions during its tenure. Schoenheight laid out a legal pad, two pens, a highlighter, and a manila folder containing a small collection of stapled papers on his table. His arguments were memorized and any reminders he would need were already scratched on his legal pad.

Once Judge Halderman entered the courtroom and ascended the bench, Rickworth struck first, without invitation hoping to take control of the proceedings to give his client any edge he possibly could.

"Your Honor, we're here on defendant's motion to suppress. The real problem with the prosecution's case is that it's based on a

190

single informant they have not identified to the defense. Without knowing who the informant is, there's no way we can question that individual's credibility and no way, your Honor, that I can represent my client adequately and prepare his defense. And I'd like to …"

The judge abruptly intervened by raising his hand, like a crossing guard directing traffic.

"Okay counsel, you can stop right there for a moment," he said calmly, "we'll get to that, but please just start by identifying yourselves for the record. One step at a time here in my courtroom."

With the wind now effectively taken out of his sails, Rickworth paused and identified himself as Casimir's attorney. After Schoenheight reciprocated, Judge Halderman addressed Rickworth once more.

"Counsel, you can see I'm a stickler for procedure. Now that we've gotten the particulars out of the way, I understand that you are challenging the search warrant based on the fact that it's supported by a confidential informant who has not been identified. Tell me why I should agree with you."

"Thank you, your Honor, as I was saying, all the evidence taken from my client, including all computers seized by the FBI, all emails, and all the hard copy materials seized from my client's home in South Africa were taken based on a search warrant supported by information from a confidential informant. But the defense has not been given the identity of this individual and so we have no idea whether he's credible or not. It is manifestly unfair to my client to be unable to test the veracity of the information supporting the warrant. Without this individual's identity, we have no way of showing this court why the individual might lie to the government to get my client arrested. Simply put, your honor, the government should not be able to rely on evidence gathered using a search warrant without providing the basis for that warrant to the defendant."

Judge Halderman sat with Rickworth's argument for a moment in silence, turning it over in his mind before asking the prosecution for its position.

"Mr. Schoenheight, your response?"

"Yes, your Honor, thank you. The fact of the matter is that the confidential informant is eminently reliable and that can be shown without revealing the individual's identity. In fact, the individual's reliability has already been confirmed, because the information the informant has provided the government is already corroborated by other sources. Further, any need by the defendant for the informant's identity is far outweighed by the government's obligation to protect the informant from harm. If the informant's identity is disclosed, there is no question that that individual will be in great danger, as this defendant has shown a propensity for violence in the past and a knack for doing away with those who stand in his way. Lastly, your Honor, there are important policy considerations here. If the court exposes this confidential informant's identity it will provide grounds for the identities of future informants in other cases to be exposed as well. Potential future informants might think twice before even coming forward if the defendant's motion is granted here."

"Mr. Shoenheight, that is well understood by this court," answered Judge Halderman, "but we are not deciding issues of policy here today. Let's try to focus on this case and our particular informant. What we need to be concerned with is whether our informant is so reliable that I do not need to expose his identity. What can you tell me about that?"

"Thank you, your Honor, that was my very next point. The critical issues here are the basis of our informant's knowledge and the reliability of the information provided. The government satisfies both requirements in spades. The informant was very close to the organization and execution of the criminal scheme at issue in this case. The defendant's operation was a diversified criminal enterprise, your Honor, that stretched to the far corners of the globe and Mr. Casimir had criminal dealings in many different types of businesses. The specific crime at issue in this case – the defrauding of Sud-Coast and Company – was one of those many operations, as was the scheme underlying the previous case against the partners of Markus Stillfield Brice.

"The confidential informant in this case was intimately familiar with the workings of the conspiracy in this case. The

192

informant's involvement in the scheme here put that individual in a singularly unique position to provide information to the government to support its case. In fact, beside the defendant himself, the government's informant may be the person most knowledgeable about the defendant's activities."

"And as to the second requirement, counsel?" prompted the judge.

"The second requirement asks how reliable the information from the informant actually was. Your Honor, the information we received from the informant was spot on in every instance. The informant not only told the FBI what types of electronic and hard copy evidence to look for at the defendant's residences in South Africa and in the United States, but told federal agents precisely what they would find, and even identified for the FBI other associates of the defendant that might have information related to this case. The FBI was able to use the information provided by the informant to obtain additional warrants and collect evidence that will all be presented by the government at trial."

"Okay, thank you Mr. Schoenheight. Mr. Rickworth, you have a response I presume."

"Yes, your Honor. We expect we know who the government's informant is and while I will not surmise here and expose that name in open court, I can say that if it is the person we highly suspect that it is, there are strong arguments the defense can make to discredit this individual. In fact, it is the government's informant, not the defendant, that we believe was actually responsible for the alleged criminal actions underlying the government's case, and we would credibly argue at trial that it was that individual that devised and drove the scheme that my client is accused of perpetrating. Mr. Casimir was an unwitting participant in the alleged conspiracy against Sud-Coast, and because it was the informant that drove the plot, the informant has a huge incentive to lie to the government to cover up that individual's role, and implicate my client instead. That being the case, we require an opportunity to challenge this witness in open court, to show why the information provided by this individual is not credible and why a warrant based on that false information should never have been issued and used to dig into the private life of my client. All we are asking for here, your Honor, is the opportunity to cross-examine this informant so that we can demonstrate to the court the informant's bias and unreliability.

Rickworth sat down in a confident huff putting on an expression of frustration to underscore the strength of the arguments he had just made. Schoenheight was now the one jumping to his feet, sure that Rickworth had scored points with his last argument.

"Your Honor, I'll just note that if the defense believes they already have the identity of the confidential informant there is nothing keeping them from calling that individual to testify." Schoenheight remained on his feet expecting that his counter would move the judge, but it did not. The courtroom fell silent again as Judge Halderman considered the arguments. Schoenheight recoiled slowly to his seat. The only sound that could be heard echoing through the mostly vacant chamber was the absent-minded tapping of Judge Halderman's pen on the ledge of his raised dark wood desk as the judge's gaze drifted down to the papers before him in focused contemplation.

"Okay, anything else?" inquired the judge, lifting his head back up to gaze at the litigants before him.

The lawyers had nothing to add.

"Okay, hearing nothing, I will say that it troubles me that the defendants don't have access to the confidential informant's identity." continued the judge. "While I agree with the prosecution that the defense has every right to call the individual they think may be an informant to testify, that would involve nothing more than guesswork on their part and if that individual was not in fact the informant, his or her testimony would be immaterial to the motion to suppress and may even be detrimental to the defense. I am going to continue the remainder of this hearing to a later date and will take the defense's request to cross-examine the confidential informant under advisement. I will issue written findings and set a date for the rest of this hearing. I'll say again, though, that it troubles me that the defense does not have confirmation of the informant's identity and I think that's likely something they should have."

He rose and was halfway out the door to his chambers by the time the bailiff exclaimed the customary "all rise."

On the way out of the courtroom, Schoenheight pulled Rickworth aside again.

"Okay, how are we looking now? Can we do a deal here? You know as well as I do that it's safer for your client to take a deal in exchange for providing information to the government instead of rolling the dice at trial."

"Not yet, old buddy, especially after that signal from the judge. We're going to confirm the identity of your informant, and then we'll be able to dig into his motives and background on the stand." Rickworth said with a smile. "We both know full well who the informant is and even if the judge doesn't grant our motion to suppress, the testimony we get from him at the hearing is going to let us have a field day with him at trial. No deal yet – we have a long way to go with this one."

Rickworth broke off prematurely to join his client who was waiting impatiently by the courtroom door.

"We'll see," said Schoenheight to himself. He headed toward the elevator and cracked his own smile when he was out of sight of the defense team.

- CHAPTER 26 -

Eve got a call from Schoenheight just at the end of a workout at the gym in the basement of the FBI's Boston field office.

"Rust here," she answered, slightly out of breath.

"Good morning, Special Agent Rust, I hope I'm not interrupting anything but we've had a development in the Casimir case that I need to run by you.

"Sure, go ahead." said Eve, as she stepped off of the treadmill she was using to take the call, and grabbed the towel draped over the side of the machine to wipe the sweat that had collected on her forehead. Her morning runs were nothing like her cross-country workouts in college where she ran dozens of miles every week, but it still reminded her of her college days and kept her sane and brought clarity to her mind and a fleeting break from the constant press of work on her many investigations.

"We had our first motion to suppress hearing this morning and the defense asked that it be given the identity of our informant and the opportunity to cross-examine the informant. The judge continued the hearing while he decides whether to make us disclose the informant's identity, but after discussing it with some colleagues here in the U.S. Attorney's office, I'm fairly sure the judge is going to make us disclose the informant's identity, so we need to be ready to do that."

Eve thought about this development as she took a long sip from a water bottle and wiped her upper arms with the towel.

"Is that completely necessary?" asked Eve. "We told the guy that we would protect him, and exposing him directly in this way will do the opposite. He will have a target on his back. I don't like putting our informants in harm's way if it isn't necessary and I don't want him to think we're going back on our word here. We need him for this case – you know that as well as I do. Is there any other way?"

"Well, if we don't give up the informant, we will likely lose the motion to suppress, and if we lose that we will lose the ability to rely on any of the evidence we got with the warrant. That includes all Casimir's computers and all the other documents we found at his homes, all the communications we were able to intercept, and all the information we were able to collect on Casimir's criminal associates that we could use to bring other criminal cases. Winning the motion to suppress is important not just to this case, but all the cases we can bring in the future based on the information we collected from Casimir. The FBI is already generating some very promising leads with that information, as you know, and if we could turn Casimir, we might be able to bring dozens of new high-profile cases. We need to win this motion, and to do that we're going to need to let our informant be cross-examined."

"Okay, understood. He's just not going to be happy about that because he agreed to cooperate in exchange for our protection. We're still going to protect him, of course, but it's going to be a lot harder after Casimir knows he's working with us. I'll have to break the news to him carefully and will coordinate with the U.S. Marshals to increase his security detail. I know he's already committed to helping us, but we should see whether we can offer him anything else in exchange for his testimony. He's really sticking his neck out now."

Eve was now stretching and working her way down to a full split on a mat in front of a long mirror on one end of the gym. She had remained fit after college and throughout her vigorous FBI field training and was in much better shape than the minimum requirements the Bureau had for its agents. She preferred running along Memorial Avenue in Cambridge with the Boston skyline in view across the Charles River, but didn't always have the time for that luxury.

"Yes, good point, I will think on that."

"Ok, thank you, anything else I need to know?" asked Eve as she rose from the stretch and headed toward the locker room.

"That's about it – we're going to need him back for the next hearing in a few weeks." continued Schoenheight. "I know we have him in a secure location, but if we could have him back in town a couple days before the hearing that would give us some time to prepare him. He may face some pretty tough cross-examination if they decide to go forward with questioning. I'm hoping that seeing him show up in court, ready to testify, will make them think twice about going forward. But I know Rickworth, and he's not going to back down from a fight if there's any chance of him winning. All we can do at this point is show up with our informant and hope that does the trick."

"Ok, understood. I'll talk to the Marshals and we'll arrange the whole thing. This case is my top priority and we'll do everything necessary to keep things moving forward. Just keep me posted if anything changes."

"Roger that."

Eve slipped her phone into her gym bag and went to shower and prepare for the rest of the day. Schoenheight stood from his seat at his desk and stretched his arms wide and took a deep breath while looking out his window at the seafood restaurant on the harbor next to the courthouse with a patio covered by a red and yellow striped tent, before digging back into the piles of information the FBI had uncovered on Casimir and continuing to prepare the case against him that had the potential to blossom into multiple indictments against Casimir's associates if the government played its cards right. The federal agents would work with their colleagues over the next weeks to bring justice upon their target.

- CHAPTER 27 -

It was sizzling hot and the air was thick with humidity on the day the motion to suppress hearing was to resume. When Casimir stepped out of the black car that ferried him to the courthouse from his ritzy hotel nearby, the hot and humid air poured into the air-conditioned interior of the vehicle like a tropical river. Each in Casimir's entourage of lawyers was dressed in a dark suit that magnified the intensity of the heat and so the group did not dawdle outside of the federal courthouse, but instead quickly ducked into the arched brick entrance and the chilly embrace of the air-conditioning inside the grand atrium at the entrance of the building.

Had they spent more than a passing moment outside of the courthouse, they may have noticed some things seemingly out of place. The first would likely have been an armored vehicle painted jet black with no outward markings sitting idle just around the corner. It was parked so that its hood, with reinforced grill and oversized tires, its bulletproof windshield, and the front end of its gun mount were just visible to anyone walking through the front entrance of the courthouse that day. It resembled a military vehicle, but belonged to the FBI and was occupied by a team of agents from the FBI's Incident Response Group. Around the back of the courthouse where an expansive curved glass façade faced Boston Harbor, one would have observed a Coast Guard patrol boat with twin outboard engines in the aft and the characteristic orange rimmed metallic hull. Even a passive observer would have seen the sailor in navy blue fatigues and life vest scanning the harbor through a pair of high-powered binoculars, and it would also have been hard to miss the large automatic machine gun mounted on the deck of the boat, and the ensign assigned to it with his hands resting on the firing mechanism. Inside the courthouse too, a keen observer would have noticed slightly more heavily trafficked corridors. The reason for that would not have been apparent, but was due to the presence of plain clothed FBI agents mixing with the civilians in the building and hiding in plain sight.

There was no imminent attack on the courthouse expected or other credible threat. The additional security was just standard procedure when a protected federal witness was making a trip to the courthouse. That witness had already arrived in the early hours of the morning so as to avoid scrutiny. Once safely inside, he would never be exposed to the public spaces of the courthouse and instead was moved through the internal halls and staircases of the building so as not to open him up to more danger than he was already in.

Casimir and his lawyers were oblivious to this covert activity. They were all focused on the single objective before them that day. They knew who the informant was, they just needed it confirmed in open court. Once the informant was in their sights on the stand, Casimir's lawyers would spend hours digging into him and tearing his credibility apart. After passing security, Casimir's entourage moved directly to the courtroom where they readied for the slaughter of their prey.

Schoenheight had arrived much earlier in the day, and had spent hours preparing for the hearing before walking down the hall to one of the small conference rooms within the U.S. Attorney's Office. When he entered, the informant was just finishing his breakfast sandwich. The food had been provided by the Marshals who had shuttled him to the courthouse that morning from a safehouse nearby.

"That was delicious, thank you," said the informat through the last chews of his sandwich after Schoenheight walked through the door.

"We're happy to oblige. It's the least we could do, really. You are the hero today and we greatly appreciate your willingness to help us out," said Schoenheight, putting on a winning smile and sitting down across from the informant. "Now, I think we've already done all the prep we need to for the questions the defense is likely to ask on cross-examination. After the judge brings things to order, I will announce that you are present and ready to testify. The Marshals will clear the courtroom of anyone not involved in the case and then they will bring you into the courtroom. Then the defense team will be free to ask you questions, if they choose. It's impossible to know

200

for sure what the other side will do, and so we'll have to be on our toes a bit, but we've prepared you well for any scenario. If they do question you, I am ready with the redirect questions we already discussed."

"Sounds good. Honestly, I'm looking forward to it," exclaimed the witness while gulping down a sip of hot coffee. "I'm happy to help – that was our deal – but just make sure they don't shoot me, okay?"

Schoenheight smiled again. "Don't worry, we've got half the FBI's Boston office here today roaming the halls, not to mention the Coast Guard and U.S. Marshals. There'll be no shooting today – we're professionals. We do this all the time. See you up there."

Schoenheight got up and with a nod to the Marshals guarding the informant in the conference room, he exited and made his way to the courtroom and arrived just moments before the scheduled hearing time. He sat and composed himself and glanced over to the defense table just long enough to notice that they were all smiles. The heavy door to the judge's chamber was thrust open and the judge ascended the bench to the chorus of "all rise."

"Okay, you all got my order, and I assume the government has followed it and that you have your witness here in the courthouse. Is that correct Mr. Schoenheight?"

"Yes, your Honor. The government has complied and we have the witness here, and he is ready to present himself as long as the Marshals have cleared the courtroom."

"Okay, well let's do that now," exclaimed the judge. Then he addressed the whole courtroom.

"Anyone not directly involved in this case must leave the courtroom. I am sealing the courtroom for the remainder of this hearing."

The Marshals reacted on queue and ushered all those in the gallery out of the large courtroom and closed the doors behind them. After the room was cleared, one Marshal stood sentry at the main courtroom doors, while the others played similar roles at the various

201

side-doors of the courtroom. Rickworth rose to his feet and readied himself for the most critical part of the case thus far. He knew Netwanye was the lynchpin to the warrant against Casimir, and thus the whole case against Casimir, and he was ready to tear Netwanye apart on the stand. He would decimate any thread of credibility Netwanye had and create doubt as to the truthfulness of the information he provided to support the warrant. He would paint Netwanye as the mastermind of the scheme and portray him as the one that recruited Casimir to unwittingly assist in defrauding Sud-Coast. With Netwanye completely discredited, the warrant would be thrown out by the judge, and the case against Casimir would be dismissed. Rickworth was ready to pounce.

What he was not ready for, was the man the Marshals walked into the courtroom. Rickworth was so focused on the task ahead that he did not initially look up to observe the small procession leading the witness into the room. Casimir was watching intently with his threatening glare ready to strike fear into Netwanye, but the confident stare was wiped instantaneously from his face when he saw the man who was striding easily between two Marshals. Shaw was alive, and there to testify against him.

Casimir began aggressively jabbing his lawyers to get their attention and his yelled whispers could be easily heard by everyone in the courtroom,

"That is not Netwanye – where is Netwanye? What is going on here?"

His lawyers had no answer for him. Shaw's name had been one of dozens on the government's list of potential witnesses for this case, but the defense team had no expectation of actually seeing the dead man alive and well and in court, as they had been informed by Casimir that Shaw had tragically passed away in a boating accident months before. As a melee was unfolding at the defense's table, Shaw made his way calmly to the witness stand.

"I promise to tell the truth, the whole truth and nothing but the truth," said Shaw calmly as he looked directly at Casimir and a wide grin took over his tanned face. The incensed defendant could do nothing but avert his eyes from Shaw's supremely confident stare. Casimir frantically tried to put the pieces together in his mind concerning how Shaw could possibly be sitting in the courtroom alive and well, and shuddered as he catalogued to himself all the detailed information Shaw knew about his business dealings.

"Okay, counsel, you have your witness, you may begin when ready," said Judge Halderman to the collection of defense lawyers. There was no immediate response as the frantic group continued to wildly open binders and reach for papers in an attempt to get their bearings, like a dray of squirrels feverishly digging for acorns they had buried months ago.

"Counsel?" continued the judge, "are you ready to question the witness?"

"Your Honor, if you could just bear with us for just a few moments," was the feeble reply from Rickworth.

"Counsel, you've had weeks to prepare for this hearing and you told me last time that you already knew who the informant was so I'm not sure what's going on here. This lack of preparedness frustrates me, to say the least. I'll give you a quick recess. We will resume in five minutes." The judge stepped off the bench again in a huff with a stern dismissive expression on his face as he headed to the door in the back of the courtroom being opened by an attentive U.S. Marshal. A loud row commenced in earnest at the defense table after the judge's chamber door closed, while Shaw sat serenely on the witness stand, enjoying the view.

***

The federal witness protection program is the pride of the U.S. Marshals Service. It has never lost a protected person who has followed the guidelines of the program, and the program has achieved a sort of mythical status amongst law enforcement. It has the mission of protecting witnesses in federal criminal cases where those witnesses' lives, and the lives of their immediate families, may be at risk due to the testimony the witness is willing to give. Often the protected witness has agreed to testify against hardened criminals ready to go to any length to avoid prison, and so the protection provided by the Marshals is often the only thing standing between these brave witnesses and certain death.

Shaw missed sailing more than anything else. He had pleaded with the Marshals to relocate him to one of the coasts, but they insisted that somewhere in the middle of the country was safer. He was moved to a non-descript condo, in a non-descript development, on a non-descript road, somewhere in big sky country. He had to drive everywhere using his government issued late model maroon Ford, and he interacted with almost no one.

"Lay low," was their direction to him at the beginning and he had followed it, but just a few months into the relocation he was already getting tired of it.

The person he spoke to most often was his handler from the U.S. Marshals, who called every week to check in. Besides those quick, impersonal conversations, he also talked to the cute barista at the coffee shop in the local strip mall, and the mail carrier when they happened to be outside at the same time. That was about the extent of his social interaction. His neighbors had greeted him perfunctorily in the beginning, but he hadn't seen them much since. The Marshals had warned against getting too close to anyone too quickly before he had established himself with a new job and more of a purpose for residing in the community. That would all take time. He should move back into life slowly, they had cautioned. He spent his days driving or walking, and eating and sleeping in between. The kites he saw in the parks reminded him of sails and made him lonely. While he did his best to forget the past months, the attempt on his life haunted him every night.

He had taken his boat for a solo sail for a few days to think and clear his head after his disagreement with Casimir about Noah's future. It was the end of the first day and he had anchored in a small cove and begun to prepare his dinner, as he had done dozens of times before, often in the very same spot.

The menu for that evening was beans and rice with cumin and paprika that would pair nicely with the striped bass he'd caught on a line trawled behind his sailboat. The fish was cleaned on the side of the cockpit on a slab of worn wood he had installed there just for that purpose and, leaving the knife in a sheath, he brought the fish into the cabin so that the birds would not snatch it while he cooked the rest of his meal. He estimated another ten minutes on the beans and rice before he would sear the striped bass filet in a sizzling hot frying pan. That left him just enough time to go back to the cockpit and smoke a cigarillo before dinner. He had acquired the habit from his days in the Caribbean. Smoking the small cigars transported him back to those simpler times.

He climbed out of the cabin and in the same movement reached for the cigarillo in his front shirt pocket with one hand and the lighter in his pants pocket with the other. He was interrupted by a firm shove on his back that sent him careening to the floor against the back wall of the cockpit. He instinctively rose and turned just fast enough to meet a fist driven squarely into his nose, dropping him back to his original position on the deck. Dazed only momentarily, he reflexively sprung back again, this time toward the cabin entrance. The move caught his attacker off-guard as Shaw's shoulder drove into the assailant's stomach sending them both tumbling back onto the deck. Shaw could tell the man was large by the resistance he felt when he tackled him. He had also noticed something fly out of the man's hand and overboard when he struck him. It may have been a gun, or some other weapon, he would never know.

As the man clambered awkwardly to his hands and knees, unsteady and unfamiliar with maneuvering around a boat rocking in the ocean, Shaw caught a glimpse of his face under long stringy black hair and recognized him immediately as one of the hitmen Casimir favored. A harsh reality became instantly clear to Shaw – Casimir had turned against him and wanted him eliminated.

The man lunged at him again, but Shaw was ready this time with the fish knife firmly in his grasp. It was all over quickly after that. The man did not even scream when the razor-sharp blade lodged between his ribs and made only a ghastly moan as his last breath seeped from his mouth.

Shaw wasted no time with the next steps. He searched the man's pockets and found a small waterproof bag that contained a pre-paid cell phone, a wad of money, and some pills. Looking at the phone, Shaw saw a string of text messages, the last of which read:

"He's sailing this afternoon. Stow away on his boat and do it tonight."

Reading up the text chain, Shaw could see that the man had been paid half his fee already and expected the other half to be deposited automatically in a numbered account after he confirmed the job was done. Shaw tapped the phone's final message and noticed that his hands were shaking as he did:

"It's done. Wire the money. I'll be laying low for a while."

Shaw knew this message would satisfy Casimir that he had met his demise. Shaw turned off the phone and slid it into his pocket. Then he weighed the body down with his second anchor and tossed it over the side knowing that in a day or two it would be completely devoured by small sharks.

He turned off his stove and sat in the cockpit as it became silent in the boat save for the rhythmic lapping of waves on the side of the hull, uninterrupted by what had just taken place. His mind was on overload. His world was turned upside down. Casimir had betrayed him, and all because he tried to keep an innocent young man from having his life decimated. He was simultaneously in shock and deeply angered by Casimir's immediate turn on him after years of faithful service. Casimir's mind could never be changed, nor did Shaw care to try. If Casimir found out he was still alive, he would just come after him again, and keep coming until the job was done. Shaw had seen it happen to others before. He had to run, and far, and fast.

Shaw pulled anchor and motored the sailboat toward shore, toward a small inlet that was less rocky than the rest of the coast and then pointed the boat back out to sea. He set his stove back on high and set the motor at full throttle before leaping off the back of the boat. As he swam the short distance to shore, he could see his prized possession puttering back out into the open ocean.

When he reached shore, he changed clothes from the dry bag he took with him and walked five miles to the nearest train station where he took the late train to the city – paying cash from a wad in the bag. He spent the night in a tiny apartment that he kept under an alias. The next day, he took another train to Portland, Maine. He spent two sleepless nights in a cheap motel outside the city. He couldn't find a motel that would let him smoke in his room, so he spent hours each night on a white plastic chair outside his room door facing the cracked grey asphalt parking lot smoking cigarillos and continuing a hopeless wander through his thoughts as headlights periodically blinded him as cars pulled into the parking lot.

He spent the days inside his room, avoiding the stains on the carpet when in bare feet and watching SportsCenter reruns. As the sun turned the sky over the parking lot a brilliant red-orange on the morning of his second long night in the chair, he realized that he had only one choice. Hours later, he found himself at the entrance to the FBI field office in Portland. He knew it was his only chance to escape Casimir completely and to have the prospect, however small, to start again.

Casimir would continue with his scheme and execute Noah and his family once the scheme was complete just as he had tried to do with Shaw. Shaw was fed up with operating from the shadows – he was ready to step into the light and work to give Noah the fighting chance he never had. He stepped through the doors and his life changed forever.

***

After precisely five minutes, Judge Halderman exploded back through his chambers' door, manifesting the frustration he felt at having to interrupt the hearing so quickly after it started. Casimir's lawyers were still scrambling when the judge climbed the three steps to the bench, so much so that they didn't even answer the "all rise" call. As the judge settled himself, Casimir and his lawyers continued to whisper aggressive exhortations at each other, but the judge stopped all the chatter with a stern inquiry.

"All right counsel, my patience is at its breaking point now. Are we ready to go or not?"

Rickworth rose feebly.

207

"Your Honor, my sincere apologies, but we cannot ethically move forward with this witness. Our understanding was that this individual was deceased and thus could not have been a part of the government's case. We believed that the informant was a different person, your Honor, and will need additional time to prepare to cross-examine this witness."

Judge Halderman glared at Rickworth, not needing to make a sound because his eyes told perfectly how he felt about the request.

"Does the government have a position on this request?" the judge asked, gritting his teeth and continuing to stare grimly at Casimir's lead attorney.

"We oppose it, your Honor. Mr. Shaw was on the witness list and, as you can see, he is alive and well. I don't know why the defense believed he was dead – and I won't speculate on that – but they did not get that information from the government, I can assure you."

"Your Honor, if I may," said Rickworth, like a preschooler now asking for permission to use the bathroom, "there may be the possibility of an agreed plea in this case. Perhaps it's best to put this case on the calendar for two weeks from today for a change of plea hearing?"

This caught Schoenheight's attention, and he figured the defense must have quickly decided to try to strike a deal in their last frantic moments of discussion. The judge was also surprised, but appeased as he immediately softened his glare at Rickworth with a perceptible relaxing of his facial muscles.

"Well, that is a bit of welcome news. I think that might be the prudent move in this case anyway, knowing what I do about it. Okay, I will put this case on for a change of plea hearing, but let me admonish counsel once more – if I get wind that this was just some sort of a ploy to buy time and that your assertion of a potential deal is not a genuine one, you will not be happy with the result – in fact you will be very troubled by it. Understood?"

"Yes, your Honor," mumbled a defeated Rickworth.

208

Judge Halderman was up and out of the courtroom again just as fast as he had arrived. The defense team quickly gathered their papers, and binders, and brief cases in a tornado of action before marching double-time out of the courtroom. It was a silent retreat, except for Casimir, who was now yelling directly into Rickworth's ear.

The clandestine sentries melted away almost as quickly as Casimir's beaten attorneys. The plain-clothed undercovers in the hallway each took their leave, stepping one-by-one without haste to the front entrance of the courthouse, onto the street, and to a group of cars parked three blocks away. The gun boat captain revved the engine and the small ship made a sharp 180 degree turn before heading to its next assignment. The armored vehicle edged its nose back from view and stood by for the time being – with no other assignments, it would stay put for the afternoon and then leave the area in the evening under the cover of darkness.

– CHAPTER 28 –

It was less than an hour later that Schoenheight got a call on his cell phone from his old friend. Rickworth had just finished discussing the hearing with his client after enduring a heated ride back to his office in downtown Boston, during which Casimir heaped on him a torrent of vile insults. After the yelling had subsided, Rickworth was able to explain to his client how bad their position really was. The warrant was based on testimony from Shaw, not Netwanye, and Rickworth had no ammunition with which to attack Shaw's credibility. Casimir tried to explain Shaw's extensive criminal history.

"The man is a career criminal. He smuggled narcotics for years from the Caribbean to the United States and ran dozens of other schemes in the islands. He essentially set up the 'Short on Law' scheme, and with a little research we will have no problem digging up other schemes he was probably running on the side without my knowledge. Surely this can all be used to discredit him in court. You're the lawyer. I am paying you well. Do your job."

"Well Casimir, let me put it this way, and please don't answer the question – it's rhetorical – but, don't you think the very next thing they will do after we delve into Shaw's criminal history in this hearing is to go to work trying to figure out who Shaw was working with when conspiring and committing those crimes. We don't really want that sort of attention; I think you would agree with that."

Casimir was quite for a moment, before erupting again, "Okay! Fine! He was a dead man, how was he in court today? I can tell you one thing for sure – he is going to be a dead man."

"Please, stop right there," interjected Rickworth, "I can't protect you if you start saying things like that. What you should be doing now is considering cooperating with the FBI and thinking about what information you have that might help them in their other investigations. That's probably your only sure way out of decades in a prison cell at this point."

Casimir sat back quietly again and his face became pale in contemplation as the reality of the situation struck him. Rickworth didn't dare ask his client why Casimir thought Shaw was dead. He was now interested only in suggesting strongly that Casimir cooperate with the government to lessen the cascade of punishment that was headed Casimir's way upon a guilty verdict at trial, and then ending his representation of Casimir as soon as possible. He had experience with his fair share of allegedly crooked clients and was not naïve and knew that the government was known to overcharge federal prosecutions at times, but so many red flags were now popping up in this case – particularly in the form of a presumed dead witness – that Rickworth knew he had to get out of it. Schoenheight was half expecting a call from Rickworth but not until some point that afternoon at the earliest. When it came so quickly, he knew there could be only one reason – they wanted to deal.

"I was going to give you a couple hours, and then try you, but you didn't last half that long. Nice going in there today, by the way. Did you learn all those moves at some special defense bar class or just pick them up along the way?"

Schoenheight did not miss the opportunity to kid his friend. Even when on opposite sides, they had always tried to keep things light between them.

"Fuck you, dude. That judge is crazy, and I'm over it – I hate when they get all high and mighty like that. But, in all seriousness, it is time to talk about a deal. My client wants to have a meeting and I think you can probably guess why – we didn't think Shaw was even alive."

"Well, your client should have done a better job killing him, I guess."

The line was silent for a moment as Schoenheight let his last comment sink in before continuing.

"Either way, we're here and I think we can put together a deal that works for everyone. Casimir is going to jail – for a long time – there's no question about that, but I'm sure he has something he can offer us that might persuade the government not to make him

211

spend the rest of his life in prison. You just let me know some times over the next week that work for you to come over to the U.S. Attorney's Office and we can have a nice long sit down and discuss your client's options."

"Well, we're ready now, if you are." Rickworth replied without hesitation.

Casimir had folded much more quickly that Schoenheight expected and he was caught off guard by the defendant's readiness to deal immediately. He didn't yet have the list of options he mentioned prepared, and while he knew significant jail time for Casimir would certainly be part of any agreed plea, he didn't yet have a sentencing recommendation that would typically be made to the court later in the case based on a standard set of sentencing guidelines, and also did not know by how much time he would lessen the recommended sentence in exchange for Casimir's cooperation. He also did not have a complete understanding from his investigators and Agent Rust and the rest of the FBI team assigned to the case regarding the extent of additional information on other ongoing criminal schemes that Casimir might have for them – the information they could demand in exchange for a lesser sentence. The options fired through his head like a line of pistons sparked into action. He could put Rickworth and his client off for a few days to give himself time to fully prepare for the meeting, but that might also give the defendant a few days to think about his decision to talk. In that time Casimir might change his mind, or even try to flee.

"I'll call you right back," said Schoenheight.

He hung up the phone, hedging that Casimir's eagerness to talk would last longer than fifteen minutes. He then made a lightening series of calls to a number of his superiors to inform them of the development and get permission to execute his plan to move forward with an immediate interview. Normally, the U.S. Attorney and FBI would work together to arrange for some sort of security for an informant coming in to talk. But, on such short notice, that would not be possible. Despite this lack of security, they felt that the decision by Casimir had been made so quickly and recently that there would be limited danger as anyone at risk of Casimir ratting on them would have no way to know that Casimir had decided to talk. They decided to bring him in quietly for what promised to be a barnburner series of meetings. Schoenheight called Rickworth to give him the news and instructed them to return to the courthouse as quickly as was convenient.

"Just tell me, though," said Schoenheight before he hung up, "what are we looking at here – just so I can be prepared and tell my bosses what to expect. Is this an initial meeting to explore options, or are we going to get a plea deal hammered out today?"

"Look, I won't make any promises, but he was thoroughly spooked by what he saw in the courtroom today – really shaken. He also has the goods on a lot of crooks. There may be fireworks today, we'll just have to see what happens."

"Ok good, looking forward to seeing you soon – you guys can just come in through the front door again and I'll meet you in the lobby and take you up."

* * *

Unfortunately, Schoenheight never got the chance. Ballistics reports and homicide scene reconstruction showed after the fact that the sniper was likely positioned on the fourth floor of an old brick building on Sleeper Street, across from the courthouse. Eyewitnesses walking along the Fort Point Channel would also later tell investigators that they heard three loud pops at around the time of the shooting. That coincided with what was found at the scene. The first shot hit the brick outer wall of the courthouse sending a spray of clay colored dust and particles off the building. The second had hit Casimir in his abdomen and the third in his chest, piercing his heart and killing him instantaneously. It was precise shooting – none in the group of lawyers following him into the front entrance of the courthouse had been injured.

The first law enforcement officials to react were inside the armored vehicle that was still sitting dormant around the corner of the courthouse. The team jumped into action the moment they heard the report from a high-powered rifle and pulled the vehicle to the front of the courthouse, but the firing was long over by the time they arrived. In a war zone, they might have returned fire or provided cover for troops advancing to address the threat. But, in the civil urban environment where they were, there was not much they could do other than ensure the others with Casimir were ferried out of the firing line and that Casimir received what little medical attention they could provide.

Days after the shooting, the investigation ascertained that the precise origin of the shots was a vacant office suite in the brick building on Sleeper Street. The door was found to be forced open and the room that hosted the sniper wiped clean. The security footage from the building that day had also been conveniently erased. It reeked of an inside job and a larger criminal force at work, but ultimately the local police had few leads after rounds of interviews. The FBI had just recently taken jurisdiction of the investigation and it would continue under the FBI's direction, likely for months.

Schoenheight didn't know what had happened until almost an hour after it occurred. The active shooter alarm had gone off in the U.S. Attorney's Office, and they had all moved as if it was a drill – because it usually was. By the time all the Assistant U.S. Attorneys and staff realized it was real, they were already outside of the back of the courthouse by the water. In all the excitement, Schoenheight had forgotten to check in with Rickworth to update him on the situation and so he called him from his cell phone. When Rickworth answered all Schoenheight could hear at first were sirens. Then he heard his friend yelling into the phone.

"Hello, Schoenheight?"

"Can you hear me?"

"Yes, barely."

"Look, the courthouse has just been evacuated. I hear sirens on the line so you must already be close. Something's going on here and I'm not sure what or how long it's going to last, so we're probably going to have to reschedule. I know you wanted to get this done today, but it just doesn't look like it's going to happen."

214

"It's not going to happen period, Schoenheight." retorted an exasperated Rickworth still struggling with the effects of shock. "I just got shot at outside your courthouse. I was right next to Casimir when he got hit. They're going to take me in for an interview soon and I need to get the blood off of my clothes. We can talk in a few days if you want, but this case is over. Casimir is dead."

Rickworth hung up before Schoenheight could react. He was worried about his friend, and not the case anymore. He wouldn't have to think much more about it, at least for now. With a deceased defendant the case would be closed. If the FBI generated any leads for other prosecutions by going through the material they seized from Casimir pursuant to the warrant, they would bring it to his attention. But, for now, the matter would be forgotten by the Assistant U.S. Attorney.

- CHAPTER 29 -

Casimir's willingness to deal confirmed for Eve and the rest of the financial crimes task force in the FBI's Boston office that he drove the conspiracy to defraud Sud-Coast and Company and was also likely the mastermind behind the scheme perpetrated by the partners of Markus Stillfield Brice. Later, when digging deeper through the emails and other physical evidence gathered from Casimir's farm in the South African wine region and also in other properties that they discovered he owned across the Caribbean, the FBI found additional information showing his direct involvement in the "Short on Law" scheme and the scheme to defraud Sud-Coast and Company. They also uncovered communications suggesting numerous other schemes taking place across the world that would keep the financial crimes unit in Boston busy for some time.

Casimir's assassination also confirmed another suspicion of the U.S. Attorney's Office and the FBI – that Casimir was part of something bigger and that he was a large cog in an even larger criminal syndicate. The collective knowledge amongst the agencies was that Casimir was killed so that he would not talk to the Feds about his criminal associates and plots that were ongoing or planned for the future. That he was killed wasn't all that surprising – informants who are found out are always in danger, and Casimir's colleagues just got to him before the government could offer him any protection. What was surprising was the swiftness of the attack. With the assassination coming so quickly after the U.S. Attorney's Office learned that Casimir was willing to talk, the obvious implication was that there was a leak, either within the FBI, the prosecutor's office, or perhaps in the office of Casimir's attorney. The government would launch a full investigation to determine if the leak had come from within its ranks.

Eve and Schoenheight, and their colleagues, had achieved the result they were seeking, just not in the way they had planned, or had hoped for. The purpose of criminal prosecutions is to make the defendant answer for what he or she has done, and with Casimir dead he would never face punishment for the horrific crimes he was responsible for. They were left with only a morbid guarantee that Casimir would never again ensnare a victim unknowingly in a complex criminal web. A rough, but effective form of justice.

With the case behind her, Eve took time to drive out to western Massachusetts for a few days to see her mother, to visit her father's grave, and to spend time reflecting on the last months. The Casimir case had been a whirlwind and she could not believe that it had ended so abruptly. Her skillset had grown immensely over the last months as she had taken the lead in what was now one of the more notable apprehensions for the Boston field office's financial crimes division. The achievement would catapult her career and she already had her next assignment, which would take her overseas to track down terrorist financing across Europe and the Middle East. With Casimir's death, she was also finally able to close the book on something that had weighed on her since the day she got that first frantic call from her mother years ago.

Shortly after Casimir's death, she had taken her own time to search through the cash of information the FBI had collected from his personal files, and late one evening she had found what she had been looking for all along and what she knew was there. It would have meant nothing to anyone without the painful memory of her father's ordeal, but to Eve it was clear. It was a short email communication from Casimir to an associate in the United States that read,

"Make sure Thomas Rust will be on the boat this week."

The email was dated three days before her father's death and she finally had her evidence. Casimir was the murderer that tore her family apart, and she had eliminated him. No one had been there to protect her family in the past, but she found some solace in knowing that she had protected Noah and his family and all those future families that Casimir would have destroyed if given the chance.

She spent days walking the gentle wooded paths in the foothills of the Berkshires, watching wildflowers sway in waves of motion with the wind and sitting with her mother and talking about anything. These conversations continued into nights that were accented by the thick smell of dried birch logs burning in the fireplace and the symphony of cracks composed by the inferno. The reprieve ended all too soon, as Eve set off to pursue justice once again.

***

Noah didn't hear about the shooting until the next day when Eve called to give him the news before the FBI's official announcement concerning the incident had been released. Noah had no reason to be at the motion to suppress hearing that day and had not been in touch with Eve for weeks. The last time they spoke had been a brief phone call in which Noah informed her that he and Alana would not be taking up the government on their offer of protection through the witness protection program. He had acknowledged that they were likely in some danger still, but explained that with Casimir staring down a likely conviction, they hoped that his criminal associates would have little interest in Noah. He knew practically nothing about Casimir except for the legal work he had done for him and the scheme Casimir was perpetrating against Sud-Coast. Everyone implicated in that scheme was now either in custody, or dead. There was no one left for Noah to tell the FBI about.

He also imparted that they were not ready to spend the rest of their lives in hiding and to subject their children to a life on the run. It was a risk, yes, but one they were willing to take to return to a sense of normalcy. When he got the call, Noah was just returning to his and Alana's apartment to deliver an assortment of snacks she had requested from the local grocery store before going back out to pick up dinner for the evening. Alana was now very pregnant and uncomfortable much of the time and Noah had focused his efforts on keeping her as comfortable as possible in the last days before her due date.

With the Sud-Coast case gone, things were tight again. While some minor work trickled in here and there, and there was some money still left over from the Sud-Coast case, the coffers were almost empty again and the nagging feeling that he had to find a way to support his family had returned as a constant thought in the back of Noah's mind.

"Our offer is still on the table if you and Alana want to take federal protection, but, off the record, I agree with you – Casimir's death makes you a lot safer – the only information you had was on Casimir and he's gone now. There's no one left with an axe to grind against you." said Eve after she and Noah had exchanged pleasantries.

"I'm happy to hear that's your assessment – and Alana will be too. We're still coming to terms with all this and I'm trying to figure out what I'm going to do for work, but we appreciate your reaching out and if there are any other developments, I'd really appreciate a heads up." replied Noah as he set the snacks down on a table just inside the apartment's front door.

"Of course – you're on the top of our call list. You split this case wide open for us and the FBI won't forget that. And confidentially, your work helped to bring closure to a cold case that was of personal importance to me and I will be forever grateful for that. Also, just so you know, we've been keeping an agent on you guys since the arrest to make sure no one is lurking around that shouldn't be. We're going to keep one on at least for the next few months until everything has really quieted down. Don't worry, we have your back. It's the least we can do."

"We really appreciate that, Eve. I just have one more question. Why did Shaw come back to testify? He could have just disappeared."

"Well, Noah, you are partially to thank for that as well. He wanted to be free of Casimir once and for all, but also knew what Casimir would do to you and your family if he was allowed to complete his scheme, and Shaw couldn't let that happen."

"Amazing – I don't know what to say."

"Well, maybe you'll get the chance to thank him one day."

"I hope I do. Thank you again, Eve. Take care."

Noah hung up and made his way back down the stairs of their Manchester apartment to pick up a takeout dinner. Alana and Noah planned to spend the night discussing what locale they might move to next to start fresh. Noah normally went to their mailbox every evening to gather the mail and see if there was anything besides bills for their perusal. He forgot that day – completely lost in thoughts of Casimir's assassination and a growing belief that a time would eventually come when he could stop constantly looking over his shoulder. If he had looked in the mail that evening, he would have found a package that would have given the young couple even more to talk about.

Sud-Coast and Company had recently received a large bailout from the South African government that allowed them to satisfy all their debts and work toward solvency. This had been widely reported in the regional press but Noah had missed it with his focus diverted to his and Alana's safety. One of the outcomes of the bailout was that Sud-Coast could settle the financial claims against it – which included the lawsuit by Undertow Acquisitions. The packet was sent to Noah's windowfront office because he was still counsel of record on the case. The packet itself was non-descript, except for a conspicuous air-mail stamp on the top right boasting the image of a Kudu leaping through the brush. When he did eventually open the package the following morning Noah would be pleased with what he saw. He was still the owner of the company that brought suit against Sud-Coast, thanks to Casimir, and now that Sud-Coast had decided to pay their debt he was the sole recipient of the windfall. It wasn't the vast fortune that Casimir had salivated over, but the one million dollars that would be wired to Noah's account would allow he and Alana to stay in Manchester for quite some time.

***

After Casimir's death, Netwanye quietly made his way back to Cape Town. He had no other obligations to the U.S. Attorney's Office or FBI, who made good on their promise to work with the South African government to ensure he would not be prosecuted in his home country. To prompt the South African government's restraint, the FBI had provided a tip about Sud-Coast and some irregularities in their accounting practices. The FBI advised the South African authorities to take an especially close look at the funds allocated to charities run by Sud-Coast. Netwanye resigned shortly after the formal investigation into Sud-Coast became public.

220

The investigation was splashed across every major newspaper in the country and Netwanye was one of many Sud-Coast executives that resigned in the wake of the allegations of fraud and so his departure did not raise any eyebrows. Apart from clemency from prosecution by the South African government, the FBI had also provided Netwanye with a handsome reward for his cooperation in the case against Casimir. Using that money, Netwanye went to work organizing a youth soccer program in Khayelitsha township where he grew up. In secure compounds he designed and built around the township, children could learn the beautiful game each day while being provided academic classes to brighten their futures, and food and shelter without the threat of violence. Netwanye was finally able to fulfill his hope of improving the prospects of the children of Khayelitsha.

***

Shaw was through with the confining restrictions of life under federal protection. He was whisked away from the courthouse after the shots reached their target and was on a private flight back to the middle of nowhere before nightfall, but he hadn't missed his small condo and felt no nostalgia in the cab ride back to his nondescript street. He sat at his small kitchen table in the darkness with a fresh Red Stripe in his hand for only a few moments before his mind was entirely made up. He had more to fear than Noah because he knew more – he had been entwined in Casimir's criminal enterprises for decades and knew some of the people that probably ordered Casimir's assassination. It was also apparent now that he had talked to the Feds, and so he knew he would always have a target on his back.

He would forever carry information in his mind that could lead to the arrest and prosecution of many powerful individuals with the means to easily order his assassination. But Shaw had decided too that he would not live his life landlocked and in obscurity. He had already dodged the onslaught of one assassin and if he was going to face another, he at least wanted to be in the midst of doing something he loved, in a beautiful place amongst people he cared for. He would return to the Caribbean and would repair and sell boats. He told the Marshals not to follow him after booking a ticket for the British Virgin Islands. The first thing he would do when he landed was to rent a cheap car and scour the island for a damaged and forgotten sailboat that he could fix up and make his own. He would begin to build a life for himself again. He knew it would be a different life – a more solitary life – but anything was better than living like a caged animal awaiting the slaughter. In the meantime, he got used to looking over his shoulder. He would be doing it for the rest of his life.

- CHAPTER 30 -

As the sun dropped toward the horizon it caused long shadows to cast off of a row of palm trees skirting the seventeenth fairway at the links style course along the western Bermuda coast. A twosome – the last group of the day – ambled up the fairway toward their drives trailed by thick plumes of cigar smoke that hung weightless in the cool, still evening air. The first was wearing coral-colored shorts and a blue quarter-zip sweater. He surveyed his lie quickly before yanking a wedge from his bag. He lined up his angle of attack with an astute examination from behind the ball before stepping up and thumping a shot onto the front of the green, which glowed in the evening sun. The second in the pair, wearing white slacks and a light blue polo shirt had a more rushed approach and didn't bother to examine his lie before choosing a club, abruptly setting himself, and contacting the ball with a downward chop of a swing, sending forth a low shot that skipped through almost the entire green before the ball's backspin brought it to a stop just inches from the hole.

"Where in the hell did you learn to do that?" exclaimed the first.

"Wish I could say I meant to do that, but I'll take it. Better to be lucky than good." answered the second.

They both continued on toward to green after picking up their cigars that had both been placed on the turf to smolder while their shots were made, each leaving a small pile of white ash where the cigar had rested.

"Okay, are we decided that we're going to leave Walker alone?" asked the second man.

"Yes, he's got no information on us and our source in the FBI tells us that he's got protection right now anyway. It's too hot to go in there and get him, and it wouldn't do anything for us. In fact, it would do the opposite. The FBI would have to look into who killed him and that, of course, would lead indirectly to us. He doesn't need to die at the moment. He's the lucky one that will escape this whole

223

mess better than when he was pulled into it."

"Okay, good. I agree, we will let him live his life in peace. Now, we need to talk about Shaw." said the second man as he grabbed a putter from his bag, removed its cover, and walked to the back of the green to assess his lie. It was silent for a moment save for the distant sound of waves crashing on a rocky shore, as both men plotted their lines and appropriate speed.

"We cannot let him go so easily," said the second man before knocking his put into the middle of the cup. "That's a three," he continued in self-congratulations.

"No question, he needs to be addressed."

The first man took two puts to finish and they both ambled to the eighteenth tee.

"All square?" asked the first man, as he pulled his driver from his bag and removed the head cover that resembled a bulldog.

"Yep, this one's for the whole fiver. Watch the wind coming off the water on your drive."

The second man snickered as the first hit a line drive down the middle of the fairway that bounced twice before settling in a perfect position.

"That one okay?" responded the first man, now showing a smirk of his own. With no response, the second man stepped up to the tee and quickly hit a hard shot that faded into the long sand trap lining the right side of the fairway and sent up a small spray of sand upon landing.

"Damn! Okay let's get going, I can get out of there okay," exclaimed the second man as he slammed his driver back into his bag and trudged down the course with purpose. The first man followed with a lighter step.

"Back to Shaw." continued the second man, "He knows too much and he is going to have to go but it's just a question of how and when."

"Agreed. He will be on guard now, and perhaps we should wait a little while until he thinks he's safe. Then we can strike easily and get the drop on him and do it quickly and quietly."

"But what about all the information he knows now. What if the FBI goes back to him for more, and what if he talks? He has already, what makes you think he will stop? The FBI will no doubt continue to pay him for information if they can find him. I don't think we want to take that risk. Why not just be done with him sooner rather than later?"

The two men split again to walk to their respective next shots. The first man lobbed another parabolic wedge shot just onto the front of the green and returned his club to his bag after taking one final pull on his cigar and then grinding the smoldering stub into the ground and leaving it for the next morning's grounds crew to collect. The second man let fly a large plume of white sand with his shot, moving the ball only a few yards out of the trap. His expletives echoed across the empty course and his thrown cigar butt exploded into a ball of yellow sparks when it struck the ground. His next shot was chipped low but too fast this time and without backspin. It skipped on the green's surface before going past the putting surface and lodging in the thick rough behind the hole.

"Fuck!" exclaimed the second man as he thrust his club into his bag and plodded angrily back onto the fairway. The two men met again on their approach to the green but were quiet as they walked together amongst lengthening shadows. The first marked his ball and helped the second to look for his in the thick tropical vegetation behind the hole. They prodded the thick rough absent mindedly for a few moments peering into the grasses as the light faded.

"I'll just drop, go hit your shot."

"You sure?"

"Yes, please, I'm about done with this hole."

The first man walked back toward the front of the green observing the back-to-front slope on the way to his ball. Lining up for a mostly straight putt with a touch of left-to-right break, he hit the ball stiffly up hill and it skirted the right edge of the hole before stopping about a foot long.

"That's good," said the second man, "and that's the round. Well played – you got me this time."

They shook hands and the second man handed a bill to the first.

"We must be about even all time now, right?"

"I think that's just about right. Good round."

They left their carts with an attendant waiting just beyond the hole and started the short walk to the grand clubhouse that glowed pink in the setting sun.

"I don't think we need to rush into this. We already know he worked with the Feds on the case against Casimir, so if he was going to spill anything, he's probably spilled it already," continued the first man, "this is really a deterrence hit now. We can't let people in our organization think they can go running to the Feds and live to tell about it and enjoy the rest of their life in paradise."

"Agreed. We don't need to rush into this, but I don't want it hanging over our heads either. We have bigger things to worry about now like figuring out how much Shaw gave the Feds and figuring out what the Feds are going to do with it. We've got one informant in the FBI field office in Boston, but we need to focus our resources on developing another mole, maybe even at headquarters in D.C. We need to figure out what was leaked and work on damage control. That includes getting rid of Shaw. Who knows when the Feds will go back to the well looking for more information from him."

"I hear you and I'm fine with just getting it done. We need to find someone good to do the job, though. Shaw killed the last man that was sent to do away with him. We cannot let that sort of thing happen again."

"I think we need to get Ruiz. He's always been reliable for us. He always gets the job done."

"Ruiz? Do you really think we need that sort of firepower for this job? Shaw isn't much of an operator, I don't think. He was on the management side for Casimir. He never did much of the dirty work. It strikes me that he's lucky to still be alive in the first place."

"We need to get this done once and for all. Let's use Ruiz and then we don't have to worry about it anymore."

The two approached a side door to the large pink stucco clubhouse perched on the side of a tall cliff facing west toward the mid-Atlantic. Sounds from a cocktail party already well underway echoed from a second-floor balcony above where the men entered the building. They walked down a short hallway leading to the locker room.

The expansive wood paneled space was a relic from a bygone era. The middle of the room was occupied by two rows of dark wooden lockers with polished brass fittings. They were surrounded by a worn sisal carpeted floor that extended to the walls of the room that were hung with old photographs of the course, past club champions, and notables that had played there. The room was empty at this time of the evening.

"It's decided then. We will take the plan to the board when we meet next week. Then we can focus on our other objectives in Boston and Washington."

"Excellent."

With their golf shoes left at the base of their respective lockers, the two men donned sport coats and headed out a different door toward the dining room. They stopped at the bar on the way. The first ordered a vodka soda and the second a rum and coke and they viewed the setting sun through an expansive glass window as their drinks were prepared.

"I can't remember, did the ladies want rum punches?"

"Yes, it must be, they love those things."

227

"Okay, good. Here's the more important question, though. Do you want to go double or nothing that the ladies order two more of these before the main course tonight?"

The two men chuckled and walked away from the bar into the main dining room that was brightly lit in pastel colors and roaring with dozens of small parties grouped around tables each concocting their own future schemes – significant and not.

Made in the USA
Middletown, DE
13 August 2021

45348239R00139